T0248057

Praise for no address

"Absolutely riveting! I wholeheartedly endorse *No Address* the book. It offers a gripping portrayal of life on the streets. Drawing from my extensive experiences serving on nonprofit boards aiding those experiencing homelessness and even sleeping in shelters alongside former HUD Secretary Cuomo, I can attest to its authenticity. My recent visits to homeless encampments and shelters further enriched my understanding and portrayal of the character I play in the motion picture. Through this journey, I've learned firsthand the importance of treating every unhoused person with dignity and respect. *No Address* is not just a story—it's a call to action and compassion that I proudly stand behind."

—WILLIAM BALDWIN, *Actor, Producer, Writer*

"The book does an incredible job contextualizing and giving color to the multifaceted challenge of homelessness, which spans the gamut of challenging life circumstances, family dynamics, personal addiction, and the realities of life with no address. If there is one thing you walk away with after reading, it is that the simple labels and quick fixes we put on homelessness are woefully inadequate and that each of us can be part of the solution in our families, communities, and our nation. Crucially, being part of the solution means amplifying holistic treatment programs for homeless, rather than just focusing on quick fixes such as providing more meals; the latter is helpful for an immediate need, but it just kicks the can down the road."

—DR. CHRISTOS A. MAKRIDIS
Professor, Entrepreneur, Adviser,
Syndicated Columnist at Forbes,
Fortune, Fast Company

"HOMELESSNESS IS one of those conversations that feels one way when you're just talking about an issue, and then it feels totally different when you say, 'That's my friend.' But the question is, what if that were me? Because life can turn on a dime. We don't know what could flip our circumstances, and we might be the person in need."

—AMY GRANT
Singer, Songwriter,
Six-time Grammy Award Winner,
Twenty-two-time Dove Award Winner

"IN THE BUSTLING streets of life, where the pavement meets the sky, there exists a hidden world—a realm of shadows, courage, and unyielding humanity. *No Address*, penned by the esteemed *New York Times* bestselling author Ken Abraham, invites us into this raw and poignant narrative. In the eyes of the homeless, we glimpse our own vulnerability. In many ways, their stories are our stories—the triumphs, the setbacks, and the unwavering will to survive. *No Address* transcends mere pages; it's an invitation to view the world anew, to recognize our shared humanity, and to embrace empathy."

—COMMISSIONER KENNETH G. HODDER
National Commander for The Salvation Army
and COMMISSIONER JOLENE HODDER
National Secretary for Program for The Salvation Army

"MY WIFE, Jet, and I lost a friend to the downward spiral of mental illness and homelessness, and the proper resources were not in place to help. Being executive producers of *No Address* is personal; our motivation is to use the power of film to bring awareness and change the status quo. The *No Address* book is an important element in humanizing homelessness—there are too many friends, brothers, sisters, parents, and loved ones on the street. Connecting with this story and rooting for these characters bring understanding and empathy to the crisis and are critical to turning it around."

—JOHN LEWIS
Robert Craig Films Foundation Board
Chairman & Executive Producer of No Address

"As SOMEONE deeply committed to understanding and addressing the complex issue of homelessness, I am profoundly moved by the narrative of *No Address*. This book, brilliantly penned by Ken Abraham and inspired by the feature film produced by Robert Craig Films, offers a riveting exploration of human resilience and community in the face of profound adversity. The story's authenticity and emotional depth highlight the stark realities faced by those without a home, making it a crucial read for anyone looking to understand or combat this pressing social issue. *No Address* not only entertains, it also educates and inspires action, embodying the transformative power of storytelling."

—KEITH DIEDERICH
President and CEO
The Gathering Inn and
Production Consultant for No Address

"KEN ABRAHAM'S *No Address* offers a poignant and powerful exploration of one of our society's most pressing issues: homelessness. Through vivid storytelling and heartfelt narrative, Abraham portrays the harsh realities faced by those who have no place to call home. With compassion and insight, he delves into the intricate web of challenges and struggles that accompany the experience of homelessness, offering readers an intimate glimpse into a world most of us would prefer to ignore. Raw authenticity sets *No Address* apart. Abraham doesn't sugarcoat or shy away from the harsh realities faced by the homeless. He boldly confronts the devastating effects of homelessness, shedding light on the human stories behind the statistics. With compelling style, he invites readers to empathize with the individuals who have come face-to-face with this crisis, and not only raises awareness but also inspires action. With uncanny skill, Abraham captures the resilience and dignity of these fictional individuals struggling against homelessness and leads a call to compassion and social change. Anyone with a heart to understand the complexities of homelessness and the need for meaningful solutions should read this book."

—BRANDAN THOMAS
Director of Leadership for Citygate Network

"THERE ARE TOO many homeless people suffering, and it doesn't have to be this way. I am grateful I could contribute by bringing artists together for *No Address* and the soundtrack to help these touching stories of survival and resilience resonate even more powerfully through music. Like the movie, the *No Address* book shows that anyone can be down on their luck and just need a hand up to change their life. This is the start of something big that will make a difference."

—GREG LUCID
Owner of Lucid Creative and
Music Supervisor for No Address

"KEN ABRAHAM does an amazing job bringing the *No Address* book characters to life in a compassionate and compelling way. His storytelling reminds all of us that homelessness could occur to any one of us, at any time. Every reader will find at least one character with whom they can and will deeply relate, whether it is Lauren fostering out of the system, or the daily challenges of Harris, or even the hard-charging Robert. The story of homelessness within the United States is a critical story that needs to be told in a realistic and compassionate way. Ken does this in a tremendous way, sharing the daily challenges of experiencing homelessness. Most importantly, the *No Address* book gives us all hope that people experiencing homelessness can recover from being homelessness and live a flourishing and meaningful life."

—ROBERT G. MARBUT JR.
Executive Producer of No Address

"WITH THIS novelization of *No Address*, you are going to interact with characters who are experiencing one of the most-challenging crises in our country today: homelessness. I am grateful for my friends at Robert Craig Films who not only tell meaningful stories like the one in this book, but they also understand the call for believers to live out our faith in tangible ways. This combination of faith and entertainment not only will touch you, it will also challenge you to be part of the solution moving forward."

—BOB ELDER
Chief Impact Officer,
Collide Media Group

"I've been on the streets working with the homeless—helping people get clean and sober, recover from addiction, start jobs, and start their lives again. I see their challenges and know the power of offering support one step at a time—whether it's recovery from addiction with a ride to the treatment center or new boots so they can get to work. It's as simple as finding a starting point to help them launch. Being part of *No Address* takes this message to a bigger audience, and I can't tell you how much it means to have this movie and book show the world that acts of kindness matter, and we can impact so many more lives if we all do this together."

—VICTOR THE GOOD BOSS
Influencer

"*No Address* exposes the raw truth of homelessness in America, reminding us that our addresses don't define us. In my opinion, through one specific character's journey, it reveals the fragile thread connecting us all to the edge of uncertainty. A compelling and eye-opening narrative that challenges us to confront our own vulnerability and the humanity we share."

—MARK S. ALLEN, *Producer, Writer, Director, p. g. a.*

"I AM BLESSED to have been able to spend many years helping people who are facing challenging life circumstances, such as serving as the Goodwill Ambassador for the International Rescue Committee, being a member of the Freedom Corps, and as an ambassador for Save the Children and World Vision. I have also seen firsthand that homelessness can happen to anyone or any family. In *No Address*, the lead character, Lauren, is kicked out of the home by her foster family just as she graduates from high school. With everything she owns in a trash bag, Lauren finds herself "fostered-out" and suddenly living on the streets. Sadly, her story is repeated in real life every day. It doesn't have to be this way! This book shows us that with the skills and resources of wonderful faith-based and nonprofit organizations there are solutions—and there is hope."

—MYRKA DELLANOS

Television Host, Journalist

no address

A NOVEL

KEN ABRAHAM

Based on a screenplay by
JULIA VERDIN and JAMES J. PAPA

Additional Materials by David Hyde

NO ADDRESS: A Novel

Copyright © 2024 by Robert Craig Films, LLC

All rights reserved. No part of this publication may be reproduced, stored in a retrieval system, or transmitted in any form by any means, electronic, mechanical, photocopy, recording, or otherwise, without the prior permission of the publisher, except as provided by USA copyright law.

No patent liability is assumed with respect to the use of the information contained herein. Although every precaution has been taken in the preparation of this book, the publisher and author assume no responsibility for errors or omissions. Neither is any liability assumed for damages resulting from the use of the information contained herein.

Published by Forefront Books, Nashville, Tennessee.
Distributed by Simon & Schuster.

Library of Congress Control Number: 2024938103

Print ISBN: 978-1-63763-263-5
E-book ISBN: 978-1-63763-264-2

Cover Design by Bruce Gore, Gore Studio Inc.
Interior Design by Mary Susan Oleson, Blu Design Concepts

Printed in the United States of America

This book is dedicated to those
experiencing homelessness in hopes
they will be encouraged, know they are loved,
know there is hope, and know there is
a God in heaven who loves them
and is here to help.

Contents

Acknowledgments

WRITING A BOOK is a journey, and like any journey, it's not one you take alone. To those who have walked alongside us on this path, we owe an immense debt of gratitude.

As we reflect on the journey that brought us here, we extend our appreciation to Rebekah Hubbell for her role in forging a connection with the esteemed author Ken Abraham. Ken Abraham's collaboration and insights have enriched every page of this book. His extraordinary talent for crafting narratives that resonate deeply with readers has elevated our project beyond measure. His presence as a leading force has been nothing short of transformative, and we are profoundly grateful for his beautiful humanity. To his beloved wife, Lisa, we extend our deepest thanks for her unwavering support and invaluable contributions.

ACKNOWLEDGMENTS

To Jonathan Merkh of Forefront Publishing and his exceptional team, particularly Jennifer Gingerich and Billie Brownell, as well as editor Jodi R. Hughes and proofreader Janna Walkup, we express our gratitude for believing in this project and bringing it to fruition with unwavering dedication and excellence.

Julia Verdin's talents as a screenwriter, producer, and director have served as the guiding light for the film *No Address*. Her wisdom and grace have been instrumental in shaping this book.

We also extend our appreciation to James J. Papa, cowriter of the *No Address* screenplay, who assisted in enriching our narrative with depth and authenticity.

Special thanks to David Hyde for his invaluable support in providing additions to the screenplay for the movie *No Address*.

We extend our heartfelt thanks to Alejandro Guimoye, Shaun Lupton, and Justin J. Clare, whose exceptional editing skills and storytelling prowess on the movie *No Address* greatly influenced the narrative of this book.

Additionally, we extend our appreciation to all those who were part of the background cast, whose presence added depth and authenticity to the world of *No Address*. Those contributions, though often behind the scenes, were essential to the film's success.

Our deepest gratitude goes to our fearless leader and founder, Robert Craig, of Robert Craig Films, whose visionary dedication to the *No Address* project has been paramount. He is strengthened by his family and beloved wife, Natascha, who support him in every way imaginable. Robert's unwavering love for the Lord and his boundless kindness toward humanity serve as the guiding light for all endeavors undertaken at Robert Craig Films. His compassion extends even further to those experiencing homelessness, embodying a true spirit of empathy and generosity toward all in need.

Our thanks go to the exceptional team at Robert Craig Films, whose collective dedication and tireless efforts have been instrumental in bringing the *No Address* project to fruition. Special recognition goes to producers Sally Forcier and Angela Lujan and associate producer Nikki Vogt for their unwavering commitment and invaluable contributions throughout the production process.

We are also deeply thankful to Victoria San Clemente, Christie O'Malior, Kerri Naber, Leigh-Anne Anderson, and Heather Atherton, whose unwavering support and vibrant energy have enriched our team and propelled us forward with renewed enthusiasm.

To the Robert Craig team's spouses and family members of everyone involved: your love, patience, and support have sustained us through long hours and countless revisions.

Heartfelt thanks to Dr. Robert G. Marbut Jr. for his invaluable expertise and insights regarding homelessness, which added authenticity to the movie set and seamlessly transitioned into the pages of this book. His dedication to understanding and addressing the complexities of homelessness enriched the narrative and brought depth to the portrayal of the characters' experiences. His contributions have left an indelible mark on the authenticity of *No Address*.

ACKNOWLEDGMENTS

To the remarkable actors William Baldwin, Beverly D'Angelo, Xander Berkeley, Lucas Jade Zumann, Ashanti, Isabella Ferreira, Ty Pennington, Patricia Velasquez, and Kristanna Loken, who each breathed life into the characters of *No Address*, we thank them for their unparalleled talent and unwavering dedication. Their captivating performances on-screen not only brought the story to life but also inspired the words that now grace these pages.

A special gratitude extends to Ashanti, whose mesmerizing voice brings the *No Address* audiobook to life. Through her beautiful narration, listeners are invited to experience the depth and emotion of this story in a truly unique way.

To my husband and our production consultant, Keith Diederich, whose unwavering support and profound insights have been invaluable throughout the creation of this project. His guidance has helped so many to understand the depth of love, compassion, and empathy that emanates from knowing individuals experiencing homelessness and their untold stories. Keith's perspective has illuminated the reality that homelessness could happen to anyone, fostering a deeper understanding and empathy within these pages.

Lastly, we acknowledge that the *No Address* project is more than just a book or a movie—it is a movement. It is a call to action to break the "no address cycle" that traps so many in our society.

Together with the support of all mentioned here and countless others, may we persist in our pursuit of a world where everyone has a place to call home.

This book stands as the culmination of countless hours of hard work, collaboration, and love. To each and every individual who has contributed, regardless of the scale of their contribution, we offer our heartfelt thanks. It is with profound gratitude that we acknowledge the presence that guided us throughout, knowing that our efforts are empowered by the grace of God.

With gratitude,
Jennifer Stolo
CEO & Producer
Robert Craig Films

Chapter 1

EXUBERANT STUDENTS, most still wearing their graduation caps and gowns, poured out of the high school auditorium and down the steps toward the welcoming arms and beaming faces of parents, grandparents, friends, and other well-wishers.

"You did it!" parents cheered. "We're so proud of you!"

"Congratulations!" others called out. "You're on your way. You're ready to take on the world!" Jubilant voices filled the street as the commencement crowd veered off in various directions, heading to parties, special dinners, or other celebrations honoring the graduates.

Slowly, the crowd thinned until Lauren—a petite, bright-eyed, slender female student, her long brown hair swirling around her shoulders—stood alone on the high school steps. No family members or friends were there to cheer for her. Nobody offered her words of congratulations, bouquets of flowers, gift cards, or positive affirmations about her future.

Nobody.

She gazed out at the deserted street, shifted her diploma from one hand to the other, and picked up the shabby backpack sitting at her feet.

Lauren ambled down the steps and glanced around hoping someone—anyone—might show up to be happy with her.

Nobody did.

She swung the backpack over her shoulders and trudged down the street by herself. Still wearing her graduation gown and grasping her cap and diploma, she walked away from the relative safety of the school. About a mile down the road, she turned into a run-down area of the city dotted with old trailers and small, poorly maintained homes and yards.

Lauren headed toward a small house with paint flaking off the window sills. She hurried through the overgrown weeds and past an old, beat-up pickup truck parked at the side of the house, its bed filled with junk. The house's front windows faced the street and were covered with cheap, dirty-looking curtains in various forms of disarray, concealing the view inside.

Lauren stopped cold before she reached the

front door. The sight that greeted her caused her expression, already sullen, to fall even further. Two large plastic trash bags and some schoolbooks sat piled on the doorstep.

What! What's going on?

Lauren ran up the porch steps and heard the faint sounds of music coming from inside. She tried to open the door, but it was locked, so she banged on it with her fist.

"Why is my stuff out here?" she yelled.

Nobody answered.

She stepped back and looked up toward a window as she thumped on the front door again. "Jade! Jade, I know you're in there! Let me in!"

Jade, Lauren's foster mom—a disheveled, haggard woman in her early forties—pulled back the curtain on one side of the window. She peered out at Lauren, then quickly closed the curtain again, blocking her face from Lauren's view. A few seconds later, the music's volume increased.

"Come on, Jade! Open the door!" She pounded harder and louder, certain Jade could hear her, even above the loud music. "This isn't funny," she railed.

She ran to the side of the house where the gate was usually open.

It was locked too. Lauren beat on the gate, but it didn't budge. "Jade! Please, Jade! Let me in."

She heard the sound of a window creaking open out front, so she ran back to the front porch.

Jade was still hiding behind the curtain, but she spoke coarsely. "Foster care cut me off. They're done paying me for you, so you're on your own now."

"What?" Lauren said. "No! I— What are you talking about? Where am I supposed to go?"

"Not my problem," Jade said. "You graduated high school. Use your smarts to figure it out. Just grab your stuff and go!" She slammed the window shut. The curtain fluttered and then drooped and hung motionless. Jade was gone.

"No . . . Jade, wait!" Lauren's eyes welled with tears as she banged on the door even harder, rapping her knuckles until they bruised. "I hate you!" she yelled toward the window, knowing Jade could hear her.

"I'll report you!" Her chest heaved as she recalled the abusive treatment Jade had heaped on her. Lauren endured it only because she was at Jade's mercy and forced to obey her foster parent's orders. "I'll tell them how you treated me like a servant. I'm going to go tell them right now!" she yelled, hoping her threat might motivate Jade to let her inside. Lauren beat on the door with her palm.

The voice inside the house snapped, "Stop with that noise or I'll call the cops on *you*!"

It wasn't that Lauren's time in Jade's "care," her most recent stop along the foster system's "orphan train," had been pleasant or even comforting. Far from it. Jade made her do all the dirty work around the house, while she sat watching television. Lauren was used to it. She'd been down that road before, since the time she was eight years old.

She banged on the door one last time, then stepped back, her shoulders drooping in despair. She knew all too well that Jade had the advantage, that the state's financial assistance ended when a foster child turned of age, and she was on her own. That was just the way the system worked. Many former foster kids were on the streets. She'd heard the stories. Some turned to prostitution just so they could afford food. Others resorted to robbery or selling drugs to survive. Many didn't survive for long.

"Please, Jade," she pleaded. "I'm sorry. I'll do more chores around the house. I'll do whatever you want. Jade, I'll do anything. Anything you want. Anything you tell me to do. Please. Please, don't make me leave."

No response.

* * * * *

Lauren's mom had given birth to her when she, herself, was quite young and not ready to take on the responsibility of raising a baby. Then her husband abandoned her, and she struggled to make ends meet as a single mother, taking any job she could find. But she loved her daughter and was determined to make a life for them.

Then one day when Lauren was eight years old, she and her mom were baking cookies in their small apartment. Lauren had been capturing the fun by snapping pictures with her new Polaroid camera.

"Ooh, that's going to be a good one!" she'd gushed as a photo developed right before her eyes.

"You and your camera!" Lauren's mom said with a smile.

Lauren moved next to her and held the camera in front of them. She pressed the button, and the camera flashed. A Polaroid selfie.

"Now we'll have one with both of us in it," Lauren cooed. She shook the photograph to make it process faster, then showed it to her mother. *"I love it! I love*

you, Mama."

"And I love you, dear. Come on, now. Let's have some fun." Mama set the temperature on the oven. *"What kind of cookies do you want to make?"*

"Chocolate chip?" Lauren pretended to beg.

"Yes, chocolate chip," Mama agreed. She pulled a large mixing bowl out of the cupboard, and she and Lauren began adding the ingredients—eggs, flour, sugar, vanilla, and chocolate chips.

When everything was mixed up just right, they scooped portions of the cookie dough onto a large baking sheet. Shaping each of the cookies so they would all be the same size, they placed the clumps of dough in neat rows until the pan was full.

"Wait, Mama," Lauren said. *"I want to get a picture of the cookies before and after, but I need more film. I'll be right back."*

She ran upstairs to get more film. That was when she heard a loud crash from the kitchen.

Lauren raced back downstairs, only to find Mama lying on the floor, and the sheet of cookie dough scattered all over the kitchen.

"Mama!" Lauren cried.

But Mama didn't respond.

Lauren crouched beside her mother, then

quickly stood up and stepped back, her eyes wide with fear, as her hands flew to her face. She screamed. *"Mama! Wake up! Mama, please. Oh, God, please help us. Mama, come on."*

But Mama lay silent on the floor amid the mess of cookie dough.

Lauren picked up the photo of the two of them, her last photograph of Mama and her together. She never found out what had happened to Mama. Someone said heart attack at the hospital, but that didn't explain why she and Mama had been having fun together one minute, and the next, Mama was gone forever.

* * * * *

Following Mama's death, since Lauren had no grandparents and didn't know her father, social services placed her in a shelter, and then another, and another. Eventually, the authorities transferred her to a foster home.

Once she was in the system, Lauren bounced around to a series of foster parents. Most possessed noble motives in trying to help, but Lauren was often unruly and difficult. As she grew into her teens, she seethed with anger. She wanted her mother back. She was mad at her father—whoever he was—and at life itself. She often lashed out at the very people who were trying to help her and lost her placement with one set of foster parents after another.

Before long, it seemed the only foster families willing to receive Lauren into their homes were those with questionable motives. They received a monthly stipend from the state meant to help pay for the foster child's needs, including food, clothing, school supplies, and other essentials, but all too often, the adults pocketed the money and the foster kids received little or none of the benefits.

The last few families with whom Lauren had lived treated her as an unpaid babysitter or maid. Some of the adults were verbally or physically abusive. Some scrimped on food, often allowing Lauren to go hungry, especially during the summer when school was out and there were no free breakfasts and lunches provided in the school cafeteria. Even when school was in session, on more than a few weekends, Lauren didn't eat after the Friday school lunch until she returned Monday morning. All the while, her foster parents received money from the state to purchase food for her. Other foster parents insisted Lauren wear worn-out, far from stylish clothes. She didn't notice so much during her early teens, but as her body matured, dressing in Ms. Rummage Sale duds was downright embarrassing.

Lauren hated her existence and trusted no one. She had long since closed off her heart to love, choosing instead to keep up her guard as a protective shield to avoid feeling the hurt of rejection again.

As she entered her upper teens, she grew into an attractive, smart, and perceptive young woman. A volcano of anger still seethed behind her pretty face, ready to erupt at the slightest crack in her emotional veneer, but Lauren learned how to play the game. She knew enough to control her temper and that it was best to be quiet and to do what her foster parents demanded. *Go along to get along.* That was the only way to stay out of their sights, to avoid trouble, and to survive.

When she failed to hold to that pattern and expressed her anger or refused to do the demeaning jobs her foster parents demanded, she landed back in the system, waiting for the next "kind soul" to take her in.

That was how she had been placed with Jade, a childless single woman and last-ditch choice by the foster system. Jade, too, had learned how to work the system, and Lauren was not her first foster child. She'd had a slew of kids before Lauren—all for limited amounts of time, until she got sick of them, bored with them, or they had rebelled against her oppressive demands. Jade also knew when the money ran out on each child she kept in her home. Her benevolence policy was simple: when the money was gone, so was the kid.

Lauren survived at Jade's house for most of her final year in high school simply by keeping to herself, which was no easy feat when Jade forced her to do so many gross chores around the house, whether it was cleaning the commode, scrubbing the floors, or mowing the lawn when city authorities tagged the house for the grass being too high.

Jade often punished Lauren with forced isolation. *"Just stay in your room and don't come out."* That was one punishment Lauren didn't mind. She actually enjoyed reading and studying. She was a good student and hoped an education might buy her a ticket out of poverty and open a door to more.

But now the doors were locked. All of them. And Lauren was on the outside, alone in front of Jade's house. She backed away and slumped down on the front steps, sobbing uncontrollably. Through her tears, she fumbled in her backpack and retrieved her phone. She pressed a button and the phone lit up. Apparently, Jade had forgotten to close the account so Lauren wasted no time. She texted a friend from school: "Can I stay at your house? Jade has locked me out."

No response. She texted a couple other people and waited.

Eventually, she tried the front door again. *Useless.*

Her eyes searched her phone messages. Nothing.

The sun was already going down and the late-afternoon sky was darkening. Lauren stood and, on a whim, walked over to Jade's run-down pickup truck. She tried the door, and to her amazement, it opened. On the floorboard she saw her ragged stuffed bunny, one of the few comforts that had accompanied her from one foster home to another. She clutched the stuffed animal to her chest, curled up on the front seat, and closed her eyes. Maybe if she could sleep for a while, when she woke up, she'd discover it had all been a bad dream.

Hours later, the sunlight bathed Lauren's eyelids, its warm rays streaming through the truck's windshield. Her eyes fluttered open and she gazed around the interior of the vehicle, trying to get her bearings. Why was she scrunched on the front seat of Jade's truck? Her sleep had been fitful and dotted with nightmares, but she must have slept at least a few hours in the darkness, because she hadn't awakened until morning. Slowly, awareness dawned on her, and she pulled herself up in the seat and slid out of the truck.

As a last futile effort, she banged on Jade's door one more time. She received no response. Lauren looked at her phone. Maybe one of the messages she'd sent the night before had evoked a friendly, welcoming response.

Nothing.

Her fingertips flew on the phone's keys: "Please respond! If I can't stay at your place, can I just leave some of my stuff with you for a while till I settle?"

Lauren removed her rumpled graduation gown. Under it, she wore torn jeans and a lilac-colored shirt. She tossed the commencement cap and gown on the doorstep, then started sifting through the trash bags Jade had put outside the front door. She found a few books and an old pair of sneakers. She swapped her dress shoes for the sneakers, stuck her bunny in her backpack, then looked hopefully at her phone. Still no response to any of her messages.

Lauren picked up her bags and headed off, awkwardly lugging the bags on each side of her. She trudged across the walkway of a long bridge spanning a wide river, one bag banging against the rail as traffic whizzed past. Looking out across the deep river below with the huge cityscape beyond, she pulled out her phone and pressed the name of another friend she hoped might help her.

The friend picked up but was reluctant to offer help, so Lauren hurriedly explained her situation, concluding, "Okay, look. I'm totally stuck here. Couldn't I just sleep on your couch? Your floor? Anywhere?"

The phone suddenly went dead. Lauren stared at the screen and shook the phone in annoyance. "Great."

She looked up toward the graying skies and yelled, "Really?"

Lauren shook her head and stared up toward heaven. "Mom was wrong about you," she cried. "You really don't answer prayers, do you?"

Chapter 2

ACROSS THE BRIDGE, Lauren veered down a narrow alleyway between graffiti-covered brick building walls. She continued onto a dimly lit street in a desolate part of the city, carrying all her earthly belongings in the bags at her sides. The street was deserted except for Lauren. A car rounded the corner and she instinctively moved closer to the building and away from the street but made no other motion to indicate she was aware of the automobile behind her.

The car slowed to a crawl and kept pace along Lauren's left side. Loud music blared from the radio as the vehicle inched closer to her. In her peripheral vision, she could see several young men boisterously bobbing in the back seat and another guy in the passenger seat. He rolled down the window and hollered, "Hey there, honey! What you looking for?"

Lauren ignored him.

"Where you goin' lookin' all sad like that? Come on, now. Don't be bashful. We'll take care of you. You might need some help . . . and we can be *very* helpful. We'll take real good care of you." The men in the back seat laughed uproariously at their buddy's crude attempts at seduction.

The car stopped and a couple of the men got out. One pointed at the bags Lauren was lugging. "Looks like you need a hand with those . . ."

She glanced at the men, then noticed a passageway between the buildings ahead, a path that looked too small for a car to drive through. She darted into the dark passage and looked around to see if the men were following her. She breathed a sigh of relief as she watched the men climb back into their vehicle and drive up the street.

Lauren made her way through the narrow path and past a group of homeless people huddled around a fire in a metal can. She quickly skirted them before they said anything to her or gave her much notice. She was simply another lost soul as she trudged up the alley. Someone was yelling profanity nearby. It sounded like two people arguing, but as she peered into the dark alley, she couldn't see their faces.

A gunshot snapped Lauren to attention. She looked around but could see no one. Tears welled in her eyes and trickled down her face. She looked up toward the heavens and whispered, "Why? Why is this happening to me?"

The only answer she received was the chaos of more frightening noises emanating from farther up the alley. She turned away from the scary sounds and headed down a dimly lit side street. Eventually, a large dumpster came into view. It stood behind a building with enough of an open angle that she could slip in between it and the building. She squeezed through and crouched behind the dumpster, shielded by her belongings. Lauren huddled on the ground and used her backpack as a pillow as she cried herself to sleep.

The next thing she heard was the blaring sound of brakes and a loud *beep! beep! beep!* A trash truck was backing up toward the dumpster. She bounded to her feet and grabbed her belongings just as the truck's back door banged open. A large forklift slid under the dumpster and a hook clanked against the heavy metal box as it caught the handles. The truck driver pulled a lever, and the machinery pulled the dumpster off the ground to empty its contents into the truck.

One of the men spotted Lauren and bellowed, "Hold it!" The dumpster jolted to a stop, swinging precariously in midair as Lauren grabbed her things and bolted from her hiding place. She hurried out of the alley without looking back.

On the main street again, Lauren walked down the sidewalk in the daylight. She glanced at a clock in a store window and was surprised to discover it was nearly noon. A neatly dressed businessman approached from the opposite direction, carrying a white paper bag from which he was eating a toasted sandwich purchased at a fast-food restaurant. He seemed to be in a hurry, gobbling as much of the sandwich as he could handle with each mouthful. The man took one last bite, then veered toward a steel, city-owned trash can only a few yards away from Lauren. He stuffed the remainder of his sandwich into the bag and tossed it in the trash as he bustled past her.

It had been more than two days since Lauren had last eaten. Her eyes widened as the man passed her, leaving behind nearly half a sandwich. Her lips tightened, pursed together, and her eyes glistened. She looked at the trash can, and then glanced around furtively to her left, then right, checking to see if anyone was watching her. She looked longingly toward the trash can and licked her lips in anticipation. Moving up to it with a desperate but determined expression, Lauren stopped and dropped her bags on the ground, then poked her head over the receptacle. She stuck her right arm inside the trash can and felt around for the white bag she'd seen the man toss.

Finding it, she yanked the bag out of the garbage, slid her other hand into the bag, and found the half-eaten sandwich. Her eyes darted around again as she pulled out the sandwich and held it before her, gazing at it as though it were a fine delicacy. She daintily picked off a soiled tomato, then raised the toasted bread to her lips and took a tentative bite. She closed her eyes, gulped hard, and began chewing. Nothing had ever tasted so good.

When she finished, she tossed the wrapping back in the trash. Then she reached down and hoisted her black garbage bags and headed farther up the street, on her way to nowhere.

* * * * *

As Lauren walked past the back entrance of an Italian restaurant, she saw a young man who looked to be in his late teens or early twenties rummaging through the dumpster. Lauren slowed and stared curiously at him.

With big brown eyes and a mop of dark curls surrounding his cherubic, dirt-streaked face, he pulled a large to-go box out of the blue dumpster and smiled. Inside was nearly an entire birthday cake—only one triangular piece was missing. He playfully stuck his finger into the frosting, then raised it to his mouth, licking the sugary delight. The young man's eyes brightened, and his smile grew larger as he took a few seconds to savor the taste. Then he carefully placed the cakebox inside a grocery bag along with several other to-go boxes.

Then he saw Lauren watching from the alleyway. They made eye contact for a brief moment. He smiled at her and nodded.

Lauren blushed slightly, embarrassed that she'd been caught staring. She hastily turned her eyes away and continued down the alley. She flopped her bags around on her back and disappeared around the next street corner.

Now on a busy city street, Lauren saw an attractive but weary-looking woman standing on the corner, forlornly waving a handwritten sign that read *Hungry. Need Food.* The woman wore tight jeans and a ripped T-shirt that showed off her muscular body. Shiny military dog tags bearing the name *Violet* jangled around her neck with her every move.

Violet held a drooping bunch of sunflowers in her other hand as she waved her sign up and down, back and forth, trying to get motorists' attention. When she held still for a moment, Lauren spotted the track marks still visible on Violet's arms.

* * * * *

"Evidence of a misspent youth," Violet sometimes told friends.

So far today, she'd received little more than snide remarks and leering catcalls from the people driving by her. A sleek, late-model BMW pulled to a stop near her as the traffic light turned red.

The driver was a man in his late forties, immaculately dressed in a classic dark business suit, highlighted with a colorful tie. He was talking on his cell phone with the window lowered and sounded frustrated.

"Come on. This is Robert. You know me. I always pay up, don't I? Yeah, I know. I know. Just put another hundred on Star Chaser . . ."

Violet had heard similar instructions, but she had no extra money to bet on the horses. If this guy did, maybe he'd pop for some flowers so she could buy some food. She boldly stepped off the sidewalk and onto the street as she approached the BMW. She leaned toward the open window and held out her flowers.

"Hello, sir," she said. "Wanna buy some beautiful flowers for your wife . . . or your girlfriend, maybe?"

The person on the other end of Robert's call hung up. Irritated, Robert turned toward Violet. "Get your dirty hands off my car," he sneered. "I just had it detailed. Can't you see I'm busy? Get off the streets and go get a real job like everyone else."

"I *did* have a real job," Violet retorted. "Protecting this country."

"Sure, you did," Robert said. He swatted the flimsy flowers out of Violet's hand, and they fell in a heap on the asphalt. Violet tried to grab the flowers, but the man quickly raised the car window, stomped on the gas pedal, and sped away before the traffic light turned green. The flowers were crushed under the BMW's rear tires.

Violet stared after the car in disgust. She plopped on the curb like a sack of cement, still trying to save remnants of the flowers that were not crushed. Few remained and those didn't look good enough to sell to people who didn't want the flowers anyway. Tears welled in Violet's eyes, and she fought unsuccessfully to keep them from trickling down her cheeks.

* * * * *

A short distance away, Lauren had watched the entire episode unfold between the man in the car and the woman selling flowers on the street. She gazed at Violet sadly, as though feeling her pain.

Violet looked up and saw Lauren staring. "What are you lookin' at, kid?"

Lauren did not answer, but instead scurried off down the street. With her bags still flapping, she tried to increase her pace as she hurried through the rough section of town.

Too late.

Like hovering vultures, two thugs—one, a muscular guy in his early twenties with a goatee and short red hair, and the other, younger than his friend, baby-faced but vicious—had spotted their prey. Both young men bore distinctive scorpion-RRR tattoos on their forearms, indicating their gang membership. They pretended to barely give Lauren a glance as they passed her, striding in the opposite direction. But then they gave each other a look, spun around, and stepped alongside her, flanking her.

"Hey, beautiful," the redhead said in his best lecherous tone. "Looking for some company?"

Lauren didn't answer, attempting to ignore him and walking faster.

He grabbed her left arm and pulled her toward him. "Hey, I'm talking to you," he glowered.

Lauren shook him off and broke into a run as best she could, weighed down by her cumbersome bags. She felt more than saw the other man run up along her right side.

"You won't talk to him because he's ugly, right? What about me?" He grabbed Lauren's arm and pulled her toward his chest, slamming her body into his.

"Hey! Get off!" Lauren yelled. "Get away from me!" She dropped one of her bags and tried to push the man away from her. He grabbed the other black garbage bag and began waving it around her head, taunting her with it. "You want this?" he asked. "Come and get it."

The heavy bag suddenly split open and Lauren's clothes, books, and other personal belongings flew into the air and spilled out onto the street.

The man howled in laughter as he and the redhead searched through Lauren's things, while still keeping her in sight.

Shocked, Lauren looked down in dismay at her possessions strewn across the pavement. She tried to scoop up as much as she could carry, but then she saw the second man sauntering toward her, waving one of the few pretty dresses she owned.

"I'll bet you look cute in this," he said, flying the dress in front of her, but not close enough for her to reach it. "Wanna put it on for us? Let's see ya."

"What's wrong with you?" Lauren railed. "Just stop it." She whirled around, simultaneously pulling her backpack straps into her hands and whacking the man with the heaviest part of her backpack.

"Ouch!" he hollered, ducking so she couldn't hit him again.

Leaving most of her belongings on the ground, Lauren ran as fast as she could in the opposite direction with nothing but her backpack, trying to get away from the thugs.

"Let's get her!" the redhead growled. Still rubbing the spot where Lauren had decked him, the other man set out after her with his buddy charging closely behind.

Lauren burst around a corner toward an encampment of homeless people. The trampled grass was covered by a variety of colored tents and a few makeshift shacks. Stacks of rubbish littered the ground. A sign on a rusty, corrugated iron fence boasted a Scripture: *"Thou shalt love thy neighbor as thyself," Matthew 22:37.*

Lauren darted through an opening in the fence and gingerly weaved her way around the tents and trash with one of the men hot on her heels. The other had held up abruptly when he saw where she was heading. He scanned the area, then split off and ran toward the side of the encampment.

Lauren ducked under a clothesline stretched between two trees. Six feet off the ground, the cord was covered with an assortment of well-worn clothes, drying in the warm afternoon air. Lauren's eyes widened with alarm as she saw a group of people in front of her sitting around a makeshift table blocking her path.

She vaguely recognized the young man she'd seen earlier digging food out of the dumpster behind the Italian restaurant. A tough-looking man in his fifties with a scruffy gray beard, craggy face, and haunted eyes sat on the ground behind the table. A beautiful woman, slightly older than the man with whom she sat, wore a long, dusty pink coatdress that had obviously seen better days. Her head was adorned with an adorable hat, like one that might have been worn by a female star in an old movie.

To Lauren, the group looked like they were eating and sharing scraps of food around the table. To the left of the table was an artist's easel with a painting of the older woman on it.

Lauren glanced behind her and saw the redheaded man gaining ground, getting closer and closer. Without slowing her pace, she swerved to avoid the table, narrowly missing the beautiful woman in the pink dress, but the move shifted her balance just enough that Lauren bumped the easel, knocking over the painting and causing her to plow through a pile of cardboard boxes stacked behind the easel, scattering them in front of a tent.

"Hey! Watch it!" several in the group called out. The older woman gasped in shock and shrank away from the table. The young man Lauren had recognized jumped up protectively. Seeing that the older woman was okay, he turned and lunged forward to block the thug's path as he charged toward them.

"Hey!" he yelled. "What are you doin'?"

The redheaded man didn't answer but simply shoved him out of his way as he continued his pursuit of Lauren. She had already run farther into the encampment and was headed toward the side street exit. She almost made it.

But not quite. Lurking on the encampment's outskirts, the other thug was watching and waiting to trap her. He tried to cut her off, but Lauren was too fast for him. She veered around him and ran across the street toward an alleyway with the redhead right behind her.

When the handsome, young dumpster diver saw the two thugs chasing the pretty young woman, he ran toward the alleyway too.

"Jimmy!" A man called from somewhere behind her. "Wait!"

"I'll be okay, Harris. Don't worry. I'll be right back."

By then, the redheaded man had caught up to Lauren in the alley. He grabbed her by the shoulders and pushed her face-first against the wall of a brick building. Lauren squirmed and flailed, trying to shove him away from her with little success. Meanwhile, the other thug reached them and grabbed

Lauren's backpack. He rifled through it, searching for anything valuable, then slammed it to the ground, causing Lauren's bunny, diploma, and a few items of clothing to spill out.

He spotted Lauren's cell phone in the back pocket of her jeans and grabbed the phone and stuck it in his own pocket.

The redhead whirled Lauren around to face him. She struggled to escape but both men leered down at her as one pressed his body tightly against hers. The other grabbed her arms to prevent Lauren from slapping or poking at them.

The redhead's voice took on a hideous tone. "You should have been nice to us, pretty girl."

Just then, the other guy—Jimmy—rounded the corner and Lauren looked at him with a silent plea for help. Without a moment's hesitation, he plowed into her assailants, yanking the redhead away from her and knocking him to the ground.

Still holding her against the wall with one strong hand, the other thug pulled out a switchblade with his other hand and brandished it in front of Lauren's face and then toward Jimmy. His movement gave Lauren the opening she needed.

Lauren kneed her captor in the groin with as

much force as she could muster. He winced and doubled over in pain. While still bent over, he glared at Lauren and swung the switchblade toward her but missed.

The redhead struggled to his feet and looked like he was about to charge Jimmy. He probably would have, but from out of nowhere, an older man appeared and jumped into the fracas. He landed a powerful punch against the redhead's nose, sending him reeling backward.

Then he grabbed the other thug's arm and twisted it behind the punk's back, causing him to release his grasp on the switchblade, the knife dropping to the ground a couple feet away. The older man leaned over and grabbed the switchblade with his left hand, while stretching his right arm up and viciously driving the palm of his hand hard into the guy's nose.

His hand flew to his nose even as his knees buckled under him, his body wobbling in the alley. But the older man wasn't done yet. He grabbed him by the hair, raised him up, and put the switchblade against his throat.

"Leave! Now!" he growled. "Before I get mad." He relinquished his grip and gave the man a shove toward the alley entrance.

Still holding his nose, the thug stumbled toward the sunlight shining in from the street. "This ain't over!" he yelled as he backed away, dragging the redhead with him. They exited the alleyway and were gone.

The older man turned toward Jimmy, his fury now directed toward his much-younger friend. "What did I tell you? You should have let me handle it, son."

"But, Harris, they were about to . . ." He looked at Lauren, frightened and disheveled as she crouched near the wall.

Harris cut him off with a wave of his hand. "Shush! Shut your mouth. You gotta be more careful, Jimmy. You could have gotten killed."

Jimmy opened his mouth to respond, but Harris stopped him. "Shut it!" he said again. "Just shut it." He turned and stomped out of the alleyway, back toward the homeless encampment.

Jimmy picked up Lauren's bunny and diploma from the ground while she shoved her clothes inside her backpack. He glanced at the diploma briefly before handing it back to her. He looked whimsically at the bunny, then offered it to her as well.

Tears trickled down Lauren's face. She stashed the

diploma in her backpack, then for several moments, she simply clung to the soiled stuffed animal.

"Are you okay?" Jimmy asked.

Lauren felt around her body. No blood or open wounds. She continued grasping her bunny as her hand felt her back pocket. Empty. She looked in her backpack but didn't find what she was looking for.

"They stole my phone," she said quietly.

"I'm sorry," Jimmy said. "But other than that, are you okay?"

Lauren nodded and sighed wearily. "Yeah. I am, now. Thanks."

"No problem," Jimmy said. "Glad to help. Are you hungry? We got some food over there." He nodded toward the encampment. "And some cake."

She slowly shook her head. "Nah, I should really get going."

"You got somewhere to go?" Jimmy asked.

Lauren hesitated.

Jimmy seemed to pick up on her uncertainty. "Come on," he urged. "We're all nice people. We don't bite."

Lauren wavered pensively for a few more seconds and then nodded.

"You sure you're all right?" Jimmy asked.

"Yeah, fine."

"Are you from around here?"

Lauren looked away and didn't answer his question.

He paused, glanced at her, and waved his hand as though trying to wipe something away. "I'm Jimmy."

Lauren returned his look with a guarded, closed-lipped smile of acknowledgment.

"Sorry if Harris came on a bit strong. He's usually pretty much harmless . . ."

Lauren looked away, then quietly said, "Thanks."

He nodded slightly. "We're over here." He pointed toward the encampment and headed out of the alley toward his friends across the street.

Lauren followed him into an entirely new world.

Chapter 3

STILL SHAKEN from her experience in the alley, Lauren looked around nervously as Jimmy led her through the encampment. They passed two white men, and Jimmy told her their names were Bill and Stevie. They appeared to be in their early thirties and were playing a game, tossing nickels against a wall near an area where several blue tents were set up.

A Black woman who also appeared to be in her thirties was pinning up laundry on the clothesline. She turned and stared at them as they passed, and Jimmy said her name was Jaycee. A skinny golden retriever bounded through some trash and over toward Jimmy.

"Come here, boy," Jimmy called. He wrapped his arms around the dog's neck, then looked up at Lauren and said, "This is Murphy. Don't worry. He doesn't bite either."

Lauren knelt to pet the dog. She placed her hands around the dog's face and looked deeply into its sad eyes. A young woman standing nearby clapped her hands and the dog obediently ran to his owner. Jimmy was on the move again, and Lauren scampered past more tents to catch up to him.

Through some circuitous route, they arrived back at the table where Lauren had first seen the group munching on scraps of food in front of the art easel. Harris seemed more at ease as he sat on a box, strumming a beat-up acoustic guitar. The woman in the pink coatdress stood nearby swaying to the music, her eyes closed, her hands raised and gently waving in the air.

"That's Dora," Jimmy said. "There's some food over there." He pointed toward the three half-empty take-out boxes containing pasta and a few slices of pizza on the table, along with a large portion of a cake. "Feel free to help yourself."

As Jimmy and Lauren approached the table, Dora stopped swaying and stared at Lauren. Harris stopped strumming the guitar and looked at Jimmy quizzically. For a long moment, nobody said a word. Then Dora broke the silence.

"I know you," she said to Lauren. The older woman peered intently at her, her eyebrows furrowed.

Dora continued speaking, more to herself

than to the group. "I do know her. Don't I? Don't I know her?" She turned toward Jimmy. "What's her name again?"

Jimmy looked at Lauren. "Umm . . . "

"Lauren," she said. "My name is Lauren."

Jimmy nodded.

"Oh, Lauren!" Dora gushed. "Thank you for coming to my birthday party."

Jimmy tilted his head slightly and smiled. "Every day is Dora's birthday," he said to Lauren but turned to make sure Dora saw him smiling.

"Oh yes!" Dora said. "And isn't the cake beautiful? Thank you, Jimmy!" She looked toward Lauren and said, "Jimmy brought me the cake. Jimmy, be a gentleman and offer the young lady a seat."

"Yes, ma'am," Jimmy said as he grabbed an old, soiled cushion and placed it on the ground by the table. "Here ya go."

"Thank you," Lauren said, plopping onto the cushion and crossing her legs in lotus position. She smiled as Jimmy sat down nearby on an overturned bucket.

Lauren looked at Dora curiously, unsure what was wrong with the older woman. Despite her current condition and surroundings, she possessed a natural beauty with clear skin and a model's perfect cheekbones. She exuded a sort of regal elegance in the way she looked, moved, and spoke, yet Lauren sensed something wasn't quite right.

"I knew you looked familiar," Dora said to her. "You look just like my roommate when I first arrived in Hollywood." Dora held up an old, scrapbook-style photo album. "I know I have a photograph of her in here somewhere."

Lauren looked around, confused, as she tried to connect the dots between Dora's disconnected statements.

"But you need a place setting for your cake," Dora said. "I've got to find you a place setting." She shuffled off toward the interior of the camp, muttering to herself, apparently in search of a plate and eating utensils for Lauren.

Jimmy started to get up to follow her, but Harris waved him off. Harris nodded in Dora's direction as if to say, *"I'll keep an eye on her."*

Jimmy relaxed and turned his attention back to Lauren. "You just graduated, right? I saw your diploma in the alley."

"Yes, I did," Lauren replied, glancing over at the table then turning her head away. "No big deal," she added sadly.

She and Jimmy traded small talk for a few minutes until Dora came back carrying an old, chipped plate and a plastic knife and fork for Lauren. The older woman also carried her tattered photo album, holding it close to her chest. She handed the plate and utensils to Lauren, then sat down without a word and began thumbing through the pages of old photos in the album. Lauren watched, but Jimmy and Harris gave no impression that Dora was doing anything out of the ordinary—and perhaps she wasn't, for her.

Jimmy picked up one of the take-out boxes of pasta and passed it to Lauren. "Here, have some," he offered.

Lauren drew her gaze away from Dora and eyed the food suspiciously, taking in every detail. She poked her plastic fork into the pasta and took a tentative bite. Except for the discarded sandwich she had retrieved from the trash can, she hadn't eaten in a while, so almost anything would have tasted fantastic at that point. She swallowed the pasta and licked her lips.

"Not bad," she said. "Pretty good, actually."

Jimmy smiled as he watched her devour the remaining pasta in the to-go box.

Jaycee came out of her tent and peered over at the group sitting around the table. "Yo, Jimmy!" she called. "Got any for me?"

"Of course, Jaycee," Jimmy replied. "Come on over!"

Jimmy smiled and Harris nodded when Jaycee hobbled over to the table. She looked much older than her thirtysomething years due to the toll her drug addictions had taken on her body. She'd survived several overdose scares within the past year, and as the unelected enforcer, Harris often warned her to stay away from the stuff. At times, he fretted to the others that it could be dangerous having Jaycee living in the encampment because she refused to obey the rules, both those spoken and unspoken. But beneath his harsh exterior, Harris was softhearted and compassionate. He didn't want to kick out Jaycee unless her staying threatened the safety of the others, and he didn't think they were quite to that point yet.

Jimmy reached out for the rest of the leftover cake and straightened the half-burned candle in the center. "Dig in, everyone," he said. "But first . . ." He turned his back away from Lauren and the others and lit the candle. He then carefully turned toward the group and held the cake with its flickering candle in front of Lauren. "I believe congratulations are in order," Jimmy said with a smile.

"Yay!" Dora yelled. "For me! Yay for me!" Dora clapped her hands and the others joined in her applause.

Jimmy leaned toward Lauren. "It's probably not what you imagined, but happy graduation, anyway! Congratulations!"

Lauren managed a slight smile as the group gathered around her and clapped as though she were the valedictorian.

Jaycee flashed her a smile, revealing two missing teeth as she grabbed another slice of pizza and chomped down on it. "Got yerself a new girl there, have ya, Jimbo?"

Lauren's head snapped up and her complexion turned red. Dora noticed Lauren's embarrassment and put her arm around her protectively, gently pushing Lauren's long brown hair away from her pretty face. Dora looked at Jaycee and then back at Lauren.

"I'm inviting her to be my new roommate," she said. "I knew you looked familiar. Yep, just like my roommate when I arrived in Hollywood." Dora picked up her photo album again and resumed searching through the pages of pictures.

Jaycee took the opportunity to reach into the box and pull out another slice of pizza while nobody else was looking. But Jimmy saw her out of the corner of his eye.

A smile crossed his face. He picked up the take-out box containing the remaining pasta and handed it to Jaycee. "Here, take this," he said. "And give some to Bill and Stevie too."

Jaycee looked back at Jimmy sheepishly. "You're a good one, Jimbo," she whispered. She nodded toward Lauren. "She's lucky to have you," she said loudly enough for the entire group to hear.

It was Jimmy's turn to blush.

Jaycee snatched the box from Jimmy's hand and waddled off to where Stevie and Bill were still tossing nickels against the wall. When they saw Jaycee carrying food in their direction, they gave Jimmy a wave.

Jimmy turned toward Lauren and pointed at Jaycee. "Sorry about that. She's a character, that one is. If she thinks it, she says it."

Lauren started to wave off Jimmy's comment but before any words came out of her mouth, Dora called out from where she was still searching through her photo album. "I know I have a photo of her somewhere." She flipped to the back of her album and frowned. She turned her head and looked up at Lauren. "Well, you really could be her twin. You're much prettier than she was, though. We lived in a lovely apartment complex." Dora leaned in and whispered to Lauren, "She was quite jealous of my career, you know."

Lauren rocked forward on her pillow as Dora continued. "I was so popular back then. I used to go to all the fancy parties and premieres. Oh, they had the best caviar and the champagne flowed like water. And they served the most delicious food you could ever imagine . . . at those parties. I attended . . ." Dora abruptly stopped speaking, tilted her head to one side, and looked around, confused about something.

"I don't know what happened to her," she said. "I lost track of her when I came back here. But oh, she was so pretty. Just like you. We were roommates when I arrived in Hollywood, you know. Did I already tell you that?"

"So you were an actress?" Lauren asked. "For real?"

"Well, I still am," Dora replied in a huff.

"Oh," Lauren backpedaled. "Sorry. I didn't know . . ."

Dora looked around at the others in the group, anxiously searching for affirmation in their faces, a slight frown creasing her own brow. "Harris!" she said. "Harris?" she peered intently at her crusty friend. "Harris, sing me my favorite song. Please get your guitar. I want to hear my song," Dora sounded like a small child begging for a piece of candy.

Harris looked at her with a kind expression on his face. He got up and moved closer to her. "My voice is a little hoarse tonight, Dora," he said. "I don't feel like singin' right now. We'll have more music tomorrow evening. For now"—his voice took on a more formal tone—"please allow me to escort you to your quarters." Harris helped Dora rise to her feet, then took her hand in his and led her to her tent.

Before closing the tent flap, Dora looked back at Lauren. "I'll get things ready for you," she called sweetly. "I'll make everything just perfect for you."

Lauren waved as Dora disappeared inside.

"Was she really a movie star?" Lauren asked Jimmy, who had started flipping through the pages of Dora's photo album. "Or is this all . . . I don't know . . . in her imagination somewhere?"

Jimmy seemed to anticipate Lauren's doubts. "There may be some truth to what she says, but who knows? Harris is the only one round here who's ever seen her in any films. It doesn't matter to us. Dora is a beautiful, sweet soul who wouldn't hurt a fly. The cops picked her up a few months ago. She wasn't doing anything wrong. She was singing in the park and dancing at the theater, over by the big fountain. But they scared her. When she came back, she was like a zombie for several days. All the sedatives they gave her, I think. It broke my heart."

"That's just not right," Lauren said, shaking her head slowly.

"Yeah, she needs to be somewhere safe with people who love her. One day, I want to start a place that takes care of people like her—and you—people who don't deserve to be out here on the streets."

Lauren raised her eyebrows. "Really?"

Jimmy's mouth formed a smile. He walked over to the clothesline and pulled down a sleeping bag. "Take this for tonight," he said, holding the sleeping bag out toward her. "You're in luck. I just washed it. You can sleep in Dora's tent. She keeps her area clean, and you will be safe with her."

Lauren looked toward Dora's tent, then at Jimmy's sleeping bag. "What will you use?"

"I'll be fine," Jimmy said. "Go on. Take it."

He nudged the sleeping bag toward Lauren again. "I know it's not home sweet home, but you'll be comfortable . . . temporarily."

Lauren gave Jimmy a slight smile as she took the sleeping bag from his hands. She leaned over and picked up her backpack before facing Jimmy. "Thank you," she said.

"Yeah, of course." He nodded, and Lauren headed toward Dora's tent. She lifted the flap and disappeared inside.

Inside Dora's tent, Lauren looked around at the woman's few belongings, all neatly organized and placed against the tent walls. Dora was already tucked inside her sleeping bag, fast asleep. Lauren crouched and scooted to the far corner, where she sat and pulled her knees up to her chest. Her eyes filled with tears.

She shook her head and reached into her backpack. Finding her favorite book, she opened its pages to where she had hidden the Polaroid photo of her mom and her making cookies, their last fateful day together. She lay down on the sleeping bag and held the picture in front of her.

"It was always the two of us, Mom," she whispered. "We were going to conquer the world. You were my rock . . . always there for me. I can still hear your voice, feel your touch." The words caught in Lauren's throat. She swallowed hard and continued talking to the photograph. "I loved to watch you cook and I loved how you used to cry at every movie we watched together. You were my heart . . . and I was yours." A large tear trickled down her face. "Mama, I could really use your help now . . ."

* * * * *

For a while the encampment seemed peaceful that night, the only sound emanating from a street sanitation truck with its lights flashing as it swept the streets directly behind the tent-lined area. Suddenly, the calm was broken by Violet, the woman who had been selling flowers on the street earlier that afternoon. She stumbled into the encampment pushing a bicycle, singing at the top of her lungs, and looking decidedly worse for wear, as if someone had attempted to match the rips in her jeans with tears in her shirt. She tripped on a root, caught herself, and then let the bicycle fall to the ground.

Unfazed, Violet sang out, "It's a beautiful day! The sun is shining down on me," despite the fact that it was pitch-black, the only light in the encampment coming from a barrel with the remnants of a fire in it. "Oh, that's the moon!" she said, looking up. "The moon shines down on me . . ."

Harris heard Violet's voice and pulled himself out of his makeshift shack. Dressed only in a T-shirt and frumpy pants, he frowned sternly at her before walking briskly toward her.

Violet saw him approaching and immediately stopped singing and began backing away from him. "Uh-oh!" she said loudly.

Jimmy had heard Violet's song, too, and popped his head out of his tent, rubbing the sleep from his eyes.

Violet continued backing away from Harris. She put her hands high in the air, as though she were being arrested. "Uh-oh," she said again.

Harris lunged forward and covered the ground separating them in a few long strides. Violet attempted to hug him. "H-hi, Harris!" she cooed. Harris pulled out of Violet's hug. He grabbed her arm, pushed up her sleeve, and stared at her needle-scarred skin. "Hmph!" He shook his head in disgust as he saw fresh track marks on Violet's arm.

"No, no, those are old marks," Violet lied.

Harris could barely contain his anger. "You wanna live here, lady, you stay clean. Those are the rules—for me, for you, and for everybody else." He plunged his hand into Violet's pocket and pulled out a small tin. Violet ripped herself out of his grasp and tried to grab the tin from him.

"No, Harris!" she cried. "No!" She slammed into Harris's chest and tried to knock the tin from his fingers, but he kept a firm hold on it. Harris pushed Violet away, but she kept coming at him, fighting to regain possession of the tin.

But Harris wasn't about to back off. Instead, he marched across the encampment to where the fire was still burning in the barrel. Violet ran after him, desperately trying to retrieve the tin. "I promise you, Harris," she cried. "Next week. I'll quit next week. For good. Please, you don't understand. You don't know what I'm going through. I really need it tonight."

"No!" Harris wasn't buying it. "I do understand. You *don't* need it!" He stopped and turned to face Violet. "Look at you!" he growled. "You're a mess." He continued striding toward the barrel with Violet charging after him, flailing at him, trying to knock the tin to the ground.

But Harris was strong. More importantly, he genuinely cared for Violet, and he was unwilling to stand by and watch her destroy herself with drugs. He walked up to the fire barrel.

"Noo!" Violet cried. "Please, Harris! Please! Don't do that to me."

Lauren peeked her head out of Dora's tent. Her eyes were wide with alarm, especially when she saw Jimmy scrambling out of his tent and breaking into a run toward Harris and Violet.

Harris stood in front of the fire and emptied the contents of the tin—syringes and drugs—into the barrel.

Violet screamed hysterically as the flames licked at her stash, melting it all in the fire. She dropped to the ground sobbing. "What'd ya expect from me, huh?" she wailed. "They let me down. People round here treat me like trash and now I don't have much time . . ."

Her words made little sense to anyone but Harris. Nevertheless, despite his concern and compassion for Violet, he refused to go easy on her. She had to beat the habit or it would kill her.

Violet turned and looked up, seeing Lauren watching her from the tents. "What's *she* doing here?"

she said to Jimmy as he joined Harris at the fire barrel. "She ain't gonna last a week out here." Violet glared at Lauren with disdain. "Go home, little girl," she called out to Lauren. "Before it's too late."

"That's enough, Violet," Jimmy said. "I don't think she *has* a home anymore. She's staying with us. That's that. Go get some sleep."

Violet stood and looked at Jimmy, surprised and taken aback by his stern words.

Jimmy waved toward Lauren, signaling for her to go back to sleep. Harris and Jimmy said nothing else. They simply moved off in their separate directions, leaving Violet standing there in the dark, alone.

Chapter 4

JIMMY MEANT no harm in his firm admonition to Violet. It was just his nature to be protective of the people in the encampment, regardless of how they had arrived. Back inside his tent, he tried to fall asleep, but his eyes kept popping open. He remembered all too well his own fear and confusion when he had first found himself without shelter.

Unlike some people who lived on the streets, Jimmy came from relatively affluent, upper-middle-class circumstances. His mother, Liz, had grown up in a wealthy family, and her parents were appalled when she married John, a working-class man who owned a struggling construction business.

Liz's parents had raised her in the Christian faith, and following her marriage to John and Jimmy's birth, she continued attending church regularly, taking the baby with her. John sometimes accompanied them but not consistently. Nevertheless, Jimmy's childhood was filled with warm, happy memories until the age of ten.

That was when John's construction business collapsed, and their comfortable lifestyle blew apart. And that was when all hell broke loose in their home.

With sparse income from construction projects and little money in savings, Liz saw no other option and sought help from her parents—much to John's embarrassment and chagrin. Her parents responded graciously, willing to help, and even paid Jimmy's private school tuition and fees—a gesture that irritated John and caused resentment to fester.

"Doesn't that Bible say that if a man doesn't support his family, he's worse than an infidel?" John railed at Liz. He hated that he couldn't support his family and that he couldn't find work beyond the occasional short-term construction job.

Before long he started drinking heavily, turning to cheap alcohol to drown his sorrows and escape reality. He refused to attend church services with Liz and Jimmy, and even became scornful of their strong, vibrant faith. *"Where's your God when we need Him?"* John taunted. *"If He could turn water into wine, why can't He turn some bricks and mortar into some green dollar bills for us?"* John grew increasingly mean and abusive to both Liz and Jimmy, at first pummeling them verbally and then matching his words with the backs of his strong hands, smacking them around in fits of drunken anger.

Throughout Jimmy's early teens, Liz lived in denial, reluctant to admit how serious the situation was and desperately holding on to the hope that they could turn things around and get back to "normal" once John found better employment.

The family received a bittersweet ray of hope when Liz's parents passed away following a tragic auto accident. Liz inherited their house, a five-bedroom structure in a nice neighborhood. It needed work, but they moved in anyway, anticipating that John could do some of the repairs himself. But he never seemed to find the time to get around to doing them, mostly because he was too drunk to function.

Jimmy loved his mom and had a good relationship with her. When John wasn't around, they enjoyed doing simple things together, such as playing board games or window-shopping in some of the uptown stores where Liz used to shop. But Jimmy could also see how blind Liz was to John's abusive personality.

By the time he turned sixteen, Jimmy had started to stand up to his father and tried to protect his mother from John's verbal and physical abuse. Their world changed again one night when Jimmy and Liz were eating a casual evening meal together and John came home in a drunken rage.

"Where's my beer?" he roared at Liz. *"Get me a beer!"* he demanded.

"You drank it all," Liz replied without even looking up from her plate.

That was a mistake.

John grabbed Liz by the arm and yanked her out of her chair. Her other arm bumped the plate and her drink, sending them flying off the table and smashing to the floor. Liz stumbled awkwardly to her feet with John's strong grip locked on her arm.

Jimmy leaped up and pushed his way between John and Liz, trying to protect his mother. The intervention took John by surprise, and he loosened his grip on Liz long enough for her to escape. Then he turned his fury on Jimmy and swung his fist into his son's stomach, sending him reeling against the countertop. Whether it was from the blow or the force of hitting the counter, Jimmy ended the night in the hospital with several broken ribs.

In another encounter John broke Jimmy's arm, and as a result of several other violent incidents, Liz, too, spent more than one night in the hospital's emergency room. Regardless of John's abusive actions, Liz refused to call the police, file a report, or take any other action against him. After a particularly horrendous outburst, Jimmy finally struck a bargain with his mom.

"If he threatens you again in any way," Jimmy implored, *"we will leave together and find our own place to live. Okay, Mom?"*

Liz reluctantly agreed. From then on they kept a getaway bag packed and ready in the kitchen pantry. *"But don't worry, Jimmy,"* Liz said. *"John told me he was sorry and asked me to forgive him. I'm sure he won't do it again."*

But he did.

A week or so later, on a rainy night as Jimmy and Liz were sitting down to dinner at home, John showed up drunk again. Opening and slamming cupboard doors, he stumbled around the kitchen, searching for a bottle of whiskey he'd been drinking earlier.

"Where's Jack?" he yelled. His face was flushed, and his voice rose in volume. *"Where's my best friend, Jack Daniels?"* John slammed his arm on the table, and swept some dishes filled with food off the table and onto the floor.

Liz grabbed John from behind. "John! Stop it! Please!"

John whirled around, his fist already balled, and struck Liz viciously in the chest, causing her to lurch backward.

Jimmy jumped in to defend and protect his mom. Trying to shove his dad away to no avail, he mustered his courage and took a wild swing at his father, connecting a strong left hook to John's jaw.

Already off-balance, John dropped to the floor.

"Mom, run!" Jimmy yelled. He grabbed Liz's hand and pulled her toward the door. As they passed by the pantry, Jimmy reached around the doorway and grabbed Liz's getaway bag. He dragged her out the front door and onto the sidewalk. Liz followed reluctantly.

John stumbled to his feet and jolted from one piece of furniture to another, banging into them as he made his way to the front door. He opened it and stood in the doorway, his arms stretched out, bracing himself against the woodwork. *"Come back here!"* he bellowed. *"Come back here right now or you're really gonna get it!"*

Liz turned to look back, barely able to hold back her tears, but Jimmy grabbed her hand firmly and tugged her up the street. *"Come on, Mom!"* he implored.

John stormed after them, his feet sloshing through rain puddles on the road as he spewed profanity at his wife and son, yelling threats about what he was going to do to them when he got his hands on them.

Jimmy and Liz rounded the street corner, and Jimmy ducked behind a dumpster, pulling Liz with him. They crouched low to the ground to avoid being seen. A few minutes later, they heard sounds of heavy breathing as John charged past the dumpster in pursuit.

"Whew," Jimmy whispered. *"That was close."* He peeked his head around the edge of the dumpster and saw John looking up and down the street, then forging off to the right. Jimmy turned to Liz, motioning with his hand. *"Okay, he's gone. This way, Mom. Quick. Follow me."* Jimmy reached for Liz's hand and tried to pull her with him as he headed in the direction opposite of the way John had gone. He felt Liz pull back, so he stopped.

Jimmy looked behind him, nervously making sure John had not changed his course, then looked at his mother. Liz stood frozen, as though she'd turned into a pillar of ice.

"Mom, what's wrong? What are you doing?"

Liz stared back at Jimmy with a scared, pained expression. *"Jimmy, I can't,"* she said quietly. *"I can't leave him. I just can't. He needs me."*

"Mom! Please!" Jimmy pleaded. "I *need you.*" He leaned toward her and spoke rapidly. *"We can get that small place together like we talked about. I'll get a job. Don't worry. I'll take care of you. We can come back and get our stuff when he's out of the house . . ."*

Tears fell from his mother's eyes as she shook her head. *"Let's just go back,"* she said. *"This was probably my fault. I shouldn't have confronted him. I got in his way, and he reacted instinctively. He's been so good lately. . . ."* She winced slightly as she continued making excuses for John's behavior. *"I'll talk to him, Jimmy,"* she said. *"He'll be better. I know he will."*

Jimmy's eyes welled with tears. *"No! No, Mom, he won't be better. Not until something changes on the inside. Mom, please don't do this,"* he begged. Jimmy pulled down his shirt collar, revealing a large purple bruise forming on his neck. *"Is this what you want for me? Last time he hit me, I thought I'd never walk again. And how many times have you been in the hospital ER?"* Jimmy reached for his mother's hands.

"You promised me if he ever did it again . . . that we'd both get out, that we'd leave . . ."

"I know," Liz said softly, but she didn't move. Her lips trembled.

Jimmy looked at her, tears overflowing his eyes and trickling down his face. *"Mom, you promised."*

Liz opened her bag and pulled out all the cash she had been hiding. She handed it to Jimmy. *"Go stay at Aunt Nancy's place across town for a few days, and I'll straighten this out with John,"* she said.

"Mom, no!" Jimmy handed the money back to his mother, but she wouldn't take it. *"Come on, Mom. You and me. Our own place . . ."* Jimmy begged. *"I don't want to stay with Aunt Nancy or anyone else."*

Liz leaned in and hugged him. She then turned and slowly walked back toward the house.

Jimmy stared after her in disbelief. *"Mom. Mom! No! Don't!"* he called to her again.

Liz did not stop walking.

The rain fell freely, mixing with the tears streaming down Jimmy's face as he watched his mother continue back toward her hellish existence in their house. He peered through the darkness for a few more minutes, but Liz did not change her course, and she did not come back.

Jimmy shrugged, lowered his head, and wiped the tears and rain from his face. With few other options, he slowly walked back home. He trudged up the steps and took a deep breath, then turned the doorknob and stepped inside.

John heard the door click shut and was all over him again in an instant. *"You're worthless!"* he roared, grabbing Jimmy by the shirt and twisting him around.

Liz ran into the room and seemed almost surprised to see Jimmy there. *"Jimmy!"* she blurted.

Enraged and drunk, John spewed another blitz of profanity toward both Liz and Jimmy. Then, still grasping and glaring at Jimmy, he yelled to Liz, *"Do you seriously think this kid is worth saving?"*

"John, please!" Liz begged.

Jimmy turned his head away from his father, trying to remove himself from John's clutches. *"Just calm down,"* he begged his dad. *"You're out of control. Take a step back."*

"You *take a step back!"* John roared. But even as he said the words, John tightened his grip on Jimmy. *"You're an embarrassment!"*

His words seared into Jimmy, spurring him on. He struggled to break free, and after a brief scuffle, was able to escape John's grip. The father and son stood staring at each other like two wild animals waiting to see who would make the first move to launch another attack.

John leaned forward menacingly. *"Get out of my sight,"* he growled.

"John, stop it!" Liz pleaded again.

Jimmy ran into the kitchen, pausing long enough to use the back of his hand to wipe away the blood dripping from his nose. He ran through the kitchen, into the main part of the house, and up the stairs to his room. He slammed the door and locked it, then grabbed his backpack, and started stuffing some clothes and other essentials into it.

He was nearly finished when John stumbled up the staircase and began pounding on the bedroom door. *"Open this door!"* he roared as he leaned heavily against it. *"Open this door . . . or else!"*

Jimmy threw his backpack over his shoulder and did as his dad demanded. He abruptly opened the door, causing John to lose his balance and trip inside the doorway. Jimmy took advantage of John's alcohol-impaired reflexes to shove past his dad and out the door. He saw Liz standing in the hallway with a terrified expression on her face. Jimmy kept moving past his mom, then stopped at the top of the staircase long enough to look back at her.

"Please, mom," he said. *"Please, come with me."*

Liz stood motionless, apparently immobilized by her fear. John staggered out of the bedroom and into the hallway. She glanced at him, then back to Jimmy, her eyes glistening with tears. She shook her head from side to side in small motions. *"I can't, Jimmy,"* she said. *"I just can't."*

Jimmy gave her one last look, nodded, and flew down the stairs and out the door. This time, he would not come back as long as John was there. He was sixteen years of age, with no money, no high school diploma, no discernible job skills, and no place to go.

* * * * *

Devastated, he didn't know what else to do but walk, so he did. He wandered the streets in the rain, alone and afraid, but too proud—and too afraid—to go home. He felt let down, rejected, and abandoned by his mother, sad she had chosen his abusive father over him. He walked for a couple hours, all the way into the city. He walked until he could stay awake no longer, and when he saw an isolated park bench,

Jimmy sat down, then curled up on it and fell asleep.

A few hours later, he felt something shaking his shoulder. *"Son, wake up,"* a gruff but kind voice said.

Jimmy's eyelids popped open and for a moment, fear gripped him as he couldn't recall where he was. Then he heard the voice again. *"This is no place to be sleeping,"* a man said. *"It's after midnight and it's too dangerous."*

Jimmy looked up into the craggy face of a gray-haired, full-bearded, slightly balding man wearing a dark work shirt and an orange neckerchief under a beige overcoat. The older man reached his hand toward Jimmy's shoulder and helped him as he slowly slid up on the park bench.

"Ooh, I was really out," Jimmy said.

The older man nodded. *"Let's get you out of here. My friends and I have some shacks and tents across the way there. You can rest and get out of the weather."*

Jimmy stood. He'd never met this man before, so he had no idea if he could trust him. But at this point, the man's offer was Jimmy's best option.

"Thanks," Jimmy said. "I'm kinda cold out here."

"I know that feeling," the man said. He extended his hand toward Jimmy. "Harris is the name. You?"

"Jimmy."

"Good to meet you, Jimmy," Harris said. "Let's get you someplace warmer to sleep."

"Okay," Jimmy said.

"Have you eaten?" the older man asked.

"Not today."

They stepped out of the street and walked toward a park area farther down the neighborhood. "We'll find you something," Harris said.

Chapter 5

HARRIS LED Jimmy to a grassy area behind some large warehouses. Shielded from the elements by the buildings' walls, numerous tents and makeshift shacks had been erected, some made from pieces of scrap wood, some roofed with cardboard or plastic. A short distance from the tents stood a barrel with a small fire burning inside. Although it was the middle of the night, several people huddled around the fire.

Harris found some food in his shack, and Jimmy gobbled it down as they talked and warmed themselves around the fire. Jimmy liked Harris immediately and for some reason found it easy to trust him. He listened intently as Harris told his story.

Born Benedict Robert Harris and now in his early fifties, Harris hailed from a middle-class family. His father had served in the US military in a fairly high position—Harris was never really sure of his father's responsibilities—but their family had moved around quite a bit when he was young, and he grew up well-educated and well-read. As a boy, he loved going to see movies at the local theater; the stories fascinated him. He also loved music and taught himself to play guitar. As he got older, he became interested in art and excelled at painting and wood carving. Even as a teenager, he sold several of his paintings—both oils and watercolors—to connoisseurs who perused his work at local high school exhibitions. Harris dreamed of one day seeing his works displayed in a bona fide art gallery.

He married his high school sweetheart and hoped to carve out a career as a professional artist, but then duty called. The United States became embroiled in the Iraq War, and with his father's legacy looming over his shoulder, Harris left his young wife and their newborn baby and went off to war.

His experiences in Iraq were horrific, leaving him with images he could not forget, no matter how hard he tried. He returned home after two years with his body intact but with a severe case of PTSD. Night after night, in bed with his wife, he awakened in a cold sweat, soaking his side of the bed. Nightmares plagued him as his brain replayed over and over again the traumas he'd encountered. Simple things often triggered strong emotional and physical reactions.

He tried support groups, professional counseling, and strenuous exercise. Try as he might, the wounds he carried within refused to heal.

Exacerbating matters further, his wife couldn't cope with his PTSD. *"Harris, I'm leaving,"* she told him one day almost a year after he'd returned. *"And I'm taking our son with me. We can't live like this."* She left with their three-year-old son and cut Harris out of her life. Within months of their divorce she'd remarried, obtained full custody of their child, and refused to allow Harris to see his son.

Her actions hurt Harris even worse than the trauma of war in a foreign land. He turned to drugs to help him cope with his anxiety and depression resulting from the PTSD, at first seeking legal prescription medications, then anything he could find that would dull the nightmares, ease the pain, and temporarily remove him from reality.

A smart man, Harris recognized he was headed in the wrong direction. It took him several years, but he finally kicked the habit, and with the help of a counselor, discovered better, healthier ways to cope with his demons. He learned to control his temper and impetuous urges. He poured his energy into his paintings and wood carvings and was able to bring in a few bucks in addition to providing an outlet for his emotions.

Just about the time things were turning around in Harris's life, his house caught fire and burned to the ground. Harris had not carried insurance on the home, thinking he'd only be living there a short time after the divorce, so with little income and no place to live, he ended up sleeping in a homeless encampment. He'd spent a lot of his time in the military living in a tent, so he actually felt quite at home. In a weird way, he enjoyed the freedom afforded by owning nothing but a tent or a shack. He spent his time painting and playing guitar, the sales from his paintings providing enough income to survive.

* * * * *

About a year after Harris became homeless, he met Dora, a beautiful woman he recognized as an actress from some of the movies he had seen during his youth, in the encampment. Dora seemed easily confused and disoriented and on the verge of dementia, so as Harris got to know her better, he became increasingly protective of her. He refused to allow anyone to take advantage of her.

Originally from Sacramento, Dora had gone to Hollywood to seek fame and fortune as an actress. She found it harder than she had anticipated to catch a break in the movie business and spent most of her early auditions fending off unwanted sexual advances from producers and film company executives.

But Dora was a good actress and once she learned the system, she landed a few roles in low-budget films based on her merits, not merely her looks. It was a start. Between roles, she worked as a waitress and took almost any kind of part-time job she could find to pay her bills.

As she got older, directors still selected Dora for roles in their movies, but she developed problems with memorizing her lines or remembering them once she'd learned them. As time went on, Dora received fewer and fewer calls.

When she ran out of money and couldn't pay rent, she hitched a ride back to Sacramento. Back home, she discovered her mother was in a memory care unit in a nursing home and could hardly remember who she was, much less remember her daughter. Dora searched in vain for former friends and acquaintances in her hometown. She found none. With no money and few opportunities, Dora soon found herself living on the streets.

When Harris met Dora, he had recognized her immediately and was stunned by her striking beauty. He turned out to be one of the few people in the encampment who had actually *seen* Dora perform on the big screen. Yet he wasn't in awe that she had once been a Hollywood star. He appreciated her quiet sophistication and realized that she was a dignified woman struggling to cope with life on the streets.

"Stay close to me, Dora," he'd told her. *"I'll help you."* Harris took Dora under his wing and cared for her deeply. They developed a strong friendship based on mutual love, respect, and genuine concern for each other's well-being.

Now in her early sixties, Dora's memory loss seemed more severe, but she maintained a sweet, kind, gentle disposition and had an almost childlike attitude. She had difficulty taking care of herself, though, and relied heavily on other members of the group to keep her from getting lost anytime she left the encampment, and sometimes, even within the rows of tents. Most people who knew Dora were happy to help her because they genuinely loved her.

* * * * *

Harris also met Violet in the encampment. A smart Black woman a few years younger than him with a military background as well, Violet had natural mechanical abilities, skills she used to fix bicycles to earn enough money to purchase food. Unfortunately, Violet struggled with addiction as Harris had in his past. When she wasn't fixing bicycles, she spent her days walking up and down the main streets, trying to sell flowers to motorists stopped at the traffic lights.

Similar to Harris, Violet came from a working-class family. Her father had served in the US Army, and she loved to hear his stories about his military career. Violet grew up surrounded by patriotism with a tremendous respect for the nation, the flag, and all things military, so her family and friends had not been surprised when Violet enlisted in the US Marine Corps as soon as she turned eighteen.

She trained hard and quickly moved up in rank. The Marines became her life. When deployed to Iraq, she joined the Lioness Program, in which the Marines attached female soldiers to combat units to search Iraqi women and children who might be trying to smuggle money, weapons, or even bombs through security checkpoints.

Friendly to a fault, Violet knew on a first-name

basis many of the children who went through the checkpoints frequently. She was devastated when she allowed a child through without searching her thoroughly. The child had carried a bomb hidden on her body under her clothing. The bomb detonated, killing the child and a number of Violet's fellow Marines. Violet survived the blast but returned home with a severe case of guilt and PTSD.

She attempted to self-medicate, numbing her feelings of despair with an increasing amount of drugs. The military police caught Violet procuring illicit drugs and she was dishonorably discharged from the service. She felt rejected and angry that the system had let her down, that despite her failures, the military had some responsibility to help take better care of her. She had risked her life for her country—and nearly died in Iraq—yet that one mistake marred her record and reputation inexorably and irrevocably.

The shame she suffered for the attack and her subsequent dependence on drugs to survive drove her away from her family, especially her father. She ended up on the streets where she met Dora and Harris. Still strong and in good physical condition, Violet's body sported numerous colorful, attention-getting tattoos—"in all the right places," as she liked to describe them. Despite her tough exterior, she had a good heart. She was sensitive and easily hurt. To mask her pain, she continued using drugs even when her bicycle repairs brought in barely enough money for food.

Dora loved Violet and didn't judge her for her actions. Harris understood her anger and tried his best to help her. He succeeded in getting her to stop using, but it was a constant battle for her to stay clean—a battle she didn't always win.

As Dora and Violet and others in the encampment became more familiar with Harris, they began to rely on him. His natural leadership skills combined with his artistic personality allowed him to exercise a much-needed authority in the camp. He laid out strict rules for the people living together in their section of the encampment, including no defecating or urinating outside near anyone's tent or shack and a no-tolerance policy for drug use. None.

That put him at odds with Violet, who, although she was functioning better by the time Jimmy showed up, still relapsed occasionally, causing Harris to get angry despite his sincere fondness for her. But Harris refused to give up on Violet and supported her through her withdrawal symptoms every time she made the effort to stay clean.

Before long, Harris developed a fatherly sense of responsibility for the people living around him. Under normal circumstances he controlled his temper, but when his street family was in danger, he was not afraid to step in and fight to protect them.

Jimmy hadn't known any of that his first night in the encampment, but he learned quickly. He grew to trust Harris as a man of integrity and saw in him the father figure he had never known, a man who offered gentle but firm guidance.

Thanks to Harris, Jimmy swiftly adapted to surviving on the streets. He found odd jobs such as cleaning shop windows or sweeping for local business owners to earn enough money for food and other necessities. Whether because of pride or his personal dignity, Jimmy avoided accepting handouts; he preferred to work for what he needed, rather than beg.

His curly dark hair, bright brown eyes, and handsome appearance coupled with his winsome, upbeat personality caused people to gravitate to him. Most people he met genuinely liked him.

Soon, Jimmy befriended a number of local

business owners who were willing to give him extra supplies to share with others in the encampment. Like Harris, Jimmy regarded the people in the encampment as family, especially Dora, Violet, and Harris. He was quick to share whatever he could scrounge. Almost every day, he boldly attempted to wrangle some extra food from local restaurants that he could pass along to his family in the encampment.

When he couldn't get donated food from restaurants, he scoured the dumpsters behind the establishments, searching for scraps of food that were still edible. He was amazed at how much food people who dined in upscale restaurants didn't eat and threw away. Jimmy grabbed those and took them back to the encampment.

On the darker side of his personality, Jimmy possessed an easily triggered temper, especially when it came to confronting injustices. He often flew off the handle and got himself into jams with some of the drug pushers and others who were looking for opportunities to take advantage of vulnerable people.

Harris helped Jimmy keep his temper under control by sharing tips he had learned and encouraging Jimmy to pause and breathe through his anger. *"Take four or five deep breaths and slowly let them out,"*

Harris taught him. *"That will gain you some time and give you some perspective."* Sometimes Harris's tips worked for Jimmy and sometimes they did not.

When he met Lauren, it had been more than two years since Jimmy had left his comfortable home for life in the encampment, but he had no regrets. He had found his family.

Chapter 6

THE SUN had barely begun to peek through the clouds still covering the encampment after a rainy night when Robert, the well-dressed man who had swatted away Violet's flowers the previous day, stood on the sidewalk on the outskirts of the tents and shacks making up the encampment. He wore a sharp, well-pressed gray business suit with a bright tie and dark sunglasses as he peered into the encampment from the street.

A late-model luxury car pulled up on the street next to where he stood. His boss, Claudia—a slim, statuesque Black woman in her forties wearing closely coiffed hair and a designer business suit with matching designer sunglasses—lowered the window.

"Get in," she said curtly.

Robert bounded around the front of the vehicle, opened the passenger door, and hopped into the seat.

"You've got five minutes," Claudia said. "Tell me what you've got here."

Taken aback by her brusque demeanor, Robert let out a sigh and spread his hands in the direction of the homeless encampment. "Well, okay. This is it. Check it out. You'll have to visualize, okay?"

He turned his body to face Claudia and pointed past her toward the encampment. "Just look at this! The possibilities are endless. It's the perfect spot for a luxury condominium complex."

Claudia twisted her mouth as she surveyed the old buildings and plot of land adjacent to it, where the homeless encampment stretched out in front of them.

"I don't see it," she said more to herself than to Robert.

Excited, Robert interrupted her thoughts. "Claudia, the possibilities here are *huge!* I've already checked. We can buy this land at the commercial property auction for pennies on the dollar, a fraction of its value."

Claudia raised two fingers to her cheek. "I don't know, Robert," she said. "Look at all that trash." She turned sideways in the driver's seat and pointed at the tents and shacks. A short distance away, smoke wafted through the air from a still-burning fire in a trash can. "No one will want to be around that mess. . . ." Her voice trailed off as she seemed lost in thought.

"I'm already working on it," Robert gushed. "I've got that under control. I'm going to have a team go in there. A cleaning crew will get it sorted out. All that debris will be gone soon." Robert rubbed his palms together. "We'll have that trash cleaned up in no time."

Claudia looked back at Robert and spoke coldly, "No, I meant the *human* trash. The people. How are you going to get rid of *them*?"

"Claudia, this is a rare find, a real gem," he said. "We can make a fortune."

Claudia stared out the window at the smoke rising from a barrel within the camp. "This is going to be a drain on time and resources," she said. "It looks to me like another one of your hairbrained schemes."

"You gotta let me run with this," Robert urged. "It's gonna be huge, I promise."

Robert fidgeted nervously in the passenger seat. He had not been performing well at work recently and was wallowing in a wash of misspent money, both his own and the company's. He knew Claudia's ruthless reputation, her demand for results. She was his boss, and he'd heard her express her views many times in the real estate office. *"It's money alone that motivates me,"* she'd often said, *"and there are no moral lines I wouldn't cross to get it."*

"Don't worry, Claudia," Robert said. "I'll talk to the city planners. Just trust me. We'll make a killing. I'm talking millions!"

Claudia removed her sunglasses and cast her eyes over the stretch of land again. She wrinkled her nose. "It stinks," she said. "I mean it literally smells around here . . . I'm not sure. This one feels too time-consuming."

Robert boldly put his hand on his boss's arm. "Just let me handle everything," he said. "Trust me. This is going to be big, really big. I promise you."

Claudia shook her head and scowled. "Yeah, yeah. How many times have I heard that?" she chided. "Get this place cleaned up within the next week, and I'll think about it. But if you mess up again . . ." Claudia paused and looked directly at Robert. "You're out. More than that, you're gone."

Claudia pressed the door locks, clicking the door open.

Robert took the cue and jumped out of the car. He started to say something encouraging and wave goodbye to his boss, but she was already driving off.

Still, she had come. She had seen with her own eyes what he'd been telling her about. That was a major development. Robert pumped his fist in the air as he watched Claudia's car round the corner.

Chapter 7

LATER THAT morning, Jimmy hastily stepped into an alleyway lined on both sides with tall brick buildings. Lauren followed him, hurrying to keep up. She wore the same clothes she had worn the previous day, a lilac top and torn jeans. The outfit had seemed cool the day before, but today it looked rumpled after she'd slept in it on the ground.

They walked through a playground where there were several large swing sets. Jimmy walked over to a swing and sat, and Lauren took the one next to him.

"Sorry about last night," Jimmy said as they gently swung back and forth. "You didn't see us at our best."

"It's okay," Lauren said. "I appreciate you being so kind to me."

"If you don't mind me asking," Jimmy ventured, "how did you end up out here?"

Lauren kicked her feet up to swing a little

higher. She looked over at Jimmy and said, "This is just temporary."

Jimmy nodded, his eyes still begging the question.

Lauren looked down at the ground and spoke quietly. "I lost my mom when I was eight," she said. "I never knew my dad, and I had no relatives who wanted me, so the state put me with some people I didn't even know."

"You were in the system?" Jimmy asked with a concerned look on his face.

"Yeah. They moved me six times in the last ten years. Until my foster parent didn't need me anymore."

Jimmy shook his head. "I've seen too much of that."

"What about you?" Lauren asked. "How did you land out here?"

Jimmy grunted. "Believe it or not, for me life out here is an improvement, compared to what I left."

Lauren scrunched her nose and looked at Jimmy in surprise but didn't probe any deeper for information. They swung in somber silence for a few minutes, and then Jimmy abruptly hopped up. "We should go," he said.

Lauren hopped off her swing and stood face-to-face with him. "So what happens now?"

"Let me show you around," he said.

Lauren cocked her head slightly to the left. "Sure. Why not? It's not like I have to be someplace."

Jimmy nodded with a hint of a smile.

They walked farther up the street, on the backside of a retail section of town. A sign, *Fresh Baked Pastries*, swung gently in the breeze behind a bakery. Jimmy headed toward the door below the sign.

"Come on. I bet you're hungry." He stepped up to the back entrance of the bakery and signaled for Lauren to wait outside as he pushed open the screen door and popped his head inside.

"Hey, Michelle!" he called.

"Hi, Jimmy," a woman in her early forties answered him. Wearing a blue-and-white striped baker's apron smeared with flour, Michelle stepped away from an oven and toward the counter. She picked up two large brown bags filled with bagels and several cheese croissants. "These are a day old, but they are still fine," she said. She handed the bags to Jimmy and smiled. "I just had one myself about an hour ago. Tasted pretty good!"

Jimmy smiled back at her. "Thanks, Michelle.

You're the best. See you next Monday." Jimmy gave Michelle a brief hug and then rejoined Lauren. Her eyes widened when she saw the two bags full of pastries.

Jimmy reached in and pulled out two cheese croissants. He handed one to Lauren and took a bite out of the other. They munched on the croissants as they made their way through the alley.

"Oh, these taste great," Lauren said.

Jimmy smiled. "Come on. There's more." They passed an open door, the back entrance to an Italian restaurant. Jimmy held up his hand to stop Lauren. "Best Italian food in town," he quipped. But he didn't step inside the door. Instead, he walked over to the dumpster behind the restaurant, where he found two take-out boxes strategically placed on the side of the dumpster where he might find them. Jimmy handed the bags of bagels to Lauren and reached up to grab the pasta-laden take-out boxes.

"You can eat pretty well around here if you know where to look," he said. He took one of the bags of bagels from Lauren.

Her eyes brightened. "Well, your food last night was better than the leftovers in my foster mom's fridge. That's for sure."

Jimmy smiled, seeming pleased that Lauren had enjoyed the food he'd provided—although rather indirectly.

"I need to make a few deliveries," he said, "and then I'll help get you get sorted out." He offered his hand to Lauren. "M'lady," he joked.

Lauren laughed and playfully swatted Jimmy's hand away. He grinned back at her before breaking into a trot through another rundown alleyway, carrying the pasta in one hand and a bag of bagels in the other with Lauren following close behind, carrying the other bag of bagels. They rounded a corner and headed toward Jimmy's route of established "rounds."

* * * * *

Meanwhile, a woman in her late thirties wearing a below-the-knee-length skirt and a drab cardigan sweater looked around nervously as she crossed the street and cautiously approached the homeless encampment. Her shoulders and her face were pinched with a pain that defied physical treatment. As she stepped into the encampment, she spotted Violet putting a new tire on an old bicycle out in front of her tent.

The woman raised her hand and waved at Violet timidly. "Excuse me," she called out.

Violet rose from where she had been working and turned toward the woman, moving closer to her and straightening her body to face her, still carrying the metal tire tool in her hand.

Flustered, Liz backed away instinctively and then regained her composure. She looked at the tire iron and then toward Violet and waved her hands defensively. "Can I have a moment of your time? Can I just ask you a question? It's ahh . . . it's extremely important . . ."

Rather than fumble over her words any further, she reached into her purse and pulled out an old photo of a much-younger Jimmy. She held the picture up toward Violet so she could see it. "Is there any chance you may have seen this boy?" the woman asked, her voice trailing off. "Have you seen him? I'm his mother."

Violet looked at the photo and although she recognized Jimmy, she held her facial expression stoically firm, giving the woman no sign of hope. "Nah. I ain't seen him," Violet said curtly. "Lots of people around here. Hope you find him, though." She turned back to the bicycle tire.

Liz sighed sadly and carefully tucked the photo of Jimmy back inside her purse. She started to walk past Violet, then spotted several used syringes on the ground and attempted to avoid walking on them. Stepping awkwardly, she lost her balance and bumped into a gas can at the side of Violet's tent. The can toppled over.

Like an acrobat, Violet leaped toward the gas can and set it upright before any of the precious fuel could escape.

"Hey! Watch where you're walkin', lady! That's our stuff," Violet huffed.

"I'm sorry," Liz said. "I'm so, so sorry." She hurried out of the encampment and back to the perceived safety of the street.

* * * * *

About that same time, Jimmy and Lauren turned into another deserted alleyway, carrying their bags of bagels and croissants and the take-out boxes. They walked farther until they neared several messy, barely put-together tents. Jimmy looked at Lauren and nodded toward the ground. "Be careful where you step," he whispered.

Lauren looked down and saw numerous empty syringes littering the ground. She looked back at Jimmy and nodded. They stepped carefully to the front of one of the poorly assembled tents. A skinny, ragged man who appeared to be in his thirties was dressed in several layers of dirty sweaters and lay stretched out on the ground in front of the tents, wallowing in his own urine. Jimmy leaned down toward him and offered him a bagel. The man made no response and didn't take the food, so Jimmy placed it on a dry spot beside him.

The man mouthed *"Thank you,"* to Jimmy but did not speak.

Two sickly looking women with grimy faces huddled together in front of another tent. Jimmy offered them some bagels as well, but they, too, ignored him. Jimmy shrugged, placed a few bagels nearby, and nudged Lauren forward. She was relieved to move on since the smell was awful. She grimaced at the stench and looked around nervously at the various inhabitants as Jimmy walked over to another tent and peered into it.

"Chrissie? Are you home?" he called quietly.

No answer.

Jimmy blinked, trying to see into the dark tent.

His eyes focused on a woman with a mop of unruly hair and a grimy face. She wore only a dirty white nightgown and was curled up in a fetal position.

Jimmy stepped inside the tent. "Chrissie, are you okay?" He gently touched her shoulder.

Chrissie rolled over slightly and looked up at him with a tear-streaked face. "Yeah, I'm fine," she said, her voice raspy. "Benny, he . . . I'm not sure . . ."

"I'm so sorry, Chrissie," Jimmy replied. "I'll say a prayer for him." He wasn't sure if Benny had overdosed or was in some kind of trouble. He may even be dead. At this point, it made little difference. He was gone. "But you need to keep warm," Jimmy said. "Where's your sleeping bag?"

"I put it over Benny," Chrissie said. "They took it away when they took him."

"Okay, don't worry. I'll find you another one," Jimmy promised. "Please take these so you have them for later, and some for the others too." He handed Chrissie the remainder of the bag of bagels, as well as a take-out box of food.

Chrissie looked at Jimmy and tears again filled her eyes. "Thanks, Jimbo." She eased herself up on her elbow and noticed Lauren staring at her from the entrance of the tent. Chrissie eyed her suspiciously.

"This is Lauren," Jimmy told her. "She's with us."

Chrissie nodded and lay back down on the ground.

Jimmy slipped out of the tent and stopped to retrieve a pencil and a small notebook from his jacket pocket. He scribbled something in the notebook.

"Who's that lady?" Lauren asked.

"Chrissie? She's got a problem with her leg and can't get around much. I try to keep an eye out . . . to see what I can do to help her around here." He stuffed the pencil and notebook back in his pocket. "This way," he said, nodding toward the open street and already walking that direction.

He guided Lauren into a dusty covered area beneath a highway overpass. Lauren looked around at several neatly lined-up tents and wooden container boxes making up small homes. She watched curiously as Jimmy interacted with the men there. Their tattoos and army–navy store garb seemed to indicate that several of the men were military veterans. Jimmy leaned down and talked to each man sitting outside his tent, then scribbled more in his notebook. One of the vets leaned into Jimmy and whispered something in his ear. Jimmy immediately wrote another note.

When he stood, he saw a man lying by himself,

so he went to him, crouched down, and offered him one of the last bagels from the second bag. When he stood, he wrote something else in his notebook.

Another man in a wheelchair wearing ragged, dirty clothing wheeled himself over toward Jimmy. They exchanged a few words, and Jimmy handed him the bag of bagels and the other take-out box. He then scribbled more in the notebook.

Lauren was intrigued by Jimmy's actions but remained silent. If he wanted her to know, he'd tell her.

* * * * *

Across town, Liz approached the front door of a large house that had seen better days. It badly needed a paint job and other repairs. She unlocked the door and carefully slipped inside her home, careful not to make any noise. She eased off her shoes and stepped over to a closet to hang up her coat. A floorboard squeaked under her step, and Liz winced and halted, listening for any sound. She tiptoed into the dark kitchen and switched on the lights.

As she turned into the room, she jumped in shock. There was her husband, John, bleary- and puffy-eyed, sitting at the kitchen table glaring at her.

For a long moment he simply stared, then he lurched up and wobbled toward her. He was wasted.

Liz looked at John nervously, then glanced toward the door where she'd kicked off her shoes. She was ready to run if he raised his fists to her.

"You were out lookin' for him again, weren't you?" he asked belligerently, steadying himself with his hand against the table.

Liz opened her mouth to voice a response, but John waved her off. She looked down at the floor and tried to disappear.

"Useless woman," John bellowed. "Where's my beer?"

"I . . . I'm sorry . . . I . . . ," Liz stammered. "I forgot."

"Forgot?" John roared. "Typical! I work all day to support you and you don't even care about me anymore, do you?"

"Of course I do," Liz replied unconvincingly. She crossed the room and looked at him.

John moved toward her, his fists balling up in an unspoken but obvious threat. "No. No, you don't. You only care about that brat, Jimmy. Listen to me! He *left* you. I'm the one looking after you. I'm the one working to pay the bills. And you've been out for three hours and couldn't even bring me back some beer? Yeah, sure; you care about me."

"Please, John," Liz implored. "The doctor said your liver is in bad shape. He told you so to your face. You shouldn't be—"

"'Shouldn't be drinking.'" John mimicked her voice. "Yeah, yeah, I know. 'The doctor said it's bad for you.' I'll tell you what's bad for me." John suddenly crossed the kitchen and grabbed Liz by the throat. He straightened up to his full height and glared down at her.

Liz trembled in his grasp as he sneered down at her. "Pathetic!" He released his grasp and pushed her away, her body banging into the refrigerator. "Pathetic! That's what you are. That loser kid of yours is not our son anymore. Give it up. *He* ran away. He doesn't want you any more than I do."

"That's not true, John," Liz said through the tears now streaming down her face. "*You* pushed him away!"

John moved forward to hit her but stopped short, his fists still balled. He glowered at her and instead of swinging his strong arm, he grabbed Liz's purse. He rifled through it and pulled out the photo of Jimmy but dropped it and snatched twenty dollars from an interior pocket.

"Give me that!" she cried, reaching for the photo.

John slammed the bag to the floor, scattering the contents in various directions.

Liz scrambled to protect the picture of Jimmy. She didn't care about anything else that John might destroy.

"I'm going out to get the beer myself," John said. "You're useless! A waste of space." He stumbled toward the door, his face seething with pent-up rage. Before going out, he picked up an empty glass beer bottle from the top of the garbage can by the door. He whirled around and threw the bottle across the room as hard as he could.

His drunken aim was off, and Liz moved out of the way in the nick of time. The bottle crashed against the wall, shattering and sending shards of glass in various directions. Liz backed up against the wall.

John gave her one more fierce look, then opened the door. Liz breathed a sigh of relief as he slammed the door behind him. Then he was gone. She got down on her knees and crawled along the floor to reach her bag and retrieve the photo of Jimmy. She held the picture gently in her palms and pressed it to her heart as tears trickled down her face.

"I'm not giving up on you, Jimmy," she said barely above a whisper. "I won't. I won't fail you again." Liz turned toward the door through which John had just exited. She screamed, "I'm not giving up on him!"

* * * * *

Jimmy continued his rounds and Lauren tagged along with him, all the way downtown to an inner-city area. As they walked, Lauren gently prodded him. "Come on, I really do want to hear your story."

Jimmy feigned a coy expression. "Well, you know . . . ," he waffled. "Bad home. Bad future. I've been out here a couple years now."

"Years?" Lauren asked, her eyes wide. "I'm not going to be here more than a few weeks."

Jimmy nodded. "Great," he said. "I've heard that before, but I hope you're right. When you figure it out, let me know."

Lauren stopped abruptly and placed her hand on her hip. "I mean, really. How hard can it be?"

"Yeah, right," Jimmy replied. "Just keep your

ears and eyes open and look for opportunities. Until then, you find help wherever you can."

They turned the corner and Jimmy stopped in front of a large stone building—the Downtown City Mission. A huge banner hung over the entrance: *God Is Here for You.* Jimmy led Lauren inside where they were greeted by another large banner in the foyer entryway: *Downtown City Mission Is Here for You Too.*

Casually dressed men and women bustled back and forth across the foyer, and several homeless people sat on chairs, awaiting the attention of the obviously overworked and understaffed mission employees. Yet everyone seemed pleasant and patient.

Jimmy didn't stop in the foyer but passed right on by to the hallway leading to the interior offices. Lauren followed him as he walked purposely down the hall until he came to a door with the name *Gabrielle Walker* on the window. Jimmy pushed open the door and peered into the office. Gabrielle, a conservatively dressed Latina woman in her early fifties whose long, dark hair and olive-colored skin made her look twenty years younger, sat working behind her desk. Her face lit up in a bright smile when she saw Jimmy. "Hey, Jimmy! Good to see you."

"Good to be seen," Jimmy quipped. "I've got a

new list for you." He walked over to the desk, tore off a page from his notebook, and handed it to her.

Gabrielle read Jimmy's notes and a sad expression appeared on her face. "Sorry to learn about Benny," she said. "I'll go check on Chrissie and get her what she needs, particularly, a new sleeping bag."

"Thanks, Gabrielle," Jimmy said, biting his lip, as though trying to control his emotions.

Gabrielle noticed Lauren still standing in the doorway and looked at Jimmy for an explanation.

"This is Lauren," he said. "She needs a place to stay. She had all of her stuff stolen."

Gabrielle got up and stepped out from behind her desk, extending her hand toward Lauren. "I'm Gabrielle," she said. "Welcome. Glad to help. Let me check the local shelters and find you a space."

Lauren shifted on her feet uncomfortably. "I'm not going to a shelter," she said.

Gabrielle looked Lauren up and down for a few seconds, then glanced back at Jimmy, as if trying to assess the situation. "You need to be somewhere safe," she said softly to Lauren. "I'm sure you realize that by now."

Lauren nodded slightly, but her eyes were glued to a box of new sleeping bags on a table in the corner of Gabrielle's office. "I'll find somewhere," she said, "but I could use a sleeping bag. Jimmy's been letting me use his."

Gabrielle walked over to the table and reached into the box. She pulled out a brand-new sleeping bag and handed it to Lauren. "This should do," she said. "Let me get you some more stuff." She reached into another box and drew out a pair of jeans, a bag of toiletries, a Bible, and a schedule of church services conducted at the mission each week. "Hopefully, you can join us." She placed the items in a large bag. "Are you sure that's all you need?"

Lauren nodded.

"Okay, here you go," Gabrielle said, as she handed the items to Lauren, along with her business card. "But if you change your mind or need help in any way, you know where to find me. My number's on the card." Gabrielle looked at Jimmy before continuing. "And, Jimmy, if she needs a phone and an EBT card"—she paused to explain to Lauren—"an Electronic Benefit Transfer card, sort of like a government-issued debit card. They replaced food stamps and other services a few years ago." Gabrielle looked back at Jimmy. "Help her fill out these forms and bring them back to me." Gabrielle handed two forms to Lauren, then turned to Jimmy once more.

"By the way, they're hiring at a tech company down the block," Gabrielle said. "I was hoping I could set up an interview for you. What do you think?"

"Oh no." Jimmy waved his hand in front of his chest and shook his head. "I'm all right. But thanks, though."

"Okay," Gabrielle said. "Be safe." She quietly whispered a prayer in Spanish.

Jimmy and Lauren exited Gabrielle's office and headed down the hall. Once they reached the foyer, Jimmy said, "Gabrielle's great. She's always looking out for us." He paused and looked intently at Lauren before asking, "So . . . do you *really* have somewhere to go? Somewhere safe?"

"I'll figure something out," Lauren replied. "I'll have to." She looked down at the pavement.

Jimmy stood silently for a few moments as he processed Lauren's admission. "Well, until you do, are you sure you don't want Gabrielle to find you a spot in a shelter? She probably could."

"How do you know?" Lauren asked.

"I've known Gabrielle for a couple years now, since I've been living in the encampment. She's a good person. She runs the soup kitchen at the mission and always goes out of her way to help the homeless."

"Why is she so interested?" Lauren asked.

"She has firsthand experience," Jimmy explained. "Gabrielle's older sister was homeless at eighteen. By the time Gabrielle found her on the streets, she was so sick she didn't live much longer. But Gabrielle saw how the homeless community had tried to take care of her sister, so that inspired her to help other people living on the streets. She really understands and is super aware of the problems homeless people face. She and I have become sort of partners."

"Partners?" Lauren asked.

Jimmy chuckled. "Yeah, I keep her informed about the needs I see, and she does what she can to help. She stands up for people however she can. She gets some heat for it, but she has guts. And she'll help you if you ask."

Lauren continued staring at the floor and fiddling with her hands. "I've been in shelters before," she said. "And I've had nothing but bad experiences there and in foster homes. I'm not interested in going back."

Jimmy waited for her to elaborate, but she remained silent. After a few more awkward moments, he said, "Okay. Well, if you're not going to stay with us, Dora will be sad. She really liked you."

Lauren raised her eyes and caught Jimmy smiling at her.

They stepped out of the flow of traffic in the foyer and Jimmy walked over to a folding table and a few chairs. A cup filled with ink pens sat on the corner of the table. He pulled out a chair for Lauren. "Have a seat."

Lauren studied him as she sat down, still holding the forms and other things Gabrielle had given her. "Well, maybe . . . if you guys don't mind, maybe I can stay with you until I figure something out."

"We'd be glad to have you." Jimmy smiled openly at her. Lauren offered a weak smile in return, then accepted the pen he offered and began filling out the forms.

While she wrote, Jimmy walked away. A few seconds later, someone began softly playing a guitar and singing.

Lauren looked up and saw Jimmy in the corner near her table. "I didn't know you could play guitar."

"You didn't ask. I don't play well, but I enjoy it. Sometimes I borrow Harris's guitar back at camp." He continued singing a familiar song, and after a few beats, Lauren joined him, softly singing along with him.

Jimmy stopped and looked at her. "I didn't know you could sing so well."

"You didn't ask," Lauren said, reaching over to poke him in the ribs.

Together, they sang softly as Jimmy accompanied them on the guitar.

He paused and looked in Lauren's eyes. A tear formed and trickled down her cheek. Their eyes remained locked and Jimmy continued singing with Lauren joining as she finished her forms.

The song ended, and they broke eye contact as several people in the foyer applauded. Jimmy waved and smiled shyly.

"Okay, enough of that," he said, doing his best to play down the emotions. "Let's get out of here." He dropped off Lauren's completed forms at the front counter, then grabbed her arm and led her out of the mission.

They walked down the street, talking about important matters and the mundane. When they saw another playground with a metal swing set, they couldn't resist. They ran to the swings and hopped on the rubber seats, swinging back and forth, high into the air. When they finally slowed down to a gentle motion, Lauren looked over at Jimmy from her swing. "Why'd you turn down that job interview, earlier? The one Gabrielle mentioned."

Jimmy's brow furrowed. "Oh, that." He waved one hand out in front of himself while hanging on to the swing's chain with the other. "I couldn't do that. I gotta look after the folks around here."

"What happened to you? Were you in the foster system too?"

"Nah," Jimmy said. A pensive expression crossed his face. "Nah, just a bad situation. A lotta people have had to deal with much worse than I did. I don't know how you women put up with it all." He blinked hard and shook his head. Looking over at Lauren, he forced a brief smile to his lips. Then he started pumping his legs so he could soar higher to the full extension of the chains holding his seat.

The swing swept backward and forward, and Jimmy soared. Then he suddenly jumped off the seat, leaving the swing's chains jangling behind him.

He landed on his feet and looked over at Lauren. "Anyway, I have a great family now. Let's go."

Chapter 8

STILL DRESSED in his impeccable gray suit but with the tie loosened around his neck, Robert pulled his BMW into the driveway and revved the engine one more time before shutting it off. It was dark outside, and he was tired but euphoric about the prospect of landing the big deal downtown. He grabbed his briefcase, got out of the car, and went inside the house and into the kitchen. He heard, rather than felt, the crunch of a toy he stepped on, one of many scattered on the kitchen floor by his eight-year-old son, Sam.

Kim, Robert's beautiful thirty-five-year-old wife, stood at the sink still dressed in her nursing scrubs and washing a pile of dirty dishes. She didn't even turn around when she heard Robert enter the room.

"You're late," she said tersely. "Sam's upstairs waiting for you to read to him."

"Me? Read to him?" Robert opened the fridge door and grabbed a plate of leftovers. He found a clean fork, sat down at the kitchen table, and began scarfing down the food. He glanced at the framed picture hanging on the wall for all to see, a photo of Kim and Robert with Sam as a toddler.

Robert shook his head as he gulped down another bite. "Sorry, I really can't, babe," he said. He took off his suit coat and placed it over the back of a chair. "I don't have time tonight. I have a hard deadline. I have to—"

"You promised him, Robert!" Kim said. "He's been looking forward to it since he got home from school today." She scrubbed the dish in her hand even harder.

Robert put down his fork and went to stand behind Kim, attempting to wrap his arms around her. When she turned away, he reached in front of her and turned on the radio, as if that had been his intention all along.

"I'm sorry, Kim," he said. "I really am." He pulled her into his arms and spun her around. He held her body close, and she relaxed as he waltzed around the room with her. "This new deal I'm working on is *huge*!" he crowed. "It is really exciting. Once I close it, all our problems will be solved." Robert stopped and tried to kiss her.

Kim abruptly pulled away from Robert. Still annoyed, she stepped over to the counter and switched off the radio. "No, Robert. No. We can't go on like this. What happened to that raise you said you were promised? Huh?" She picked up a pile of overdue bills stacked on the table and waved them in Robert's face. "We need to deal with these things, now! Why haven't they been paid? Are you gambling again?"

"Honey, please," Robert begged. "Please don't start. I'm under a lot of pressure. The raise will come through once I close this deal."

Kim flipped through the bills. Her frown deepened as she pulled out the electric bill and gas bill, both with big red stamps on the envelopes. "Oh, come on, Robert!" she cried. "Just tell me the truth. I thought you paid the electric and gas bills? What's going on here?" She waved her arms, leaned her head back, and looked at the ceiling. "They'll just cut us off, you know. Then what?"

"Stop worrying, Kim." Robert tried to speak calmly. I just need this one big deal to go through." He placed his hands on his hips as he spoke. "You never believed we'd live in a house like this . . . and look at us now."

"Yeah, true," Kim replied. "But we've already refinanced the house and taken out a second mortgage on it. You got lucky once, but we can't afford to live like this."

"Don't say that, Kim! This deal is going to come together. I promise. I can feel it. And when it does . . ." He paused and smiled. "Then I can really be here for you and Sam like never before."

Robert stepped forward and kissed Kim on the lips. This time, she let him kiss her, but she didn't kiss him back. Then without another word, Robert walked out of the kitchen.

Kim stared silently as she watched him disappear into the next room. She sighed as her face creased with worry. She understood Robert all too well. She knew about his poor family background and how kids made fun of him while he was growing up because he wore old hand-me-down clothes. His junior high haircut looked like someone had put a bowl over his head and trimmed around it. As Robert entered his upper teens and early twenties, he craved material things, money, and the appearance of success—even if he couldn't really afford any of it.

He did work hard, and he had enjoyed a fabulous streak of beginners' luck in the real estate market after he finished college and secured his license. He was smart and perceptive, knowing what people wanted. He was also a charmer who smooth-talked his way into people's hearts, including hers.

Their life together had been so good—talking until all hours of the night, laughing together, slow dancing in their living room, loving each other passionately. When Sam was born, he brought even more joy to their lives. But then things fell apart.

Kim had often expressed a desire for a larger home in a better section of town, so after Robert closed a big real estate deal a few years earlier, he was convinced he was on a roll. He placed a down payment on a house they couldn't really afford without even consulting Kim. He also leased an expensive BMW he'd practically salivated over on the dealer's lot. Then the economy soured, and real estate took a plunge. His boss put Robert on a straight commission basis, making it even more imperative for Robert to close sales, simply to keep up with the mortgage, car payment, and basic household expenses.

When he failed to make his monthly quotas, Robert turned to gambling, trying to hit it big in one fell swoop. He cashed in on a few small payouts, but for the most part he threw good money after bad.

When rejection and loss overwhelmed him, rather than seeking help, Robert turned to alcohol, digging himself even deeper into a hole.

Hailing from a more conservative, simple background, Kim's parents had disapproved of Robert from the outset. They regarded him as arrogant, flashy, and vulgar. Kim, however, saw a different side of him. To her, Robert was ridiculously good-looking, glamorous, and fun. Most importantly, she loved him passionately with her whole heart. She had worked hard to earn her RN nursing status, and it had proved to be a wise decision when she had gone back to work and kept working even after Sam was born.

Lately, Kim had been more realistic and blunter with her husband. *"Robert, it is my income that is keeping our family afloat,"* she'd told him. *"But not for long."*

Robert had paid no attention. That night, he peeked into Sam's room and saw that it was dark. Sam was already asleep in bed, his book lying closed on the floor. He quietly closed the door and tiptoed down the hallway and into his office. He flipped on the light switch and went to his desk. He turned on his computer, then opened the large, deep desk drawer.

He pulled a thick file out of the drawer and plopped it onto his desk. With the file removed from the drawer, Robert's eyes immediately fell on a bottle of booze and a glass tumbler he kept hidden in the drawer beneath the file. Robert looked longingly at the alcohol, paused, then slowly shut the drawer.

He sat down in his chair and turned his attention to the computer screen displaying a horse-racing gambling site. Robert took in the attractions on the site and gave a little nod. He clicked off the site and opened a spreadsheet for work.

Kim walked by his office door. She paused, looking in at Robert with a quizzical expression.

Robert looked up and saw her. "I'll be there in a bit," he said.

Kim nodded. "I have two eight-hour shifts tomorrow," she said. "Please don't wake me when you come in."

"Yeah, sure," Robert replied. "Right. Good night."

"Good night, Robert," Kim said, moving past his office toward their bedroom. Robert barely acknowledged her leaving; he was already poring over his "big deal" files.

Neither Kim nor Robert was aware of the time when Robert finally crawled into bed that night. Dawn came too quickly, and it was time for him to get to work. He walked into the kitchen and poured a cup of coffee before going back into his office. He hadn't slept much despite staying up so late, and his face bore a troubled expression as he opened the drawer containing the large file and the alcohol. This time, he didn't even try to resist. He grabbed the bottle and emptied the contents into his coffee.

He sat down at the desk and pulled up the horse-racing gambling site. A countdown clock was ticking off the remaining seconds before bets would be closed on the next race. He hastily toggled the computer to display his bank account. A few more clicks, and he saw that his checking account showed a balance of $295.54.

Robert quickly clicked back to the gambling site. Time was running out, so he hurriedly typed *$295.00* and clicked the button "Place Bet."

He took a swig of his spiked coffee and sat back, waiting, watching the live footage of the race, sipping his drink anxiously. He moved his face closer to the screen . . . then closer still, intently staring, desperately watching every nuance of the race.

His face suddenly dropped, and Robert slammed his cup down on the desk, splashing the remaining liquid onto the floor.

"No! No!" Robert furtively looked around, hoping he hadn't awakened Kim or Sam.

His horse had lost.

Again.

Chapter 9

VIOLET AND Harris were *looking good!*

They had just left the Salvation Army where they both had a hot shower and changed into fresh, clean clothes. Harris had enjoyed a shave—with real shaving cream—and both had washed and conditioned their hair, something they rarely did in the encampment.

"We need to get back. Dora is going to be afraid something happened to us," Harris said as he headed toward the encampment, striding down the street ahead of Violet and carrying a plastic bag full of clean towels and clothes.

"Hey, slow down!" Violet called from behind him. "Haven't you forgiven me yet?"

Harris stopped and turned toward her. "Five years sober, and I still have to watch out for you. That's crazy. You gotta be willing to do things differently, Violet. Talk to me next time you're tempted to use. I might be able to help. But I'm not going to hang around and watch you kill yourself with drugs or anything else."

"I know, I know, Harris. I'm sorry," Violet said. "How many times do I have to tell you?"

"Don't tell me," Harris's voice softened. "Show me, Violet. Please. I want you around." He hugged her and softly kissed her forehead.

She pushed his chest. "Aww, Harris, you old softie." They walked on together, side by side, toward the encampment. When they arrived on the street adjacent to their homes, they saw a sharply dressed man standing outside the encampment holding a clipboard. As they drew closer, they saw that he was soliciting passersby to sign a petition.

Harris and Violet were about to walk past the man when he marched over to them and extended the clipboard toward them. "Excuse me, folks. Got a quick minute?"

"Sure. Nothin' but time," Harris answered. "What's up?"

"Do you live in this neighborhood?" the man asked.

Harris nodded. Violet pulled back, looking at the man suspiciously, her eyes narrowing as she recognized him as the driver who had knocked the flowers out of her hands a few days ago.

"Mind signing this petition?" he asked Harris.

"Sure. What's it for?" Harris asked.

"Just to do some cleanup around here," the man replied breezily.

"That sounds good. I'm all for beauty and order." Harris took the clipboard and pen and was about to sign it when Violet pushed up next to him. "Cleanup, huh? What type of cleanup?" She grabbed the petition from Harris.

"Well, I need to get enough signatures so the city council will get that trash over there cleaned up," the man said, pointing at the encampment. "I'm sure you—"

"Oh, yeah?" Violet interrupted him. "Where are we supposed to sleep? Are you gonna let us crash at your house?" Violet lifted the clipboard in the air and then brought it down hard over her strong thigh, snapping it in half. She pulled the halves apart and threw them on the ground.

Stunned, the man backed away as though uncertain if Violet might do something even more violent to him.

"Get outta here!" she yelled at him. "And you better not show your face around here again. Ya hear?"

The man turned and ran toward his car as Harris and Violet watched. Harris then turned to Violet. "What was that all about? I can't believe he thought we were going to fall for that nonsense."

"I gotta bad feeling about that guy," she said. "He is up to no good."

* * * * *

Robert drove a short distance from the encampment to a municipal building downtown, where the city council was conducting a town hall meeting and receiving suggestions, grievances, and complaints as they made decisions regarding the city's new development plans and budget. The room was filled with people voicing their opinions, so Robert got in line to present his case regarding the removal of the homeless encampment. He had lobbied hard the previous week to jam the issue on this month's meeting agenda, and this was his opportunity to speak his mind.

The council members sat at long tables elevated on a platform above the visitors and staff members. Comprised of several businesspeople, the council was chaired by a stern-looking, no-nonsense Black woman who fielded the comments offered by citizens and firmly guided the council's responses.

Nattily dressed in a blue suit and tie, Robert stood behind a blonde woman who was making her case regarding something Robert cared nothing about. Adrenaline surged through his body, and he shifted his weight from one foot to the other as he waited impatiently for the woman to conclude, ready to present his case to the council the moment she vacated her spot at the podium.

The woman in front of him stepped aside and Robert immediately moved into position, but before he could begin speaking, the chairwoman at the center table banged her gavel and declared, "That's it for today. Thank you for coming." She started to collect her notes and stand.

"No! Wait!" Robert called out frantically. "You're not done here. We need to discuss what *you're* going to do about all the homeless people in this area."

The councilwoman looked down at Robert and continued to gather her papers. "That will have to go on next month's agenda," she stated.

A sharp-looking young business owner leaped to his feet, the veins nearly popping out of his neck. "No!" he shouted. "You get these people off our streets *now*! It's out of control. There are tents and shacks everywhere, along with the filth and junk. They're ruining our businesses!"

Robert's adrenaline was pumping wildly. "Yeah! Come on! It's on this month's agenda! Look. Deal with it!" He glanced across the room at the virulent business owner, then back at the chairwoman. "There's a huge encampment right around the corner. You gotta clean it up. Get the cops to go in and get them out. It needs to happen. Now!"

The room was abuzz with people agreeing and disagreeing. An elegantly dressed Hispanic woman rose to her feet in the audience and pointed at the councilwoman. She spoke rapidly and emotionally. "Yes!" she cried out. "You need to do something. I pay my taxes and a lot of money to live in this area—"

"We all do!" Robert yelled in agreement.

"Now it's disgusting," the woman said, wringing her hands. "I found feces on my doorstep just yesterday! Needles and trash all over the streets. Why should we have to deal with that?"

The chaos was starting to get out of hand, and the chairwoman attempted to placate the people. "There are laws we have to follow," she said. "It's not that simple."

More citizens stood and started shouting, waving their fists. Flustered, the councilwoman prepared to leave the room.

"Yes, it is that simple!" someone shouted.

Someone else yelled, "That's right!"

"Enough!" a loud voice boomed. "Get the vagrants off our streets!" The meeting quickly degenerated into cacophony with a multitude of people simultaneously yelling and nearly screaming their opinions. Others in the room looked on, shocked, as the noise level escalated.

Suddenly, a female voice pierced the din. "Stop it!" she yelled. All eyes in the room turned toward the area from which the voice had emanated. "I am Gabrielle, director of the Downtown City Mission," she said. "And I work with these people every day of my life." Dressed demurely in a flowing flower-patterned dress with a gold cross around her neck, Gabrielle's demeanor commanded attention.

"Come on, folks," she addressed the crowd. "You should all be ashamed of yourselves!" The room fell silent. Turning slightly sideways so she could speak to the council and the assembled citizens at the same time, she continued. "Those 'vagrants' are human beings. Where are they meant to go? That's what we need to talk about. We need real solutions! Housing with drug counseling. Mental health care. They need *help*."

A young woman seated in the row behind Gabrielle popped up. "Yeah! She's right," she said. "You've left enough problems for my generation. Get real about this issue and have some heart. Things aren't working the way they are."

A homeless preacher, wearing layers of colorful but dirty, shabby clothing, with a scruffy beard and a knit cap stood up and roared from the rear of the room, "This is the end!"

He waved his arms in the air as he moved forward up the center aisle, past Robert, and planted himself in front of the council before turning and continuing his rant. "These are the final days, my friends." He looked around the room at the surprised expressions on people's faces. "It's coming!" the preacher railed. "The day of reckoning is coming." He extended his arm and pointed at various people. "We are all sinners! *You* are all sinners!"

Most people in the audience cringed. Some smiled, amused; others shook their heads in disdain. A few may have felt spiritually convicted, but all began to move away from the disheveled preacher.

The room quickly cleared except for Robert and a few others.

Robert sighed in frustration, flopped down on a chair in the third row, leaned forward, and put his head in his hands. Under his breath, he groused, "This is ridiculous."

A hawk-nosed man in his mid-thirties with an old-fashioned, military-style crew cut leaned over from a chair next to Robert. He spoke quietly, covertly attempting to conceal his comments from any remaining council members. "You won't get anything done down here. You want action? You gotta do it yourself."

Intrigued, Robert turned toward the man who had interrupted his reverie, and the man leaned closer. "There's a bunch of us residents and business owners who are fed up with what's going on," he whispered. "We've already done a few cleanups around here. If you need help, call me. I'm Carl." He handed Robert a business card.

Robert looked at the card for a few seconds, considered what Carl was implying, and pocketed it. Then he got up and started back down the aisle toward the exit.

But he didn't move fast enough.

The preacher lurched into Robert's path, got in his face, and pushed up against him so closely that Robert nearly retched at the reeking smell.

"You'll all rot in hell!" the preacher spat at Robert. "Sinners! Sinners! Your day will come!"

Unnerved, Robert pushed the preacher away and ran out of the town hall meeting room.

Later that night, Robert sat at his kitchen table, frustrated over the ever-mounting stack of bills and his inability to earn enough income to pay them—especially in light of his heavy drinking and gambling. He fumbled in his pocket and found the business card Carl had given him after the council meeting.

Robert stared at it for more than a minute, then picked up the phone and dialed the number.

"This is Carl," a voice answered. "What do ya want?"

Robert spoke quietly into his phone. "Carl, it's Robert from the council meeting today. Hey, ah . . . I'm calling about that help you offered."

Chapter 10

LATE THAT afternoon, a clean-shaven Jimmy and a beaming Lauren walked out of the Salvation Army building wearing clean clothes and carrying freshly laundered towels under their arms. They spotted a Salvation Army food truck on the street and ran over to join the line of other individuals awaiting a free meal and a special treat. While waiting, they talked about some of their favorite things—food, school subjects, animals.

"Okay, so what's your favorite color?" Lauren asked.

"Green," Jimmy responded without hesitation. "Yours?"

"Purple," Lauren replied with a hint of smile. "But not dark purple. More like a lilac-ish, lavender sort of purple."

Jimmy nodded, noting Lauren's lilac-colored sweater. "Yep, I can see that."

A girl who looked a few years younger than

Lauren joined the back of the line. She was all alone, her face dirty and tear-streaked.

Jimmy noticed her first. Then Lauren. Neither said a word, but Lauren carefully watched the girl, taking in her condition. It was impossible to avoid the obvious—it could just as easily have been her a short time ago. "I wonder if she has a safe place to stay," Lauren said aloud, more to herself than to Jimmy.

Jimmy let Lauren stew in her thoughts for a few moments. They both watched as a Salvation Army officer approached the young girl and began speaking to her. "I think she's in good hands now," Jimmy said. Then he cocked his head to one side and spoke softly. "Everything happens for a reason. I've been trying to figure out why you ended up with us."

"Good luck with that," Lauren quipped.

Jimmy grinned, then turned to face the man in the Salvation Army food truck who handed them each a bag of sandwiches. They thanked him and drew the sandwiches close as though they had received a priceless gift. Their hands brushed slightly as they walked away. They quickly resumed bantering lightheartedly all the way back to the neighborhood where the encampment was located.

When they turned the corner near the encampment, Jimmy gasped. "Oh no!" An ambulance was parked in front of the tents, and paramedics hurried past a pack of onlookers. Jimmy bolted toward the ambulance, running as fast as he could, and Lauren rushed after him.

Once inside the area, they saw Jaycee lying on her side, one knee bent over the other, her face pale and clammy. She wasn't wearing shoes, and her toenails had turned blue. Gurgling sounds came from her mouth.

A male paramedic carefully moved Jaycee onto her back and rubbed his fist hard in circular movements on her sternum. A female paramedic leaned over Jaycee's face and put her ear to her mouth. She looked at the other paramedic and shook her head, then tilted Jaycee's chin up and put the mask portion of an Ambu bag, a manual resuscitator, over her nose. She squeezed the bag part, trying to jump-start Jaycee's breathing.

Jimmy and Lauren stood nearby, horrified at the sight. Harris approached them and put his arms around their shoulders. "Don't worry," he said. "They got here quickly. She'll be fine."

The male paramedic reached into his pack and

drew out a Narcan nasal spray. He pushed down on the container, forcing the spray into Jaycee's nose. Jaycee bolted upright, spewing vomit all over her clothes.

Lauren jumped back a bit in shock. Violet joined them but didn't say anything. Her eyes remained fixed on Jaycee.

"Narcan always does the trick," Harris said quietly. Then he added, "I just worry about the one time no one's around to help."

Jimmy shook his head. "She needs to be in a treatment place, not out here."

Violet turned away and put her head in her hands.

Harris nudged her lightly. "Hey. You okay?"

Violet turned back and stared at Jaycee, who was struggling to stand up while the paramedics attempted to keep her sitting down.

Violet looked Harris in the eyes. "Yeah. I'm okay. Maybe I needed to see that."

Harris wrapped his arm around Violet and drew her to his side. "Maybe we all did," he said. "It's getting dark. Let's get Jaycee settled and call it a day."

* * * * *

By ten o'clock that night, a full moon beamed down on the encampment, and the trees in the park swayed gently in the wind. The area was quiet and dark with only a few embers flickering in the rusty barrels where people had warmed themselves earlier in the evening. Most of the residents had already gone to bed because the air held a chill, as if a storm were soon approaching.

One was.

Robert, Carl, and other vigilantes surreptitiously approached the encampment. They were all dressed in dark clothing and wore black balaclavas—knit ski masks that covered their heads and faces with an opening only for their eyes. Carl looked around, surveying the scene. He put his finger to his lips and beckoned the men into a tight huddle, whispering instructions.

Two additional vigilantes moved over to a chained city water spigot. One man expertly cut through the chain with a bolt cutter. Another man attached a high-pressure nozzle to a hose while the other screwed the opposite end of the hose onto the spigot. The first man fed the hose over the fence. Then the men crept toward the tents and makeshift wooden shacks, dragging the hose with them.

When they reached a heavily populated portion of the encampment, the vigilantes aimed the high-pressure hose at a tent and signaled to the man who had stayed behind to turn on the spigot. Instantly, a powerful stream of water slammed into the first tent, then into another, flattening them both. The men heard frightened cries from within the tents as they collapsed on top of the people sleeping in them.

The first man turned the hose on another tent, and a half-naked burly man stumbled out. He grabbed a piece of tarp to shield himself from the onslaught of pressured water.

A woman hurried out of her tent, and the night-clothes on her body were soaked to her skin as she ran through the powerful spray, trying to escape.

The burly homeless man charged the man holding the hose and knocked it out of his hands. The water shot high into the air, and the homeless man grabbed the hose and turned it toward the vigilante, who turned tail and ran off, tearing at tents as he passed them. A second vigilante saw what was happening and tackled the homeless man, wrestling him to the ground, preventing him from turning the water off.

Another vigilante, accompanied by Carl and Robert, marauded through the encampment, ripping down tents and pulling tarps off shacks. One man picked up a pallet and heaved it against a flimsy tent, flattening the tent on top of the people inside.

Carl ran from tent to tent cutting the strings and ropes securing them and laughing hideously as he watched the simple structures cave in. Robert looked around, astounded at the devastation, and a bit uncertain what he should do.

"Come on!" Carl shouted at him. "Don't just stand there. Man up!"

Robert nodded, took another quick look around him, and pulled up several tent stakes, sending the tent to the ground. He grabbed a small table in front of the tent and hurled it against the roof of a shack, puncturing the tarp.

The first vigilante found a pile of dishes on a small pallet. He stomped his heavy boots on the plates, smashing them to little pieces.

The second vigilante laughed uproariously as he knocked over a shopping cart filled with someone's possessions, causing the items to roll across the ground.

People were shouting and crying in the darkness. Several women and children screamed in fear as the third vigilante kicked over milk crates that served as a table. A tattoo-covered man crawled out of a collapsed tent with an armful of his belongings. He held them tightly to his chest as he ran into the night.

A long-haired young woman ran out of a shack, clutching a dog to her chest. Her father followed closely behind her, urging her forward to somewhere safer.

* * * * *

In a separate section of the encampment, Harris was fast asleep when the commotion began. He was stretched out in his shack, surrounded by his wood carvings and paintings. In one corner was a pile of brushes and paints on a small stool, and his guitar leaned against the opposite corner.

A piece of debris fell through the tarp on his roof and landed on Harris's face. He bolted up with a start as the rest of the tarp was ripped off.

"What the—" He jumped up and peered out the top of his shack. He could see the men rampaging through the encampment, destroying everything they could with their bare hands, the bolt cutter, and knives. People ran yelling and screaming in every direction.

He glanced toward Violet's tent as she opened the flap to see what was going on. When she turned toward him, Harris called out to her, "Grab essentials. Meet at the park. Go!"

Violet nodded, then ducked back inside her tent to do as he'd said.

Harris worked feverishly inside his shack. He gathered as many of his wood carvings and art supplies as he could and tossed them into a large cloth shopping bag. Then he started to grab some of his paintings, but suddenly the side of his shack was yanked off and Carl barged in.

Carl grabbed Harris's guitar and hurled it outside.

"Time to go, buddy!" he yelled deviously.

Carl locked his arms around Harris's shoulders, knocking him off-balance. He dragged Harris outside and slapped the paintings out of his arms.

"Please!" Harris cried. "Not the paintings. I need them for my show." Harris fell to the ground, desperately attempting to salvage his work, but Carl savagely kicked the artwork out of his reach.

"No one's gonna want that trash!" He grabbed Harris and yanked him to his feet. Harris twisted his body and elbowed Carl in the face. Carl's body recoiled, and he cried out in pain as he lost his grip on Harris and fell backward into the mud.

Harris grabbed as many paintings as he could carry, along with his bag of supplies. He left Carl on the ground and ran to find Dora and Lauren. He spotted them stuffing some of their possessions into their bags. Harris ran to help them. Dora looked up at him with childlike confusion in her eyes.

"Harris, what's happening?" she asked. "Why are they doing this?"

Harris gave her a quick hug. "It's okay, Dora, but we gotta go. Hurry now." Harris waved at Lauren, indicating that she and Dora should follow him as he led them through the mess toward the back exit. Others hurried out behind them, stumbling and not knowing where to go.

* * * * *

Back in the encampment, Jimmy awakened from a deep, contented sleep. He looked outside his tent to see what all the noise was about, and his jaw dropped. Still rubbing his eyes, he spotted Dora, Lauren, and Harris moving toward the exit. Behind them, a man pushed another homeless man in a bent wheelchair, his bag of belongings in his lap.

Then the men wreaking havoc raced past him, and Jimmy lurched out of his tent.

"Stop!" Jimmy yelled. "Stop it!"

Across the way, Violet, too, screamed at the men ripping apart the camp. "This is my home!" she yelled furiously.

She continued yelling as Jimmy scanned the area looking for anyone he could help, but he was surrounded by chaos.

"These are *my* things! Show me some respect. Get your filthy hands off—"

Jimmy turned back to see what sort of trouble Violet was encountering.

An enraged Violet, with a bag of her stuff in her hand, glowered at a masked man who had grabbed her bicycle workbench and was about to throw it upside down.

"Who do you think you are?" Violet shouted at him. "Destroying our homes like this. You—" She flung her body forward and slugged him. She hit him again and again.

Attempting to deflect her frantic blows, the man grabbed Violet's arms, trying to restrain her.

"Get away from me!" she yelled.

Jimmy started toward Violet to help her, but someone jumped him, grabbing the back of his shirt collar and yanking him backward, constraining him in a strong grasp as Jimmy squirmed to get away.

Violet continued struggling against her assailant, flailing at him wildly. She clawed at his face and caught him off guard, then kneed him in the groin and pulled off his balaclava.

Momentarily stunned, Violet stared at the man and narrowed her eyes as Jimmy watched surprise fill her expression.

The man doubled over in pain and looked back at Violet in shock. He was no longer anonymous.

Violet recognized Robert and punched him again. "I knew you were bad news!" she yelled.

The man reeled back, howling in pain, but his cries were drowned out by the sounds of sirens approaching. He struggled to put his balaclava back on to conceal his face as he limped off to rejoin his fellow vigilantes.

Violet screamed after him, "You're gonna pay for this! Mark my words. What goes around comes around!" She took off running in the opposite direction.

The men in black took off, too, heading toward their vehicles, but the one who had latched on to Jimmy refused to let go. When he realized his buddies were fleeing, he violently pushed Jimmy to the ground, then viciously kicked him with his heavy black work boots before running off, leaving Jimmy groaning on the ground as the sirens grew louder.

A police cruiser with its blue lights flashing and siren still wailing whipped into the encampment and came to an abrupt stop. Two officers stepped out—one female and one male—and gazed in shock at the destruction all around them.

"What a mess," the female officer said. She pulled out her walkie-talkie. "Unit 74. Cleanup and a caseworker needed at a downtown homeless camp."

The male police officer saw Jimmy moaning on the ground and tried to pull him up. "This mess is your doing, huh?"

Jimmy flinched in pain and jerked away from the officer. "Are you crazy?" he lashed out at him. "I ain't done nuthin', so get your hands off me." He shoved the police officer away from him.

"You touch this uniform again, kid, and I'll arrest you," the officer threatened.

The female officer cocked her head to the side

and looked at her partner skeptically. "Come on," she said. "He didn't do this. He's a homeless kid. Probably lives here. Let him be."

"Yeah," Jimmy retorted. "What are you gonna do about the group that attacked us? Where's our protection? Find those guys and arrest *them*."

"Do you have any idea who they were?" the female officer asked.

Jimmy looked at her in disgust. "Isn't that your job?" He took a breath and tried to calm down. "Truth is, no one wants us in their neighborhood."

The two cops stared silently at Jimmy, so he went on. "But you're not going to do anything anyhow, are you? As always, we just have to fend for ourselves. Right?" Jimmy stormed off toward where he'd seen the others go.

"Come on," the male officer said as he left. "Let's wait inside the car for that cleanup unit."

* * * * *

An hour or so later, Robert emerged freshly showered from the bathroom at home. He dried his hair with a towel in one hand as he walked into the hallway while holding a glass of whiskey in his other hand. He went to the living room and took a long swig of his drink before turning on the television and flipping through the channels until he found the late-night local news.

A newscaster sat at the studio desk with large, full-color images of the wrecked homeless encampment behind her on the screen. The woman spoke tersely: "We've had a report of a group of vigilantes attacking a homeless camp tonight. Reports of this type of activity have been increasing in recent weeks, and this attack appears to have been especially severe. Viewer discretion is advised since some of these scenes may be disturbing."

More images of the wrecked encampment filled the screen. The newscaster continued, "According to the police, minor injuries were reported as well as extensive damage to the makeshift homes and other property. The city authorities are working to find shelter for the individuals affected as the investigation is ongoing."

Robert stared in disbelief at the footage on his television screen. His own actions had been horrific, but he hadn't seen the devastation caused by the others. The cameras panned over the encampment, showing the total destruction. The glass of whiskey in his hand began to shake as Robert watched, his chest heaving. He was putting the drink on the coffee table in front of him when a young man appeared onscreen, being interviewed by a reporter who referred to the young man as Jimmy. Robert recognized him.

"We're people, just like everyone else," Jimmy told the reporter. "We just want to be left alone. We're not hurting anyone. We live here, that's all." Jimmy paused and looked around at the destruction and then back toward the camera. "We have to live somewhere."

The newscast shifted back to the studio, and the woman behind the desk continued her report. "The police are reviewing security camera footage from the area, and we've reached out to the city council for comment. Anyone with information is encouraged to contact city police." The screen flashed back to Jimmy standing in front of the remains of the encampment, where the destruction looked as though a bomb had detonated, leaving fragments of clothing, pots and pans, and a mess of plastic and shards of wood and metal everywhere.

Robert leaned in toward his television and glared at Jimmy's image. "Take the hint, kid," Robert hissed. "And get off my corner."

The front door rattled, and Kim walked into

the entryway, weary after a long night of work at the hospital.

Robert lunged for the television remote and quickly changed the channel so Kim couldn't see the story on the screen. In his haste, he knocked over his drink, spilling whiskey across the table and onto the floor. He scrambled to contain his mess, slapping paper towels all over the table and the floor beneath it while pressing the button on the remote to turn off the television.

Kim stepped into the TV room and set down her purse and jacket but hesitated at the doorway. She stood with a quizzical expression on her face, her lips pursed suspiciously, as she watched Robert on his hands and knees, moving around the floor, attempting to clean up the mess.

"Everything okay here?" she asked.

Robert looked up at her. "Yeah, great," he said. "I just had a slight accident."

Kim nodded. "Uh-huh," she said, showing no concern or emotion. "Is Sam okay?"

"Sam? Oh, yeah," Robert said. "He's sound asleep. Go kiss him good night if you wish."

Kim looked at Robert and cocked her head to one side. "What's going on, Robert?"

He rose from his knees, holding the batch of booze-soaked paper towels. "What?" he asked. "Nothing's going on. I just spilled my drink. I was working late and must have dozed off . . . and the sound of you coming in startled me. That's all. Clumsy me."

Kim shook her head slightly and didn't bother to respond. Instead, she turned and walked toward the hallway. "I'm going to bed," she stated flatly. She turned slightly and eyed Robert once more before continuing down the hallway toward their bedroom.

Robert dropped the wet paper towels into the kitchen trash can. "Right. Um . . . I'll be right there. I'm going to lock up." He watched and listened, then peered down the hallway to make sure Kim had gone into the bathroom to get ready for bed.

Robert stepped back into the center of the kitchen and leaned heavily on the island countertop. He exhaled deeply. The mess in the living room was minor compared to the one looming larger every day in his life.

* * * * *

Shortly after daybreak, under cloudy skies, Harris, Dora, Violet, Lauren, and Jimmy trudged back to the encampment. The sight that greeted them brought tears to their eyes. They looked around in shock at the devastation. The tents and shacks that had previously been their homes and those of their friends were smashed, torn, and broken. Possessions and debris were strewn all over the place. Some burned remnants smoldered on the ground where the barrels had been tipped over.

Dazed and confused, Dora gazed around, muttering. "All gone," she said. "It's all gone."

"How can they just come in and destroy your tents and stuff?" Lauren asked.

Violet snickered and gave her a look. "Wanna call the cops, Lauren?"

Harris flicked the side of Violet's head. "Knock it off, V."

Violet shook her head as she looked at a bent bicycle that stood in the place where she had formerly worked to repair bikes for others. "Now I ain't got no transport. How am I gonna make a living?"

Jimmy looked at Dora, who was still spinning around, distraught. "All gone," Dora repeated. "All gone!" Jimmy clenched his fists as he walked away from the older woman. He paced as he forced himself to breathe and count.

Harris walked over to him and laid his hand on his shoulder, while Violet and Lauren tried to calm Dora. Jimmy looked into Harris's face.

"We can't move again," he said. "Look at her." He nodded toward Dora. "She gets worse each time. It's like her brain steps down another level every time we have these kinds of incidents and have to find a new location to live. She needs stability."

Harris nodded. "I know. But we don't have an option." He waved his arm in a broad sweeping motion. "Look at this place. I doubt any of the tents are still usable."

They walked over to the dumpster. It was filled with people's possessions that had been tossed into it following the attack. Harris spotted his guitar case sticking out of one side. He pulled it out and then saw two of his prized paintings. He retrieved them and a small smile crossed his face. The paintings were not seriously damaged.

Jimmy pulled out one of the tents and examined it. Totally useless. He shook his head and threw it back in the dumpster.

They moved on and pored over the remains of what had been the hut where Harris slept and kept his belongings. Everything was trashed.

"We're not going to just pack up and leave," Jimmy said. "We can fix this. We can put this back together."

Harris surveyed the area briefly, looking down at the ground and then at Jimmy. "Jimmy. We can't fix this, son. It's not fixable. We gotta go."

"But we live here!" Jimmy protested. "We can't just leave."

Harris shook his head violently. "We have to move on. There's nothing left for us here."

A car pulled up on the street and parked next to the encampment. Joanne Bartwell, a kindly social worker around forty years old, got out and took in the destruction for a moment. Harris and Violet knew her, and she started walking toward them.

"I'm so sorry to see this happen, folks," Joanne said. "We can get you all taken care of. I've got two places in a shelter only five minutes from here and three more places in a shelter downtown." Joanne glanced around the encampment. "Is there anyone else who might need some help?"

Jimmy spoke up. "Yeah, maybe a few. There were plenty of others. But we don't know where they got off to or if they'll come back or not." He looked toward Dora, Lauren, Violet, and Harris. "We're family," he said. "Find us a place where we can be together or we're staying right here."

"Hmm, I see," Joanne replied. She pulled out her phone and scrolled for a minute. A frown crossed her face. "I'm afraid that's not going to be possible."

While Joanne continued looking at her phone, Gabrielle's car pulled up behind Joanne's. Two Downtown City Mission volunteers jumped out, carrying tents, blankets, and other supplies. Jimmy's face lit up and he looked back at Joanne. "Then we're staying here."

The volunteers began distributing the tents and some bottles of water, coffee, and snack bars to the encampment residents who were slowly gathering again, and Joanne's kindly demeanor turned sour. She was not happy. Harris eyed her as she marched over to Gabrielle, who was getting more items out of her car.

"Gabrielle, this is *not* the answer," Joanne whispered loudly. "We've got to get them off the streets. You *know* that."

"Come on, Joanne," Gabrielle said, waving her hand toward the encampment. "You know how hard it is to split up these street families. They've been through enough trauma for one day. Let them alone.

My church group will take care of them." Gabrielle and Joanne had worked together before in similar situations. They were both trying to help but from two separate perspectives.

Joanne shook her head slowly. "Fine. I'll let it go this time. The city is working to provide more shelters and housing. These people can't stay on the streets forever." She went back to her car and drove off.

With the help of Gabrielle's volunteers, Harris and Jimmy got busy putting up the new tents where the now-destroyed ones had been located.

"I can handle my own," Violet said. She took one of the tents and began unpacking it. Harris grinned at her.

"Stubborn to the last." He knew Violet was more than capable of putting together her living space.

Lauren stayed close to Dora as the others worked.

When he finished one tent, Jimmy walked over to Gabrielle to get a tent for Dora and Lauren.

"You're the best," he said to Gabrielle. "Thanks for always being there for us. Anytime you need help, you know I'm always there for you too."

Gabrielle gave him a quick smile. "I'll take you

up on that, Jimmy. And I'm sorry about this." She looked around the junk-riddled encampment. "This should not have happened." She sighed deeply. "We're working on better solutions. We're raising funds to buy an old motel to help house people around here. I'll need your input on what's needed. We're hoping the city will help us too."

"For real?" Jimmy asked. "I'd be honored." Gabrielle and Jimmy walked over to Dora and Lauren to start setting up their tent so they could rearrange their living space.

The sky had been socked in by clouds earlier in the day, but it began to brighten as a few rays of sunshine pierced the darkness. Soon the clouds broke up and drifted away completely. It had been a tumultuous night and a difficult morning, and Harris was relieved his family was still alive and intact. He could only hope that the vigilantes who had attacked them had drunk their fill of evil and violence and would not return anytime soon.

Chapter 11

THE FOLLOWING morning brought a peaceful calm to the encampment—or what was left of it. Harris sat on an old beach chair with a painting canvas balanced on his lap as he sketched a picture of Dora. Violet sat nearby braiding some paracord, a lightweight rope thread, into a colorful bracelet. Jimmy and Lauren shook out a dirty carpet and laid it in front of Dora's tent to give her entryway a touch of elegance.

When they finished, Jimmy moved over to his tent and sat on a milk crate as he put on his shoes. Violet tucked the paracord bracelet inside her pants pocket and walked past Jimmy to retrieve a bucket and cloth.

"I'm heading out to the street to see if I can convince a few friendly car owners to let me wash their windows," she said. "If I make some money, I'll bring us back some peanut butter."

Jimmy gave her a thumbs up. He knew how

much Violet loved peanut butter. He hopped to his feet as Lauren came out of a tent wearing clean pants and a clean shirt. "Does this look okay?" she asked. "It's the only clothing I managed to salvage from the attack."

Jimmy looked at her and tried not to smile—too much. "You look great," he said. "Let's go downtown to the mission to feed some homeless people today." The irony of his words didn't escape him.

Lauren nodded. "That sounds good." The two of them headed toward the exit and passed by Harris, still sitting on his beach chair with a different canvas balanced on his lap. He was painting the landscape in front of him.

"Sure you don't want to come along?" Jimmy called to him.

Harris didn't answer for a few seconds, his gaze focused in front of him. Then he looked up at Jimmy. "Nah, why don't you pray for me?" he said, only half joking.

"Okay, we will. See you later." Jimmy waved to Harris and Dora, who had come out of her tent to sit beside him. "Don't forget to keep an eye on our stuff, er . . . what's left of it."

Harris gave Jimmy a thumbs-up as he and

Lauren stepped out onto the busy street and headed away from the camp.

"Where are we going?" Lauren asked.

Jimmy smiled. "You'll see. Come on. But first, I have a short detour in mind."

She shot him a questioning look but shrugged and followed him.

"I thought you could use a break," Jimmy said after they'd walked a few blocks. "This street is alive!"

They were approaching a corner where a street performer was putting on a show. They listened and applauded when the performer concluded, then continued walking down the busy city street. Jimmy took her to a vintage record store, and they rummaged through old albums, holding up one after another, showing each other their favorites and unusual artwork on covers.

An acoustic guitar was propped in the corner of the store, and Jimmy pointed at the guitar and asked the clerk, "May I?"

The clerk shrugged and nodded.

Jimmy picked up the instrument and began playing. When he finished, he put the guitar back where he had found it. The store's owner alternately scowled at his clerk and eyed Jimmy and Lauren the whole time they were inside, looking like he was ready to call the police if they attempted to pilfer anything.

They didn't. They soon waved a thank-you and went out the door to explore more of the city. They found an art gallery that was free to the public, so they went inside and perused the paintings, wandering through one hallway after another, admiring the works and making comments as if they were professional connoisseurs.

After leaving the art gallery, they walked toward the downtown area and came upon a food cart. Jimmy had a few coins in his pocket and a couple dollar bills, so they purchased two hot dogs and sat on a park bench enjoying the food.

"Thanks for showing me around," Lauren said. "This was fun."

Jimmy nodded. "Sure thing. I want you to know this life out here isn't all dirty backstreets and alleys."

Lauren chuckled. "Maybe not, but that music store guy didn't seem to want us in there."

"He was just jealous of my amazing guitar-playing skills," Jimmy quipped.

"You played two chords," Lauren replied sardonically, rolling her eyes in jest.

"That's two more than he knew," Jimmy said.

Lauren laughed so hard she nearly choked on her food. "You know, it is kind of sad, but in the little time that I've known you, you're probably the *realest* person I know."

"Realest?" Jimmy feigned an insulted expression. "Why not *best*? Or *most loyal*?"

Lauren couldn't keep from laughing. "Loyal? What are you, a dog?"

Jimmy shrugged. "*Realest* works for me."

"Yeah, me too," Lauren said, elbowing him in the arm. They fell quiet as they gazed straight ahead and watched the people walking past. It was a good quiet and Jimmy smiled to himself as he enjoyed the moment.

* * * * *

Several hours later, Dora was resting in her tent and Harris was still painting, the landscape in front of him nearly finished. He was so intent on his project that he didn't notice the three men tramping across the encampment behind him.

A local gang leader, Duke was a greasy-haired, six-foot-two tough guy in his early twenties who had earned a reputation around the city and was not to be messed with. Wearing his usual tight jeans and a tight T-shirt that showed off his taut muscles, Duke presented a menacing presence, even when he was trying to be nice—which he rarely was.

Following Duke were Red and Q, the two miscreants who had attacked Lauren a few days earlier. Q still wore a large bandage over his nose as a result of the altercation. Both men struggled to keep up with Duke's long strides.

"You two knuckleheads better watch and learn," Duke said with a raspy voice. "You gotta let 'em know who's boss. Those vets usually have some income. They make good bank . . . and that's what we want."

Duke stopped walking and raised his hand. Red and Q pulled up beside him. The three men looked around the encampment. All was quiet. No sign of anyone else nearby.

Then Red spotted Harris and pointed him out to Duke. The leader nodded silently and waved, indicating for Red and Q to follow him. They crept up behind Harris until they were standing right behind him, peering over his shoulder at his beautiful, nearly completed painting.

Duke shoved his elbow, causing Harris's brush to streak across the canvas, smearing his work. Duke burst out laughing.

"Hey!" Harris yelled. "What's goin' on?" He whipped around in the chair, startled and angry. "What did you do that for?"

Harris quickly tried to paint out the odd streak on his canvas.

Duke moved closer and grabbed the chain Harris wore around his neck, from which his dog tags dangled. Duke twisted the chain, almost choking Harris as he pulled hard, and Harris dropped the canvas and paintbrush on the ground.

"'Harris,'" Duke read. "'Harris, Benedict R.' Dang!" He turned toward Red and Q, who had drawn up behind him. "How 'bout that?" Duke continued reading from the military tags. "'Blood type: A positive. Protestant.'" Duke shoved his face right in front of Harris's. "Did you like killing people?"

Harris's face turned a deep red, partly from anger and partly from Duke's grip on his chain, but he remained silent. He breathed deeply, trying to maintain his composure.

Duke continued his taunt. "How many people did you kill? Huh? How many? Did you kill kids too? I'll bet you did. I know your type." Duke poked Harris hard in his back. "Did you paint pictures of those dead kids?"

That did it. Harris leaped to his feet and shoved Duke hard, sending him reeling backward. "Get lost!" Harris roared, his usual peaceful demeanor giving way to rage. "Unless you want to end up looking like your buddy over there." He nodded toward Q.

Q glared back at Harris but didn't say anything.

Duke regained his balance and got right back in Harris's face, drawing his switchblade at the same time. "You shouldn't have done that," he growled.

Harris looked Duke right in the eye. "Oh, it's okay," Harris said. "Now, let's all forget about it and move on." He chuckled slightly at his juxtaposition of the situation. "I don't want to hurt anyone."

Duke held the switchblade close to Harris. He jabbed at him with the knife, teasing him. He ran the blade along various parts of Harris's body, laughing. "*You* don't want to hurt anyone?" Duke asked. "You're a funny guy, Harris, Benedict R. What does the *R* stand for, anyhow?"

In his peripheral vision, Harris saw Dora peering out of her tent. He gave her a stern look, trying to send a message to her to stay hidden. He looked back at Duke and deflected his question.

"What's it matter? Look, man, I've got nothing for you except this painting. You can have it for a hundred dollars."

Duke wasn't buying the painting or anything else. "Funny. Real funny, Harris, Benedict R. But don't try my sense of humor." Duke suddenly pulled the switchblade away from Harris and in a swift motion slashed it across Harris's painting, leaving the canvas gaping in the center.

Just as quickly, he had the blade back at Harris's neck. "Hold still," he commanded.

Duke stuck his other hand in Harris's pocket. Nothing.

"No money?" he asked belligerently. "No EBT food cards?"

"I got nothin'," Harris said. "Go rob a bank or somethin' if you're so desperate."

"A real comedian," Duke spat. "Well, then, we'll just have to go search. If we don't find some money or EBT cards, you'll have to rob the bank for us."

Red and Q howled with laughter. Duke motioned them toward the tents while he kept Harris at bay with the switchblade. Q ran over to Dora's tent and pushed inside, then tugged Dora out. She held on to her purse for dear life, refusing to let go. She started loudly muttering, "I'm not here. I'm not here!"

Harris tensed. Knife or no knife, he moved toward the tent to help Dora. Duke grabbed him by the shoulders, tightening his grip against his neck so Harris couldn't escape.

Q struggled with Dora, but the older woman had some weapons of her own. She glowered at the man with owl-like eyes and hissed at him like a snake.

Freaked out, Q let her go and ran back to Duke. "That woman's crazy!"

Red went into Harris's tent and came out waving two paintings, a small handful of money, and a plastic EBT card. He handed the stash to Duke, who tossed the paintings aside and pocketed the cash and card.

Duke spoke loudly into Harris's ear. "It's the first of the month coming up soon. We'll be back for more then." He shoved Harris hard, causing him to stumble to the ground. "You and your friends better have some more to give me, or we'll destroy this place. Again." Duke snapped his fingers and headed toward the exit. Red pushed Harris over as he passed him, and Q gave him a hard kick in the stomach before the lapdogs joined their leader and strutted off toward the street.

Looking horrified, Dora ran over to Harris and cradled him in her arms.

"I'm okay, Dora," Harris reassured her. "They can't hurt us. They're just punks. We'll be fine."

* * * * *

After people-watching on the bench downtown, Jimmy took Lauren to the church service conducted by the Downtown City Mission. It was primarily held for people staying at the shelter, but they also welcomed anyone else who wanted to attend. More familiar with a liturgical form of worship, Lauren found the freedom and exuberance of the mission service exhilarating.

Afterward, they passed through the foyer into a large room filled with folding tables and chairs. A long serving table ran the length of the wall on one side and dozens of people were lined up going through the serving area cafeteria-style. Jimmy paused just inside the doorway and leaned close to Lauren.

"So . . . guess what?"

Lauren looked back at him curiously and

shrugged. "Got me. What?"

"I scheduled the job interview," he said. Lauren's expression brightened immediately. "Now, don't get your hopes up on me getting it."

Lauren smiled at him broadly. "Oh, stop, Jimmy. You've got this! You'll do great."

He spotted Gabrielle wearing a white apron and standing with a volunteer behind the serving table with several large, steaming containers of meat, vegetables, and rice and a big salad bowl. Gabrielle scooped out generous portions of food to each of the men and women as they reached her part of the table and then continued down the serving line. She looked up and saw Jimmy and Lauren.

"Jimmy! Lauren! So glad you came. Good to see you both in church this morning too."

"Told ya I'd be here," Jimmy said. "Don't have much, but I always got my word."

Gabrielle nodded and smiled at them. "No more trouble, I hope?"

Lauren and Jimmy shook their heads. "We've been doin' okay," Jimmy said.

Gabrielle reached into a box on the floor behind her and pulled out two clean aprons and handed one to each. "Here ya go, your work clothes." She smiled.

As Jimmy put on his apron and tied it in the back, Lauren leaned closer to Gabrielle.

"Um, Gabrielle?" she said quietly.

Jimmy moved behind the serving tables to get to work and give the women a moment to talk. He picked up a large spoon and began dishing out food to the people passing through the line, smiling broadly at each person as he handed back their plates.

Lauren looked into Gabrielle's eyes as she spoke. "I just wanted to thank you for the sleeping bag and everything. I'm sorry I was so . . . you know . . ."

Gabrielle smiled at her warmly. "Oh, don't apologize. I'm just happy you've found some good people. And I'm always here if you need help."

"Thanks, Gabrielle," Lauren said.

"Anytime." She nudged Lauren toward the serving line. "Now get that apron on and help us serve some food." She pointed at the long line of people stretching all the way out the door. "We got a lotta hungry mouths to feed."

They all plunged in wholeheartedly, serving food to people of many races, some dressed fairly well, others in layers of shabby rags, some who looked healthy and well, and others who appeared emaciated, either from lack of nutrition or heavy drug usage. The volunteers fed them all, no questions asked—except one: "Can I get you anything else?"

As people exited the serving line, other volunteers guided them to seats at the tables spread out all around the room.

Jimmy and Lauren stayed until the last person was fed. It felt so good to give to others who had no real way of repaying them for their kindness beyond a thank-you and a smile.

As they walked back to the encampment in the dimming light, Jimmy and Lauren shared stories about some of the people they'd met that day.

* * * * *

When they arrived back at the encampment, Jimmy and Lauren learned that Dora and Harris had experienced a totally different sort of day. As they gathered around a fire barrel that evening, Harris told them and Violet—who had earned a few dollars washing windows that day and had brought back some peanut butter—how he had been attacked by Duke, Red, and Q and how they had stolen his money and EBT card.

"Luckily, I'd spent most of my benefits for

this month," Harris said, putting a positive spin on the situation. "So there's not much left on my card for them to get. Still, we probably need to leave this area, and we gotta keep a watch out for them. They'll never be satisfied, no matter how much they steal from us."

Dora nodded enthusiastically. "I know who they are. Horrible, really horrible, nasty hooligans. I've never had to fight a gang before. I was a nurse in a play once and my line was, 'The nasty hooligans are here!' It's those nasty hooligans who . . . ," Dora's words faded into absurdity.

Violet was furious. "I'm not letting them take what little money I make, and that's that."

"Yeah," Jimmy said loudly. "I agree. I say we stay and fight them."

Harris slowly shook his head from side to side. "Look, these clowns are bad news. It's been a long day. How about me and Jimmy keep watch tonight. Let's sleep on it and come up with a plan tomorrow. We'll have a clearer picture in the light of day. Sound good?"

The group agreed, and the women soon drifted off to their respective tents. Jimmy and Harris remained by the fire in silence for a few minutes.

Then Harris looked at him. "Long day. You got first watch?"

"Sure thing, Pops," Jimmy replied. He warmed his hands over the fire and gazed intently around him in each direction.

What a day.

Chapter 12

WEARING HIS Sunday best, including a blue dress shirt and an old sports jacket he'd found in a dumpster, Jimmy walked alone toward a tall, gray, corporate office building looming over a narrow street, alongside other tall buildings. He slowed his cadence as he looked up nervously at the gigantic structure lined with windows reflecting the sun all the way to the top. He suddenly stopped, turned around, and walked away in the opposite direction.

With his palms sweating, he stopped again. He took a deep breath, braced himself, and turned around once more, walking back toward the high-rise. He stepped up to the thick glass doors and walked inside, holding his handwritten resume.

He found Ms. Leonard's name on the wall registry and punched the elevator button that would whisk him to her floor. Good thing the elevator made no stops along the way, or Jimmy may have gone back to the first floor and out the door.

Instead, he stepped out of the elevator and slowly walked down a brightly lit hallway until he found Ms. Leonard's office. He stepped inside and told the receptionist his business.

"Um, hi. I'm here for an interview with Ms. Leonard," he said much louder than he'd intended. Other people sitting in the waiting room raised their heads and stared at him.

"Just have seat over there," the receptionist said. "She has someone in with her right now, but she won't be long, I'm sure."

"Thank you," Jimmy said, then walked across the room, sat down, and immediately began fidgeting. He waited nervously for about fifteen minutes, then nearly bounded out of the chair when his name was called. The receptionist smiled at him as she ushered him in to Ms. Leonard's office and nodded toward the chair in front of the desk. Jimmy sat down quickly and looked up at Ms. Leonard. Her hair was wound into a tight bun, and she wore a starched beige shirt and a dark blazer. She sat tall and erect in her chair, looking down her nose at Jimmy.

He offered her his crinkled, handwritten resume and she took it without a word. She looked at the resume and shook her head dismissively as she

At the age of eight, "Lauren" tragically witnessed the unexpected death of her mother and enters the foster care system.

"Lauren" finds her belongings from her foster care home stuffed into trash bags and left outside the front door.

OPPOSITE PAGE: Lauren sets out on her own not knowing where she might sleep or find her next meal.

"Jimmy," portrayed by Lucas Jade Zummann, is a runaway youth with an abusive father. His mom posts signs around town, hoping to reunite with her son.

MISSING
JAMES (JIMMY) MURPHY
AGE: 19 HEIGHT: 5 '11 WEIGHT: 150
LAST SEEN ON 21ST AND MAIN ON APRIL 2ND, MAY BE TRAVELING WITH A GROUP
IF YOU HAVE ANY INFORMATION CALL OR HAVE SEEN JIMMY PLEASE CALL (916) -293-2834 OR 911
IMMEDIATELY
PLEASE - INFORMATION NEEDED

Alisa Schulz portrays a heartbroken mother of a runaway youth who is now homeless.

Opposite page: The cast and director, screenwriter, and producer Julia Verdin pose in front of "Jimmy's" house in Sacramento, CA, after filming a dinner scene.

Harris, a gifted painter and battle-scarred veteran, is constantly warding off a harassing gang.

Opposite page left: This scene illustrates how, for those experiencing homelessness, a simple visit to a local park can quickly become a dangerous situation.

Opposite page right: "Harris" champions his street family to get their lives back as they deal with the tension from an unforgiving community and local authorities.

In a flashback scene, actors Kristanna Loken, Keenan Moran, and William Baldwin enjoy happier times before they learn the reality of their financial situation.

Opposite page: Behind the scenes: the movie crew stages a heartwarming family dinner scene in a Folsom, CA, home.

Above: Producer Robert Craig enters as the character of a prison guard in William Baldwin's jail cell scene.

Opposite page bottom: William Baldwin portrays "Robert," a once-successful businessman in the throes of financial ruin due to his gambling addiction.

ABOVE: Beverly D'Angelo plays the role of "Dora," a former star actress who is now grappling with mental health challenges.

RIGHT: Beverly D'Angelo portrays "Dora," whose storyline is inspired by true events. This film is a testament to the enduring human spirit and the transformative power of community.

Filming Ty Pennington as "Mr. Mills," the hardware store owner who offers "Jimmy" a break when he misses his interview.

handed it back to him.

"This is a mess," she said coldly. "You should type it up properly."

Jimmy shifted uncomfortably as Ms. Leonard eyed him up and down. Embarrassed, Jimmy leaned forward and placed his hands under him, then leaned back and sat on them.

Ms. Leonard looked down at another form Jimmy had filled out while he had been waiting for her. "You need to put a proper address on here," she said.

"I did," Jimmy responded. "Downtown City Mission."

"But that's not where you live, is it?"

"No, but . . ." Jimmy really didn't want to tell her he had no address, other than the encampment where he and the group lived.

"Well, I need an actual address," Ms. Leonard insisted in a huff. "You can't have 'no address.' You have to live *somewhere*. Please fill it in properly and then bring it back to me if you want to be considered for a job with this company."

Jimmy sat silently for a long moment. Ms. Leonard simply glared at him. After a few more seconds of uncomfortable silence, Jimmy got up.

"Thanks for your time, ma'am," he said. "I'm clearly not a fit here." He gritted his teeth and walked out the door.

* * * * *

Lauren stood in front of a bowl of warm, soapy water, washing some dirty dishes. Violet was sorting through cans and plastic bottles on her worktable, keeping count on a scrap of paper.

Jimmy appeared and trudged toward his tent, walking right past them without saying a word.

Lauren called out to him. "Hey, how'd it go?"

Jimmy didn't turn around, and he didn't stop walking. "Waste of time," he groused. He took a piece of paper out of his pocket, crumpled it, and threw it on the ground, and then dove through the front flap of his tent.

Lauren stared after him, her eyes wide. She dried her hands, walked over, and picked up the ball of paper. She pocketed it and went back to cleaning the dishes.

Harris walked toward them, licking chocolate off his fingers from a protein bar he'd just finished eating. He dropped the wrapper into the fire barrel and turned to watch them. After a couple of minutes, he spoke quietly.

"I don't think the gang will be back before the first of the month, but keep on alert, just in case."

Violet gave him a sharp salute, and Harris went on his way.

Moments later, Jimmy emerged from his tent. Now dressed in casual clothes, he passed by the women and walked right out of the encampment without saying a word to anyone.

A little while later, Dora stepped out of her tent wearing a long, flowing, slightly tattered pink evening dress set off by a colorful scarf encircling her neck. She held an old beat-up mirror in one hand and her makeup bag in the other.

"It's a beautiful day!" she said cheerily.

"Hello, Dora," Violet called.

"Hi, Dora," Lauren said. "You look lovely."

Dora sat down near Lauren and Violet and started to apply her makeup. They all looked up when a woman ran into the encampment. She spotted Violet and rushed toward her. Violet glared at the woman, her mouth gaping in surprise.

"I'm sorry to bother you again," the woman said. She held out the picture of Jimmy. "But someone told me they'd seen my son around here." She took a breath. "I wondered . . ."

Lauren ambled over, curious. Violet looked at the photo, then cocked her head slightly as though thinking.

"Look, lady," Violet said. "How many times do I gotta tell you?"

Lauren craned her neck behind Violet, trying to see the picture, but Violet pushed her back. Violet looked directly at the woman and said, "I ain't seen that dude."

The woman lowered her head and sighed. "Sorry. I was just hoping . . . He's been missing for quite a while. It's been more than two years. I miss him so much."

She started to walk away, but then stopped suddenly. She turned back toward Violet and Lauren and handed Violet a clear plastic bag containing freshly baked brownies.

"Here," she offered. "Please take these so they don't go to waste. They were his favorite."

"Thank you," Violet replied. "We'll keep our eyes out for him."

The woman nodded sadly. She turned and trudged back out toward the street.

Lauren reached over and grabbed a brownie. “Was that Jimmy she was lookin’ for?”

Violet nodded and looked off into the distance.

“Why’d you lie to her?” Lauren asked.

Violet simply shrugged. “Why? You gonna report me to the principal?”

Lauren looked at Violet quizzically. “No.” She paused for a few moments before going on. “But she seems like she really loves him. Why didn’t you tell her?”

“Just drop it,” Violet said, harsher than necessary. “We don’t know that lady.” She looked at Lauren. “And we don’t owe her nothin’.”

“But if his real family is looking for Jimmy, who are we to get in the way?” Lauren asked.

Violet bristled. “*We* are his real family,” she said. “And we protect each other. Always. Remember that.” Violet turned on her heels and disappeared into her tent, leaving Lauren standing there dumbfounded.

Dora danced up next to Lauren. The former actress had finished putting on her makeup and now wore a pink bow in her hair. She leaned in toward Lauren.

“She’s had a rough life,” she said, nodding toward Violet’s tent. “Went through a lot in Iraq.”

Dora shook her head, her eyes full of sadness. "Four surgeries. Gave her drugs for the pain and she became addicted to them. They discharged her without benefits. That's why she's the way she is."

Dora smiled at Lauren for no reason as she picked up a coat. "Anyway, I've got to go. I have a date with a friend."

"A date?" Lauren asked, pretending to be astonished without revealing her skepticism. "Want me to go with you?"

"Oh no, dear," Dora answered kindly. "I have to go alone. Have a good day."

"You sure?" Lauren said, attempting to mask her concern.

Dora didn't answer. She simply turned and wandered off toward the main entrance of the encampment. Lauren watched her go, not sure what to do about it. Harris was gone. Jimmy was gone. Violet?

She turned toward Violet's tent and called out to her, trying to keep Dora in view. "Violet! Violet! Dora's leaving . . ."

She knew Violet heard her, but she didn't answer. Lauren shrugged and stepped closer to the encampment exit, trying to spot Dora.

But Dora was gone.

* * * * *

Inside her tent, Violet sat with her head in her hands. She stared at the ceiling for some long moments, then placed a set of cheap headphones on her ears and turned the music up full volume so she could hear nothing else.

A tear trickled down Violet's cheek. Then another. And another.

Chapter 13

LATE THAT afternoon, as the sun began to set, Jimmy returned to the encampment. He seemed to be in better spirits and was carrying several take-out boxes from the Italian restaurant. He placed the food on the table near where Lauren was sitting, reading a book, then walked over toward Dora's tent.

"Dora!" he called. "Dinnertime. I scored some of your favorites."

Dora didn't answer, but Violet looked up and hurried over from her worktable where she'd been hard at it, trying to repair a beat-up bicycle for more than an hour. She and Lauren had ignored each other since Dora had left, neither of them saying a word to the other.

"Dora! Come on out," Jimmy called again.

No answer.

Jimmy sat down with Violet and Lauren, and they began to eat without Dora. Harris joined them and looked around, then walked over to Dora's tent.

He opened the flap and peeked inside. Seeming puzzled, he stepped back to the table and stared at Jimmy, Lauren, and Violet.

"Where is she?"

Nobody answered. They exchanged sheepish glances. Lauren coughed, the words getting stuck in her throat.

"She went to meet a friend," she finally said.

"What? You let her go alone?" Harris asked, immediately growing agitated.

The question caught Lauren off guard. "Well, yeah," she answered. "I asked her if she wanted me to go with her, but she said she wanted to go alone."

Harris was clearly worried. "You all shoulda kept an eye on her."

Violet flashed Lauren a dirty look. "Yeah. You should have."

"I didn't know I was supposed to babysit her," Lauren protested.

"Oh, come on!" Violet said. "Anyone can see that she's not all there. Stuck in her own little fantasy world, all those imaginary friends she has—"

"I'm sorry," Lauren said. "I didn't realize . . ." her words trailed away as she covered her mouth with her hand.

Violet glared at Jimmy, who remained silent as if trying to process the situation. "This is all *your* fault, Jimmy," she said. "Told you not to let outsiders in. I knew we shouldn't trust her." She nodded toward Lauren.

Lauren's body recoiled, stung by Violet's verbal attack. She looked toward Jimmy, hoping he might defend her or at least offer a bit of solace. But Jimmy was lost in his own thoughts and paid no attention to her.

Harris weighed in instead. "It's not her fault," he said, looking at Lauren. "Maybe it's time to get Dora somewhere safer. Her memory is getting worse."

"No!" Jimmy yelled. "We can take care of her. Dora doesn't want to live like that, okay? She's family and she needs to stay with us." Jimmy turned to Lauren and asked, "What was she wearing?"

"A long pink dress and her coat," Lauren replied.

"Okay. Let's go. I think I know where she is." He sprinted off, out of the encampment and down the street. Lauren, Violet, and Harris looked after him, confused, but then quickly followed.

Jimmy led the way as Harris and Violet tried to keep up, trailing him as he ran through a courtyard with a fountain in the center, out the other side, and toward an old, ornate theater. Lauren lagged behind even though she was easily the fastest runner in the group. She felt awful for letting Dora go out on her own, but also hurt by Violet's words.

Jimmy spotted Dora first. "There she is!" he called to the others. They hurried toward the woman, then slowed to a crawl as they got closer. Dora, in her flowing pink dress, was doing a swirling, ballet-style dance in front of the theater entrance. People on the street stopped to watch her gracefully performing to music only she could hear. A few clapped as they passed. Others stayed longer, enjoying the show. A few laughed, shook their heads, and walked away.

Lauren ran up behind Harris, Jimmy, and Violet. She breathed a sigh of relief at seeing the woman safe, then turned, backed away from the group, and started slowly walking down the sidewalk.

* * * * *

Jimmy and the others inched closer to Dora, ready to embrace her and welcome her back into their care.

"Dora." Harris spoke her name softly so he wouldn't alarm her. But for some reason, Dora pulled away from them, as though afraid. The trio stopped and stood in place, staring at her.

"No! No! Don't take me away!" Dora cried. "This is my home. The theater is where I belong."

She looked up at her friends, making eye contact with them, then extended her arms toward Harris.

"Dora, we're here for you," he said. He quickly moved to her and wrapped her in his arms, then Jimmy and Violet embraced her as well. It was an odd yet beautiful moment as the four of them stood with their arms around each other in front of the theater.

As they gently led Dora away and started heading back toward the encampment, Jimmy turned and looked around for Lauren. He spotted her in the distance, walking back toward their tents, her head down. He started to run ahead of the group to catch up with her.

Violet suddenly grimaced and her body spasmed with pain as she began coughing violently. Jimmy stopped and turned back.

Violet bent over in the street, clutching her stomach and clenching her teeth. Perspiration dotted her forehead and she wiped the droplets away using her forearm.

"V, that sounds bad," Harris said. "Are you

okay? Maybe you need to go to a doctor."

Violet glanced at Dora and then at Harris and Jimmy. She pulled herself upright and tried to put on a happy face. "I'm fine," she said, clearly lying. "I must have eaten something that didn't agree with me." She waved her hand. "Let's go home."

Jimmy eyed her but decided to let it go for now, then turned and hurried to catch up with Lauren.

When he reached the encampment, Jimmy saw Lauren coming out the tent she had been sharing with Dora. She carried her sleeping bag and her backpack.

Jimmy ran to her and grabbed her shoulder. "Hey, what are you doing?"

"Everyone hates me," Lauren said. "So I'm leaving."

"Are you crazy?" he replied. "Where are you going to go?"

Lauren looked around, unsure, and bit her lower lip nervously. "Maybe Gabrielle can . . . find me a place in a shelter—"

"Wait," Jimmy interrupted. "Stop. You told me what happened in the shelter. You don't want to go back there. And you can't blame yourself for Dora wandering off. It wasn't your fault. It's hard for all of us together to keep a close watch on her. I know.

Believe me, we all try, but sometimes we blow it. And we worry about her getting picked up by the cops again." Jimmy sighed heavily. "Lauren, nobody meant to blame you. Don't mind what Violet says. We were all just concerned about Dora."

Tears welled in Lauren's eyes. "She's so sweet. If anything had happened to her . . . I don't know . . ."

"Well, it didn't," Jimmy said. "Come on. We need you. Dora needs you here . . . and so do I."

Lauren looked at him and studied his face. He hoped she saw his genuine affection for her. But after a few seconds, she shook her head hard and continued walking away.

"Lauren!" Jimmy called.

"Leave me alone." She reached the exit and increased her pace as she headed down the street away from the camp, but Jimmy caught up to her.

"Lauren, stop," he said. "Please come back."

"Why? Why would I?" she asked, her voice quivering with emotion. "Nobody wants me here. Violet said it earlier and she nailed it."

Jimmy grabbed Lauren's hand, bringing her to a halt. "You know that's not true," he said quietly.

"Then why is everything always my fault?" Lauren asked. "'She doesn't belong here,' is what

Violet said. 'She won't survive a week,' and 'She should have watched Dora' . . . Violet's right. I should have watched Dora."

"But we found her," Jimmy said. "She's all right. Lauren, we're family. We look out for each other—"

"No. *You're* a family, but I'm not," Lauren said. She stood stiffly and tried to turn so Jimmy couldn't see her face. "No one has looked out for me. Not since . . . ." A tear trailed down her cheek.

Jimmy stepped forward and wrapped Lauren in his arms, drawing her tightly to his chest. Lauren didn't return the hug at first, but she didn't resist the embrace either.

"I look out for you," Jimmy said, still holding her close. "You know I do. The others do too. You can't take Violet too seriously. She just gets grumpy sometimes. You're part of this family now." He smiled. "Whether you like it or not."

Lauren softened in his embrace, then wrapped her arms around him, hugging him back. "Thanks," she whispered. "I'm not sure I really know what family is anymore."

Jimmy pulled back and gazed into Lauren's eyes. After a few seconds he nodded slightly, then said, "Wait here a second, okay?"

Lauren didn't respond, but she didn't move away.

Jimmy gingerly stepped backward, keeping his eyes on her as he moved.

"Okay." She sighed.

"Promise? Don't move." Jimmy turned and bounded back toward the camp.

When he reached it, he ran over to Harris's tent and grabbed his guitar and a lantern. He slipped the guitar strap over his shoulder and hurried back to where Lauren was waiting.

"Come on," he said. "I want to show you something."

Lauren looked at him quizzically.

Jimmy smiled. "Just follow me." Sleeping bag tucked under her arm, she went with him to the top of a parking garage. When they reached the highest level, they walked toward the edge of the wall. Jimmy turned and looked at her.

"This is my secret spot," he said. "I come here when I need to get away."

Lauren looked around at the empty parking area. "It's . . . ahh . . . great."

Jimmy set the guitar on the ground and then lit the lantern and placed it nearby. The light of the flame created a soft ambience against the hard concrete. Jimmy took the sleeping bag from Lauren's arms and spread it on the ground near the lantern. Then he reached out to take Lauren's hand.

"Okay, close your eyes," he said.

She hesitated. "What are you up to?" she asked with a laugh.

"Just close your eyes. Trust me."

Lauren closed her eyes and Jimmy took both of her hands in his. He turned her around and led her to the parking garage wall overlooking the city lights below.

"All right," he said. "Now open your eyes."

"Whoa!" Lauren gasped at the beauty of the twinkling lights spread out as far as she could see. "That's incredible!"

"Pretty amazing, isn't it?"

"You aren't kidding," Lauren replied. "It's like the whole city is lit up for us."

Jimmy smiled and they gazed at the view for a few minutes. Then he walked with Lauren back to where he had set up the lantern, guitar, and her sleeping bag. They sat and Jimmy idly plucked the guitar while Lauren looked up at the stars.

After a while, she asked, "Do you have any

happy memories?"

"Happy memories?" Jimmy pondered for a moment. "Yeah, fourth grade choir."

"So you were a singer way back then too?"

"Yeah, I could really rock 'Twinkle, Twinkle, Little Star.'" He laughed and plucked a few notes of the song, then added a few power chords as if he were a rock-and-roll star.

Lauren giggled.

Jimmy continued strumming the guitar, softly picking out a familiar melody as Lauren relaxed. They were quiet for a while, both enjoying the music and the moment. From time to time, Jimmy quietly sang a familiar song and even dared to play one he had written. Eventually, he put the guitar aside.

"Thanks for the music," Lauren said, rubbing her arms to warm up. The late spring evening had turned chilly, and Jimmy removed his jacket and put it around her shoulders.

"You're welcome," he replied as he scooted closer and wrapped an arm around her.

She pulled the coat snug to her body, then they eased back to lie on the ground and look up at the sky.

"Look at all those stars," Jimmy said. "Wow!

It's spectacular. There are even some planets visible tonight." He pointed toward the night sky. "See that one? That bright one on top—that's Jupiter. And over there, that's Mars. And there's Venus."

Lauren gazed at the stars above them as Jimmy continued pointing out various constellations.

"How do you know so much about astronomy?"

He smiled. "Oh, I used to read about it with my mom. She was really smart. I don't think I gave her enough credit. She'd tell me all sorts of stories. I still remember most of them." He paused and stared into the heavens. "I miss her."

Lauren reached over and gently took Jimmy's hand in hers. The moment their fingers touched, he flinched as if he'd been zapped by electricity, but the sensation drew a warm smile to his face and he squeezed her hand in reassurance. He glanced at her and caught her smiling at him too. Fingers laced together, they gazed into each other's eyes silently for several delightful moments—hers twinkling with excitement in the dark. Then they looked back to the night sky. She laid her head on his shoulder and smiled when he reached his arm around her and held her tightly.

Chapter 14

THE WEEK passed quickly—too quickly for Robert, since he had made little progress on his anticipated big deal. Late Saturday night, he wearily stumbled through the front door of his home, trying not to awaken Kim or Sam. He flipped on the lights in the kitchen and saw that Kim had left him a plateful of food on the table. Beside it was a pile of unpaid bills with a handwritten note placed on top.

Sam's school called. They said they haven't received his tuition yet!

He tensed. Robert took a bite of the cold food and winced as he read Kim's note again. Another paper was on the table beside the pile of bills. It was Sam's math test. Robert looked at it and smiled. Atop the page the teacher had written "97% Great work, Sam!"

Robert quickly finished his dinner, then placed the plate in the sink. He turned the kitchen lights off and walked down the hallway toward Sam's room. The door was slightly ajar, and the room inside was dark except for the light shining in from the hallway. Robert peeked in and was surprised to see his son awake and staring at the ceiling, watching the shadows from a moving constellation night-light.

Robert walked over to Sam's bed and sat on the edge, facing the boy.

"Hey, bud," he said quietly.

Sam did not respond. He simply looked at Robert, almost as if he were a stranger.

Robert nodded slightly. "Your mom said you're doing great in school. I saw your math test score too. Way to go. I'm so proud of you."

"Thanks, Dad," Sam said sadly.

"Is everything okay?" Robert asked.

Sam looked up at his dad and a tear rolled down his cheek. "When are you going to be home, Dad?"

"I don't know, buddy," Robert said. "Dad's been extremely busy lately."

"You're busy a lot," Sam said with a sniffle.

"I know, son. I know. I'm going to change that. Soon. Real soon." Robert reached out and softly stroked Sam's hair. "Go to sleep now, okay? I love you."

"I love you, too, Dad," Sam said. He pinched his eyes shut and rolled over on his side.

Robert tucked the covers in around him, then stepped to the doorway and stopped. He turned back and took a long look at his son, concern creasing his forehead as he closed the door behind him.

* * * * *

The following day dawned with inviting sunshine flooding down on the Downtown City Mission, giving the building a bright, inviting appearance. It was Sunday, church day at the mission, so Lauren helped Gabrielle organize some simple but lovely flower arrangements in the worship area.

"Just because we don't have a lot of money doesn't mean we can't do things with excellence," Gabrielle said with a radiant smile.

Lauren and Jimmy placed the service order cards around the church, then cleaned the windows before people arrived. Soon, a ragtag assortment of guests poured into the room—vagrants, homeless people, a few known drug addicts, and several people in serious need of mental health resources. The mission welcomed them all and conducted an encouraging church service reminding each person of their worth and dignity in the eyes of God.

After the service, Lauren reached for Jimmy's hand and said, "Come with me. I want to show you something."

They walked back to the mission's office area, and Lauren stopped in front of a table with several computers and a printer on it. She pressed a few keys on one of the computers, and a resume printed out—Jimmy's much-improved resume. She nodded toward the printer, indicating that Jimmy should retrieve the paper.

He picked it up and his eyes widened with surprise. "Wow! This is great! Where did you learn to do this?"

"I took a business class at school," Lauren said. "They wanted to prepare us for the future." She smiled and then broke into a laugh.

"I appreciate you helping me out. I really do," Jimmy said, "but that job interview was just too humiliating. I'm not smart like you. I don't even have a high school diploma. You could easily go to college, get a good education, and get a decent job. Not me."

"Come on, Jimmy," Lauren said. "Stop that. You're smart, too, and people love you. You just need to have confidence in yourself. You gotta start somewhere—make some contacts with people who can help and keep building relationships if you want to start a rescue mission someday." She looked at him with open admiration. "Please. Just try one more time."

"Okay, fine," he reluctantly agreed. He looked into Lauren's beautiful face. "I'll do it for you, but right now, I gotta figure out where to find dinner for everyone." Jimmy headed toward the mission's exit with Lauren at his side.

"Maybe you could ask that caseworker woman if you can put your name down for an apartment," Lauren said. "If you get something, you could live there."

"No," Jimmy replied. "I couldn't leave Dora, Harris, and Violet. They're *family*. And they need me."

Lauren stopped and placed her hands on her hips. "Jimmy, we can't stay on the streets forever." She paused and tilted her head. "Maybe we can find a place for them too," she said hopefully.

"No, we stay together," Jimmy said firmly. "Family should always come first. You can do what's best for you, but I'm not leaving them. I can't leave them."

Lauren looked down at the ground. She spoke

quietly, almost in a whisper, "Jimmy, we shared a special moment when we were stargazing. Did that not mean anything to—"

She heard a shuffle and looked up, but Jimmy was gone, already striding out of the mission's office area.

* * * * *

On Monday afternoon, Robert sat at his desk at Gipmar Real Estate, searching online for potential deals. Posters and photos of high-end properties adorned the walls of the sleek office complex. He'd been at it for hours and looked up in surprise when Claudia stormed into his office.

She stopped right in front of Robert's desk without a word and tossed a handful of eight-by-ten, full-color photographs in front of him. The photos were all of the rebuilt homeless encampment on the property Robert had so confidently declared a done deal. He stared at the photos in shock.

"*Why* are they back?" Claudia fumed. "Are you planning to build the high-rise on top of them?" The veins in her neck looked like they might pop through her skin, she was so angry. The photos clearly revealed that not only were the tents, shacks, and debris back, but it seemed that *more* now covered the ground Robert had planned to develop. Following the vigilante attack, Robert's contacts on the council had confided to him that it might take a while longer before the city could move in with bulldozers . . . but nobody had predicted *this*.

Flustered, his words caught in his throat. "I didn't know . . ." he said hoarsely. "How did this happen?"

Claudia raised her eyebrows and glared down at Robert. "The fact that *you* don't even know just shows me that you can't be trusted with this or any project."

"B-but, Claudia, p-please . . ." Robert stammered. "I'll handle it."

"Like you 'handled' the last project?" She paused as though replaying Robert's recent list of failures in her mind. "I've given you"—her voice softened slightly, then quickly grew harsher—"I don't even know. How many chances?"

When he failed to answer, she spoke quietly but firmly. "It's over. You're fired, Robert."

Robert jumped to his feet, his eyes pleading as much as his voice. "Please, Claudia. I h-have a family

. . . I h-have a wife and ch-child." His voice cracked with emotion. "I need this job."

Claudia made a disgusted face. "Have some self-respect, Robert. Don't beg. Just pack up your things and get out." She spun on her heels and marched out of the office.

Robert slumped in the chair with a devastated, desperate look in his eyes. He flopped forward, holding his face in his hands.

After a long while, he retrieved a box out of the supply closet and set it on his desk. He tossed his personal items into the box: a photo of Kim and Sam, a trophy he had received as one of the company's highest achievers, another award for outstanding sales as well as recognition certificates, letters of appreciation, and other career accolades. His suit rumpled and disheveled, he carried the box out to his BMW and heaved it onto the front passenger seat.

He walked around the car, opened the door, sank into the driver's seat, and stared out the windshield. At nothing. Absolutely nothing. His eyes glazed over. Then, as if a dam of emotion had broken within him, Robert let out a howl of pain and frustration. He slammed the steering wheel with his palms as he continued to scream. When he was done, he reached over and grabbed the armrest of the door and jerked it closed.

Before pulling out of the company parking lot, Robert grabbed his award certificates and other personal papers from the box and tossed them out the window. Then he jammed the gearshift into position and stomped on the gas pedal. The car lurched out of the parking spot, leaving Robert's most-cherished career reminders swirling on the ground. As he sped away, what was left of Robert's loftiest goals and achievements were strewn across the parking lot.

He kept his foot pressed firmly on the gas pedal, racing from one traffic light to the next, speeding recklessly through the green lights, then slamming on the brakes at the red lights. In a seedy part of town, he pulled the car off the road and parked, then walked into a dingy-looking bar. The dim lighting made it difficult to see, but Robert found his way to a barstool and ordered a drink . . . then another, and another.

The bartender refilled Robert's glass several times, and then stood back against a row of whiskey bottles and watched Robert from a distance. No doubt he'd seen Robert's type before.

From the stool in front of the bar, Robert raised his glass and looked toward the bartender. "Another," he said, much louder than necessary.

The bartender ambled back over to him and stood in front of him on the other side of the counter. "You all right, buddy?" he asked, his eyes never leaving Robert's.

"Yeah, yeah," Robert said, nodding over his glass. "I'm fine. Never been better. Just keep 'em flowin'. Pour me another, please."

The bartender pulled a half-full whiskey bottle off the shelf and refilled Robert's glass again. "That'll be forty bucks, for this and the ones you've already had," he said.

Robert reached in his pocket and pulled out his wallet. He found a couple of twenty-dollar bills and threw them on the bar. "There ya go," he grunted. "Let's keep this party going!" He raised his glass high above his head, toasting himself.

The front door of the bar opened and in walked a tough-looking man. The man sauntered over to where Robert was perched on his barstool and moved in uncomfortably close to him.

Robert looked at him through his bleary eyes and turned back to his drink. Without looking up, he groused, "What do *you* want?"

The man didn't hesitate. "You owe me money," he growled.

Robert looked up from his drink and turned toward the man. "And who might you be?"

"I'm the guy who didn't get paid for that little cleanup project I did for you."

"I didn't hire you," Robert retorted. "Go talk to Carl. Your deal was with him, not me."

"We did." The man snarled. "Why do you think we've been looking for you?"

Robert turned and looked at him, then glanced over at the bartender who was watching their every move. "Yeah, well, you didn't finish the job, did you?" Robert said sarcastically. "So I'm not paying you a penny."

The man's face reddened, and he pressed in even tighter to Robert. "Maybe you didn't hear me," he said icily. "We did a job. I expect to get paid."

Robert pushed his feet off the barstool and spun around. "No!" he yelled. "Maybe you didn't hear *me*. You didn't do the job. They're still there. All those vagrants! They're still there and because of your incompetence, because you botched it, I got fired." He turned abruptly back to the bar. "So the joke's on you. Get in line," Robert said with a drunken laugh. "I owe money to everybody in town." He sat back down on the barstool. "Go tell your friend he can pay you if he wants. I've got nothing to pay you with."

The man leaned back, seeming to soak in this new information. Then he recoiled and was right back in Robert's face, even closer. "You better not be lying to me," he threatened. "You wanna know something? I'm going to get paid what I'm owed . . . one way or another."

Robert chuckled aloud. "Humph," he grunted. He lifted his glass to take a drink, but the man swiftly pushed his arm down on the bar, splashing the whiskey across the counter.

"Hey!" the bartender yelled as he quickly came over to where the two men were. "Beat it!" he commanded.

The man pressed against Robert's shoulder to make his point one more time. He glared at the bartender, then at Robert, then turned on his heel and strutted out of the bar.

Robert looked at what was left of the whiskey in his glass. He picked it up and tossed back the remaining liquid. He slowly lowered his arm, placed the empty glass in front of him, and stared aimlessly into the emptiness of his life.

* * * * *

The encampment was quiet and peaceful in the middle of the afternoon. Harris sat outside his tent cleaning his paintbrushes.

Across the way, Lauren brushed her teeth, holding a cup of water from a water bottle.

Jimmy crawled out of his tent wearing a brand-new suit he'd gotten with the help of the Salvation Army and popped some chewing gum in his mouth. He stood and straightened out his clothing, then carefully folded his typed resume in thirds and placed it inside his interior jacket pocket.

"This is my day, guys!" he declared.

Dora crawled out of her tent, and Jimmy helped her stand. He smiled at her and Dora hugged him in return.

Lauren finished brushing her teeth, then walked over to Jimmy. She sidled up to him, face-to-face, and looked into his eyes. She straightened his collar and smiled. "There ya go. Perfect."

Jimmy shuffled nervously in front of her.

"You are going to do great," Lauren said. "You're going to nail this interview."

Jimmy didn't have time to respond before Dora came up and grabbed his arm. "Where are you going, Jimmy?" she asked. "Please don't leave us."

"I have a job interview at a hardware store. You know what they say: twenty-third time's the charm!" He laughed at his own joke, then looked at Dora reassuringly. "But don't worry, Dora. I'll be back. Don't you worry about—"

"Yo! Benedict R.!" A loud voice interrupted him.

Harris looked up, shocked. His face blanched as he saw Red and Q approaching fast from the edge of the encampment. Rage instantly surged within him, and he stood up tall and clenched his fists, ready to confront the jerks.

Jimmy grabbed Harris's shoulder, holding him back. "What did ya always tell me?" he said. "Take some deep breaths. Count to ten. Let's get outta here before they start trouble."

Dora, Violet, and Lauren stood aghast, their mouths open with fear.

Jimmy took the lead and tugged on Harris, pulling him with him as the women followed.

"Quick!" Jimmy said. "Run as fast as you can."

Red saw them going and took off after them. "Move it, Q!" Red yelled. "Don't let them get away. We'll get it from Duke if we don't deliver." The men chased after the five homeless people who were frantically fleeing out the exit toward an alley.

Just as Jimmy, Violet, Lauren, Harris, and Dora made it across the alleyway, a car pulled in and stopped right in front of the exit. Red and Q skidded to a stop. Red angrily beat on the roof of the car with his fists.

"Get outta the way!" he shouted. "Move it!"

The driver gawked at him in fear. Red banged harder on the roof, then both he and Q jumped over the hood of the car and continued their chase.

A few steps in front of the others, Jimmy ran down the street, dodging passersby as Violet and Lauren assisted Dora and Harris stayed close behind them to prod them along. Then, instead of Dora falling behind, Violet turned away from the others. She buckled over, clearly in pain, her breathing deeply labored. Harris grabbed her and pulled her along.

"Come on, V," he said. "You can't stop now."

Violet looked up and saw Red and Q gaining

on them. "We gotta do something," she gasped.

"I got an idea," Jimmy said. "Follow me." He ducked around a corner and darted down another alley as the group struggled to keep up. He stopped next to the dumpster behind his favorite Italian restaurant. The others soon caught up with him.

"Jimmy, you crazy? We can't hide back here. We'll be cornered, for sure," Violet said.

Jimmy pointed at the dumpster.

The others watched, puzzled, as he reached up and flipped the heavy lid all the way open. "Hurry! Get in."

"What!" Lauren blurted.

To show the way, he climbed up the side of the dumpster, jumped inside, and then popped his head out. "Come on!" He reached his arm down the outside of the dumpster. "I'll help you. Put your feet on these bars going across the back, then climb on over." He looked at Dora. "Don't worry. I won't let you fall."

The others looked at one another reluctantly, but the sounds of Red's and Q's footsteps drawing nearer got their adrenaline pumping. Harris helped the women climb up the side of the dumpster, and Jimmy helped them get in. Once Harris had climbed in, he put his fingertip up to his mouth. "Shh!"

Jimmy quickly pulled the heavy lid down on top of the dumpster. It was pitch-black inside, but nobody said a word, not even Dora. They all froze just in time as Red and Q reached the area—and ran right past the dumpster and down another alley.

"What did I tell you?" Jimmy whispered.

"Jimmy, I'm scared," Dora said. "It's so dark in here, and the metal wall is cold." Jimmy moved his hand around in the dark until he found Dora's hand. He squeezed it and held on to her.

"All I know is it smells like crap in here," Violet said in a sardonic attempt at lightheartedness.

Jimmy chuckled and sighed. "It beats getting stabbed," he said.

"Maybe you're smelling the pizza," Harris quipped. He held out a box of trashed pizza. "Anyone hungry?"

"Eww! Gross!" Lauren said, coughing as if she were choking. The entire group laughed, the tension relieved.

But then suddenly they heard footsteps outside, approaching the dumpster. A hand opened the metal lid above them, and they all cowered back into the farthest corner. Someone tossed a large bag of trash into the dumpster, and it landed right on top of Violet. The heavy lid slammed shut.

"That's it!" Violet hissed. "I'm getting out of here!" She brushed the mess off her shoulders and stood on her tiptoes, pushing the lid open a few inches and filling the dumpster with light.

"Wait!" Jimmy whispered. "Hold on." He stood up next to Violet and peered out at their surroundings.

"Okay," he whispered. "Let's go. But keep the noise down. They aren't that far away."

Violet jumped up on the metal crossbar on the interior of the dumpster and pushed the lid up with her shoulder. She swung her leg over the side and hopped out, landing on her feet on the ground. She then reached up to help Dora as Harris and Lauren lowered her carefully over the side while Jimmy held up the lid. Once the women were all safely out and breathing fresh air, Harris and Jimmy jumped out too. They all breathed sighs of relief that they had given the thugs the slip.

They headed back toward the encampment as the sun was lowering on the horizon. When they rounded the corner closest to where their tents were located in the encampment, they stopped short and simply stared.

Nobody said a word.

The encampment had been trashed—again. Tents had been torn down or sliced apart, and apparently the entire area had been doused with water, turning the ground into mud.

Dora broke away and ran into the encampment where she found her favorite "angel" in the mud. She picked up the doll and hugged it tightly to her chest as tears welled in her eyes. The others followed and started picking through the mud, trying to salvage their tents, tarps—anything that wasn't ruined or cut to shreds. A dark shroud of sadness covered their faces like a heavy, wet blanket.

None of them had any question about who had vandalized their stuff. Jimmy looked at Harris. "We gotta find a way to get that gang arrested." He spat out the words derisively.

Harris looked down at a smoldering pile of his possessions and found his Bible with the cover burned but the interior still intact. He brushed the crud off his most prized possession, shaking his head at the disrespect, yet thankful it had survived the attack.

"Right now, we gotta find a place where they can't find us, son."

Violet's brain lurched in a different direction.

"What I wouldn't do for a nice apple, some peanut butter, and some chocolate right now," she said. The others weren't sure if she was serious.

Violet walked off and looked around the area where her tent had stood only a few hours earlier. She searched for her bicycle and her repair table, but both were gone. She looked like she was going to let loose a litany of profanity, but she didn't. Instead, she started coughing. Then she doubled over and grabbed her side, obviously in severe pain. She stumbled over to an old beat-up sofa, plopped down on the filthy wet cushions, and lay back, looking up at the sky.

Lauren and Jimmy were cleaning the mud off the salvageable items and packing the remnants of the group's possessions into a grocery store shopping cart. There wasn't much worth packing. As they worked, Lauren looked at Jimmy's now soiled and stained suit that he had donned for his job interview.

"Do you think you can reschedule?" she asked.

Jimmy shook his head. "No. This was a sign. That job wasn't meant to be. I need to stay with the group. I need to focus on protecting everyone."

"Jimmy, that's crazy!" Lauren said louder than she had intended. She raised her hand to her mouth as though doing so would quiet the sound. "I care about everyone here too," she said. "But we can't just spend the rest of our lives out here."

Jimmy shot her a less-than-complimentary look but didn't answer. He simply went off to gather up whatever else he could find.

Harris was about to do the same, but first he walked over to Violet and gazed down into her face.

"You okay, V?" he asked. "You don't seem yourself lately. As a matter of fact, you look kinda pale. Especially for you." Harris forced a smile.

"I'm fine," Violet responded.

Harris cocked his head and squinted. "Come on, V," he said. "It's me you're talking to . . . What's going on?"

Violet mustered her strength and looked Harris in the eyes. "I got stomach cancer," she said bluntly. She raised her hand up to her face. "But don't tell the others. I don't wanna worry them, and really, there's not much to be done, anyhow. It's pretty far along."

Harris was flabbergasted, somewhere between mad and crushed at the news. "Why didn't you tell me, V?" he asked, his voice shaking with emotion. "They got cures now. We can . . . People can live after cancer."

"Get real," Violet said, attempting to hide the

fact that Harris's words had hit a chord in her heart. "That all costs money . . . lots of money . . . money I don't have with no way of getting." Violet bit her lip. "It's been so hard, Harris . . . I can't . . ." She winced in pain again.

Harris knelt next to her and took her hand in his. He held it tightly as Violet continued to explain. "I've worked so hard to stay clean," she said. "Trying to pull myself together. But I'm in so much pain. I don't know how much longer I can do this."

"Don't talk like that, V," Harris said. "Maybe you can get some type of aid. Maybe the military will help. There are programs for stuff like this. We'll figure it out. Please, promise me you won't start using again."

Violet looked up at Harris kneeling on the ground, his face above hers. She couldn't miss the pleading look in his eyes. She knew he cared for her, and in her own way, she truly loved Harris.

"Promise," she said, the word barely audible. "But don't worry about me too much. I'm okay with going soon . . . so it's all good." Her facade of toughness fell away for a moment as she looked at Harris. "I'll miss you lots, though," she said as a tear formed in her eye.

"No, no, no. That's not going to happen," Harris said. "You are singing at my art show where I'm planning to exhibit some of my paintings—some of the paintings I've done of Dora, and Jimmy, and you." Harris paused and stroked his chin. "Looks like I need to do one or two of Lauren as well." He smiled at Violet. "But you and me. We're going on that bike ride to LA that we've always wanted to do. And we're going to have our beach picnic that we've talked about." Harris's eyes filled with tears. "I can't lose you, V," he said softly. "You're my rock."

Violet squeezed Harris's hand and looked into his face. "Don't go gettin' sentimental on me," she said. "You know how I hate that." She wiped the tears from her eyes and bit her lip. "Okay, enough of this," she said, waving her hand in front of her. "Let's start packing." She looked at Harris and a firm expression crossed her face. "And remember. Not a word to the others." Her tone softened. "Promise?"

Harris nodded and stood. But then he sat back down with Violet on the couch. She leaned over and put her head on his shoulder as he wrapped her in his strong arms, comforting her, both of them lost in silence.

Chapter 15

IT TOOK several weeks, but Harris found the family a new home. The reflection of an old abandoned building covered in graffiti wavered in a moonlit puddle. The image suddenly broke apart as a large shopping cart careened through it with Jimmy behind the cart steering as the group walked ahead. Harris opened the door to the office building and heaved in a box of the group's possessions they had collected recently.

Violet, Dora, and Lauren followed Harris inside, and Jimmy wheeled in the full shopping cart with an assortment of bags tied to it with ropes. They carried their meager belongings into a spacious, open area where they found a discarded couch and a few broken chairs. Jimmy went back to stand guard outside, checking and double-checking to make certain they hadn't been followed. Once everything was in the building, he stepped inside too.

"I think we'll be safer here and less visible,"

Harris said as he looked over the group's odd assortment of belongings. "This building is up for demolition, but it will probably take them a while to get around to it. Till then, welcome home." He smiled. "Not too shabby, huh?"

The change seemed to be wreaking havoc in Dora's brain. She wandered around in circles, talking to herself, confusion coloring her face, her eyes wide with fear.

"This is not my home," she said repeatedly. "There must be some mistake. This is not my home." She continued moving in circles and mumbling as she inspected her new surroundings. "But it is beautiful. Can we have a housewarming party? I know my friends will love it."

"Of course, Dora," Jimmy said as he eased up next to her and took her hand. "But for now, it's time to rest." They walked over to the old sofa in the middle of the open room and sat down on it. Lauren brought over Dora's pillow and sleeping bag and wrapped them around her. "You can sleep here for now," Jimmy said. He looked toward the loaded shopping cart. "It's late. We'll sort everything out in the morning."

Harris, Violet, and Lauren pulled out their own

pillows and sleeping bags and did their best to find comfortable spots on the office floor to sleep. When Dora finally drifted off, Jimmy joined the others, placing his sleeping bag on the floor near Dora. Now that his family was safe, Jimmy closed his eyes and was soon fast asleep as well.

* * * * *

Across town, Robert had no such luck. Sleep had eluded him on this dark night. He'd finally made his way home, and his hands shook as he drew a glass of tap water from the sink faucet. He sat down at the kitchen table and stared at a notice of sale. His face felt swollen, and he knew dark bags filled the spaces under his eyes. Piles of bills, most stamped *Overdue!*, were spread out across the table.

The front door clicked open, followed by the quiet footsteps of someone entering the house. Robert turned and looked up as Kim walked into the kitchen and plunked her bag down on the table. It was late and she had worked two shifts at the hospital. Fatigue weighed heavily upon her. Likely not wanting to wake up Sam, she merely waved at Robert and quietly said, "Hey."

Then she spotted the notice of sale and her brow furrowed as she picked up the letter from the table. "What's this?"

Robert snatched the notice out of her hand and crumpled it up into a ball. Kim grabbed it back and unfolded it, glaring at him. On top of the paper in bold print, she read: "Notice of Sale."

"What! The bank wants to sell our house?" She looked at Robert. "This is serious!" She read down the page and her eyes widened in despair. "Robert!" she hissed in a loud whisper. "*Sale?* What is going on here?" She waved the letter in Robert's face. "And why haven't you told me anything about this?" The volume of her voice rose, but Sam waking up was the least of their concerns. "You can't hide these things from me," she said. "Especially when we're living off *my* salary!"

"I'm dealing with it," Robert said loudly. "I'm working on it. I'm talking to them."

"The bank must have found out that you lost your job," Kim said. She flopped down on one of the kitchen chairs, sighed, and looked at Robert with a beseeching expression. "Robert, I don't know how much longer I can keep doing these double shifts," she said quietly. "You have to get a job. We're not going to be able to handle this on just my salary alone."

"I've been trying, Kim, for several weeks now, going from agency to agency. I've been rejected by the best of them," Robert said sincerely. "The market is down. I can't find anything that will pay enough."

Kim bristled. "Oh, come on, Robert! You can't afford to be picky anymore. *Any* job is better than none. Somebody said, 'There's a four-letter word to use when you're broke. It's called *work*!' How many weeks do we have?"

Robert didn't answer. Instead, he put his head in his hands and leaned on the table.

Kim snatched up the notice of sale again and looked at it more carefully, reading the fine print. Her face went pale . . . and then flushed red.

"*Three* weeks!" she yelled. "Robert! You better fix this. Please. Figure this out."

Robert looked up at Kim with tears in his eyes as he watched his wife storm out of the room.

Frustrated, he violently shoved the entire pile of bills onto the floor.

* * * * *

At the abandoned building, now the temporary home of the displaced group from the encampment, life slowed to a wonderfully nondescript normality. With no attacks from the gang for more than a month, while living in their new location, Harris, Dora, Violet, Lauren, and Jimmy enjoyed the relative peace of scrounging enough money to survive. A marvelous sense of contentment pervaded their new digs, where they had set up five small tents inside the biggest room.

Violet sang as she swept dirt into a corner of the room. Jimmy and Harris carried in a comfortable-looking chair they had found in the dump. They placed it near the couch as if it were a prized piece of expensive furniture, which it may have been at one time.

Meanwhile, Lauren hung some clothes on a makeshift clothesline attached catty-corner between two walls. She and Jimmy finished up their tasks and headed off to Sunday morning worship service at the Salvation Army. The chapel was crowded with churchgoers, some of whom had spent the night at the Salvation Army and were freshly showered and wearing their Sunday best. Others were fresh off the streets out of the homeless camps, along with a few folks dressed in Salvation Army uniforms. Lauren and Jimmy found seats together in one of the rows near the front.

After a rousing service with an emphasis on the freedom, healing, and deliverance that faith in God could facilitate, the congregation filed out the back exit of the chapel. Many people stopped at the door to shake hands with the major, the minister who had preached the encouraging sermon that morning.

A woman also stood at the back of the chapel greeting each person. She had been tacking "Missing Person" notices with Jimmy's picture on telephone poles all around town, and she passed out flyers bearing Jimmy's photo as people passed her.

"Have you seen my son?" she asked person after person. Most shook their heads. Some said, "No." Most said nothing at all.

"Have you seen my son?" she asked another woman exiting the chapel. The woman stopped and peered at the picture, but then shook her head and continued out of the chapel.

Jimmy and Lauren left the aisle where they had been sitting. They exchanged pleasantries with a few people but didn't dally. Gabrielle was counting on them to help her serve lunch at the Downtown City

Mission that afternoon. They pressed through the crowd, moving toward the chapel exit.

At almost the same moment, Jimmy's mom stepped inside the back of the chapel. Her eyes lit up when she spotted Jimmy heading in her direction. "Jimmy!"

Jimmy turned when he heard his name. His mouth dropped in shock when he saw his mother standing in the doorway of the Salvation Army chapel.

She rushed toward him and threw her arms around him. "Oh, thank God! It's you, Jimmy!"

"Mom?" Jimmy managed to say. Lauren stepped back to give them space but watched curiously.

His mom eased back and looked at Jimmy in awe. "You're so tall now," she said. "You look like you've grown several inches since I last—"

"Mom." Jimmy pulled back, his body language clearly indicating his discomfort. "What are you doing here?"

She stepped closer to her son. "Please, Jimmy. Come home." She paused, as if guessing what was on Jimmy's mind. "He's gotten better."

Jimmy tipped his head back and looked at the ceiling before responding. "So you haven't left him." He turned and started to walk away from his mother, obviously unimpressed and unconvinced that anything had changed during the years he'd been gone.

His mother followed him, trying to grab his arm, but he shook her off. "Please, Jimmy," she said quietly. "Please come home. He's trying to change. It will be better, I promise."

Jimmy moved farther away as she tried to stay close to him. "Same old story," he said, shaking his head.

"Please, Jimmy," she begged. "My car is right over there." She pointed toward a parking lot located across the street. "Please come with me. I miss you so much." She latched on to his arm and tried to lead him toward the car.

Jimmy recoiled and stepped away from her. "Stop!" he said loud enough that other people nearby turned to stare at them. "Why'd you even come here?"

"Jimmy, we're family . . ."

"I have a *new* family now," he said flatly. "People who actually care about me." His demeanor softened and a sadness covered his face. "You shoulda left with me, Mom. We could have gotten a place together and—"

"We have a place, Jimmy. Do you know how long I've looked for you?"

A tear trickled down her cheek. He gently ran his finger over the bruise highlighted by the moisture on her face. "You can still leave if you want to, Mom," he said tenderly. "I know people now . . . people who could help you."

"I can't leave," she said. "He needs me."

He shook his head. "*I* needed you! I was just a kid." He turned away from his mother, then looked back at her. "If you want me in your life again, you know what to do."

It was her turn to look away. Hurt and silent, she appeared to be looking at something far off in the distance.

Jimmy stood there for a long moment, his fists clenched, anger surging through him as well as sadness—all of it probably showing on his face.

Liz tried again, stepping toward Jimmy. She reached her arms around him and tried to hug him.

Jimmy's entire body stiffened, but then he relaxed a bit and allowed Liz to embrace him. Sunshine reflected on the stained-glass window above them, casting rays of light all around.

Still wrapped in his mom's arms, Jimmy spoke

softly into her ear. "Mom, be careful."

She looked into his eyes. "I do love you, Jimmy," she said. "I'm glad to know you're okay. Do you need money? Anything?"

Jimmy shook his head. "No." He clenched his jaw and walked away from the chapel.

She called after him, "You still know how to reach me."

Jimmy did not respond but continued walking. Lauren ran past his mother and hurried to catch up with Jimmy. Liz remained in the same spot, devastated, waiting, it seemed, in case Jimmy changed his mind.

He didn't.

The Salvation Army major walked over to Liz, said a few words, and gently led her back toward the front of the chapel where they could talk privately.

Jimmy kept walking away from the entrance, then stopped, his fists still clenched as he seethed. He counted to ten, just as Harris had taught him, trying to process and get a handle on his emotions.

Lauren caught up to him and tentatively touched his arm. "Hey. What was that about?" she asked.

Jimmy shook his head. "It's too difficult to

explain. I don't know where to start."

"I've seen her before," Lauren said, nodding back toward the Salvation Army chapel. "She came by the other day looking for you."

Jimmy looked shocked and alarmed. "What?"

"Don't worry," Lauren hastily added. "Violet told us not to say anything."

Jimmy breathed a sigh of relief. "Good."

"It seems like she really loves you, though."

"Not enough," Jimmy answered sadly. He took a deep breath to settle his emotions. "Anyway, mind your own business."

Lauren remained undeterred. "Okay, but maybe we could get her some help?"

Jimmy whirled to face her. "You think I didn't try? I had it all set up. She was supposed to leave with me. We were going to get a place of our own, together. But she chose to stay with my drunk, abusive dad." Jimmy's eyes scrunched up in pain at the memory. He shook his head rapidly and brushed his hand across his forehead, as if doing a mind sweep to make the thoughts go away.

"I'm sorry, Jimmy," Lauren whispered.

He pretended he didn't hear her. "Come on. We need to go help Gabrielle. She'll be overwhelmed trying to feed everyone if she doesn't have enough help."

He headed off toward the Downtown City Mission with Lauren hurrying to keep up. More words were unnecessary. They both seemed to understand that the best thing they could do right then was to help someone else.

Chapter 16

ON A SUNNY day three weeks later, a sheriff's cruiser pulled up outside Robert's home. Sam was at school and Kim was working the day shift, but Robert was at home and he heard the car door slam and the rough knock on the door. He pulled open the curtains on the front window and peered outside. He flinched when he saw a deputy sheriff in full uniform standing at the front door.

Robert opened the door to meet the sheriff just as the officer finished placing heavy blue tape on a sign positioned at eye level on the door. The officer turned without saying anything and began walking back to his car. Robert ripped the notice off the door and read it.

EVICTION NOTICE:
You have three days to vacate.

His eyes widened.

"No, no, no! Hey! Wait!" he called after the sheriff. "Just give me a few more days . . . please, I'm begging you." His voice was shot through with desperation, but the officer continued walking toward the police cruiser without looking back.

"I have a wife and a kid!" Robert yelled.

The sheriff turned momentarily and nodded. He got in his squad car and drove away, leaving Robert standing in the doorway. Robert ran his hands through his hair in frustration and despair. He went back inside, sat at the kitchen table, and began making frantic phone calls.

"Listen, I'm in a jam. I need a favor. I need a place for Kim and Sam and me to stay for a few days, just about a week."

One person after another turned down his requests for help.

"How ya doing, brother? It's Robert. I need a favor. I was wondering if—"

Click.

"Please, Dave," Robert said when one friend answered and consented to hear his plea. "You have to help me," Robert insisted.

Dave hung up.

Robert rolled his eyes in frustration, then

dialed another number. Another so-called friend. No answer. He dialed another number, that of a business associate with whom he had done some deals in the past. He moved the phone away from his ear as a voice shouted at him, "Where's my money? You better get over here and pay up right now or—"

Robert quickly hung up. Then dialed another number. Again and again. He had long ago burnt his bridges with his own family members, so he knew better than to call any of them for help. But his friends—

"Geoff, this is Robert. Can Kim, Sam, and I stay with you for a few days?" he asked. "We're, ah . . . we're doing some construction work on the house, and they tore the kitchen apart. The place is a total mess. I thought we'd be able to stay, but we can't. Could we come to your place and crash for a week? Is that okay with you?"

"Sorry, Robert. Always glad to help, but we have Jan's folks staying with us right now."

Robert's face fell. After ending the call, he threw his phone onto the living room coffee table and looked up at the ceiling in despair. Unwittingly, his hands drew together, and he mouthed a prayer as the painful reality of his situation hit him.

* * * * *

It was a perfect day for a stroll in the park. Birds fluttered from tree to tree, chirping happily. Squirrels leaped between branches and rabbits bounded through the bushes. Harris and Dora walked arm in arm along the idyllic paths with Dora stopping every few minutes to smell a flower. Dressed in a long, seventies-style pink dress, she held a badly wrapped gift.

"I hope you'll like my friends," she told Harris.

"Oh, I'm sure I will," Harris replied.

"I can't wait to see what they serve us with tea today."

"I hope it's chocolate cake," Harris said, playing along.

"Mm, yes. Me too," Dora cooed. She gazed up at the sunshine filtering through the tree branches in a secluded, isolated area of the park. "Look how beautiful—"

Suddenly, Red appeared in front of Dora and Harris. They stopped short on the path.

"Duke ain't happy you skipped out on us," he snarled.

Dora looked at Harris nervously. She whirled

away from Red and bumped right into Q, who was standing behind her, leering at her.

Feeling pinned in, Dora freaked out. She pushed past Q and bolted.

"Dora, wait!" Harris called. "Stop. Please! Everything is okay. Come back!"

But Dora kept running.

Red laughed.

Harris tried to push past him to go after Dora, but Red grabbed him by the arm forcefully and pulled a switchblade, putting it up to Harris's neck. Q came up behind Harris, grabbed his arms, and held them behind his back while Red searched his pockets. He found two quarters and held them up in front of Harris's face.

"Two quarters? That's all you got? You're pathetic." Red threw the quarters in Harris's face. "Let's go get his lady friend, Q. I want her EBT cards and yours, too, old man. If you try anything, you'll either end up dead or wish you were."

Harris kicked Q hard, knocking him backward. Red countered with a gut-punch to Harris's stomach. Doubled over in pain, winded, and clutching his midsection, Harris mustered his strength and lashed back at Red, kicking him hard and sending him flying backward to the ground. Harris looked in the direction Dora had run, and he staggered after her.

Reaching the street, he spotted her running down the sidewalk far ahead. "Dora! Dora! Stop. I'm coming!" he yelled as loudly as he could.

Dora continued running, panic-stricken, her face flushed with fear.

A group of pedestrians was walking toward her, not really paying attention as they talked. They appeared to be business associates, all stylishly dressed. Flustered, Dora tried to weave through them but bumped into a man. He pushed her away.

Dora stumbled and started to hyperventilate, her eyes darting right and left erratically, her panic continuing to build. She regained her footing and slammed into one of the women. The woman shoved Dora off her, causing Dora to fumble the present she carried. The package tumbled out into the street.

A car sped down the lane closest to the sidewalk, directly on target to hit the gift. Dora ran into the street to retrieve her present without even looking for traffic.

Out of breath and still a distance behind her,

Harris called out, "Dora! No! Come back! It's me, Harris!"

The car's brakes screeched as the driver tried to stop.

Too late.

A horrific, sickening *thud* filled the air as pedestrians screamed at the sight of the car slamming into the elderly woman who never saw it coming.

Shocked, Harris stood in disbelief for a few seconds, unable to process the awful sight he had witnessed from a distance. Then he took off in a sprint toward Dora. His legs pumped harder, faster, as he raced to get to her.

He pulled up short and nearly retched when he reached her and saw Dora's body lying on the ground, motionless.

"Quick! Call an ambulance!" Harris hollered to anyone who could hear. "Call 911! Please, help her!"

He frantically pushed his way through the gathering crowd of onlookers to get to Dora. He knelt on the street and felt for her pulse.

An ambulance siren sounded in the distance, getting closer.

There was no pulse. Dora was gone.

Harris sat on the pavement and pulled Dora's dead body into his arms, holding her as tears streamed down his face.

How could this have happened?

Chapter 17

JIMMY SAT alone atop the parking garage roof, staring out at the city lights later that night. He was so overcome with grief, he didn't hear Lauren approaching until she was only inches away.

"Hey," she said cautiously. "I thought I might find you here. I've been looking all over for you. What's going on?"

Jimmy didn't answer. Nor did he turn to look at her. He continued staring out at the city.

She came alongside him. "Jimmy?" Concern filled her voice. "Are . . . are you okay?"

When he finally turned to look at her, his face was wet with tears.

"Jimmy! Wha—" She knelt beside him and rested a hand on his shoulder. "Hey. What's going on? What's wrong?"

Jimmy choked on his first attempt to form a sentence and finally said simply, "Dora."

"Dora?" Lauren repeated. She wrapped her arm

around Jimmy's shoulder and hugged him tightly.

"She was hit by a car."

"What! Is she okay? Where is she?"

"No. Harris tried to get to her. . . . Those thugs attacked him in the park. She ran," Jimmy said. "He tried to stop her."

Lauren let go of Jimmy and rocked back, shocked.

"She's gone," Jimmy said.

"Gone? Gone where?" She turned his face toward hers and looked him in the eyes.

"She's . . . gone." Jimmy struggled to get out the word again.

Suddenly Lauren realized what he meant. Dora was dead. Her eyes welled with tears, and she threw her arms around Jimmy. "Oh, Jimmy! I'm so sorry. She was so . . . so good." Jimmy nodded in her embrace.

For a long time, they simply held on to each other. Finally, when they had regained some composure, Jimmy said quietly, "We should go. Harris . . ."

Lauren nodded but said nothing as they stood and trudged back to the abandoned building to join Harris and Violet in mourning Dora.

* * * * *

Dora's funeral service was simple but fitting. Harris sat on the sidewalk with his head in his hands, occasionally looking up at a sketch of Dora he had been working on. With no next of kin to notify, the city had dispensed with Dora's body, so Jimmy, Violet, and Lauren placed a small candle and some flowers around the bottom of a signpost to which they had attached Harris's sketch, creating a sort of memorial on the sidewalk. All of their faces were wet with tears.

Jimmy stood before the group and, his voice shaking with emotion, asked, "Okay, who wants to go first? Who wants to say something?"

A brief silence followed as each family member's eyes focused on the ground and the sketch of Dora. Violet bit her lip, wanting to speak but unable to find the words to express her feelings.

Harris slowly rose to his feet, his demeanor rather surprising. His eyes were filled with rage, his fists clenched. He stomped the ground with his sneaker-clad feet, making sounds similar to those of a wounded animal. The sounds turned into deep, guttural sobs.

"Dora," he said over and over again. "Dora, oh, Dora."

The group stared at him, not knowing how to comfort or console him, or if he even wanted them to. Jimmy moved toward him, but Violet caught his arm and gave him a look.

"Leave him be," she whispered. "Let him get it out so he can deal with it."

Jimmy stopped in his tracks, nodded toward Violet, then turned back and knelt to face the sketch of Dora and the simple memorial they had made honoring her life.

"Dora, you were like a second mother to me," he spoke with deep emotion. "I should have protected you better . . . I'm so sorry." He paused and wiped the tears from his face. "I know you believed in God and in Jesus and that you are in a much better place now, but I sure miss you . . ." Jimmy's voice cracked, and he could no longer hold back the tears.

Lauren went to him and pulled him into a tight hug. Her eyes quickly flooded as well.

Violet took a shaky breath and faced the others. "When I got kicked out of military housing," she said slowly, "everyone abandoned me." She looked at the sketch of Dora. "Everyone but you. You didn't judge me . . . you just held me when the memories got bad . . ." Violet's body began shaking as she tried to control her grief and her rage but was unable to contain either.

Lauren let go of Jimmy and reached toward Violet, pulling her into a hug. Violet remained rigid for a few moments before she broke, dissolving in tears and sobs in Lauren's arms.

"I'm sorry, Dora," Lauren said, looking at the sketch through her tears. "This should not have happened to you."

Jimmy wiped away more tears as they continued streaming down his face. Lauren, Violet, and Harris joined him kneeling on the ground as Jimmy led the group in prayer, thanking God for Dora's life and the legacy of love she had left for them.

Later that evening, they returned to the abandoned office building, leaving Harris's charcoal sketch of Dora and the memorial to wave in the wind.

A light rain began to fall, smudging the charcoal and streaking Dora's image. A street sweeping machine rolled by and the operator saw the tattered sketch. He stopped the machine, pulled the sketch off the sign, and put it in the street sweeper's cab. He then swept away the flowers and the candle.

* * * * *

Three days later, Robert and Kim stuffed their suitcases and other belongings into Robert's BMW, packing it so full, there was hardly room to sit inside. Eight-year-old Sam carried his box of toys out of the house and handed it to Robert. Sam pulled out his stuffed dino and held it tightly in his arms.

"Dad, where are we going?" Sam asked.

"I'm working on that, son," Robert replied.

Sam stood looking back at his home and burst into tears. Kim came around the car and tried to comfort him, to no avail.

"It's okay," she said, wrapping her arm around Sam. "We're just going for a little while. We'll figure it out. Come on, now. Let's get in the car." Her tears continued to flow as she helped Sam find an empty corner in the back seat.

Robert struggled to tie the toy box on top of the car with some other suitcases. Kim ran back inside the house and returned carrying a houseplant she crammed into the front passenger seat along with herself.

Without ceremony or even a last look back, Robert climbed in and started the car and pulled away from their home. He eased out into traffic and stomped on the gas pedal. The thrust caused the poorly secured box of Sam's toys to wobble on the roof and then crash onto the road.

"No!" Sam cried as he looked out the back window and watched his favorite toys scatter across the asphalt.

* * * * *

That night, the moon beamed down on Robert's BMW with boxes still strapped to the top, the car sitting in a deserted parking lot. Inside the vehicle, Robert sadly watched over his wife and son as they tried to sleep under a stack of coats and towels. Fast-food wrappers dotted the floorboards. Robert sighed, pulled his coat closer to his chest, and wriggled his body in the driver's seat, trying to find a position comfortable enough to sleep. He closed his eyes, then opened them a few moments later, staring straight up in despair.

* * * * *

At daybreak, across town, Jimmy, Lauren, Violet, and Harris folded up Dora's tent and gathered her few belongings. Harris busied himself sketching Violet as she posed for him, and Lauren sat in front of her tent, reading another book she'd found somewhere. Jimmy walked over and sat beside her.

They looked at each other warmly but didn't speak. They all felt Dora's loss deeply.

Chapter 18

THAT NIGHT, the abandoned office building where Harris and his friends had taken refuge appeared especially eerie in the moonlight. Inside, they had created an organized living area. There was no electricity, but the moonlight streamed through the large-pane glass windows, revealing two shadowy figures on the opposite wall.

Violet snuggled in her sleeping bag inside her tent, nearly asleep, when the sound of someone stepping on a can pierced the silence. Her eyes popped open and she sat up, her heart pounding. She leaned forward, all senses on high alert. Footsteps and whispering voices came from the office area. She quietly slipped out of her sleeping bag and peered out of her tent into the darkness, then slowly crawled out on her hands and knees.

Already accustomed to the darkness, Violet detected movement behind a pillar. She grabbed a saucepan and moved toward the pillar, her eyes scanning the area. She heard a light rustling sound, and she froze. Wings fluttering captured her attention as a pigeon flew away above the pillar. Violet breathed a sigh of relief and chuckled to herself.

Then Lauren screamed. "Aaaah! Help! Somebody help me!"

Violet spun and saw Red and Q dragging Lauren toward the door as Q held a switchblade close to her neck.

"Let me go, you creeps!" Lauren yelled. "Help! Jimmy! Harris! Violet . . . anybody! Help me, please!"

Violet was on her feet, running through the dimly lit room. "Jimmy!" she cried out. "Harris!" But she wasn't waiting for cover.

She furiously charged through the door and whacked Red with the saucepan. She pulled Lauren out of his grasp and wrestled him to the ground. Q held on to Lauren and continued dragging her on the floor as she kicked her feet and flailed her arms against him, screaming.

Jimmy burst through the doorway. His eyes widened when he saw Q dragging Lauren toward the exit leading to the alley. "Hey!" he shouted.

"Help!" Lauren cried.

Rage flashed through Jimmy as he charged at

Q, pushing him away from Lauren and knocking him down. Lauren scrambled to stand and moved to the side, watching nervously. Jimmy twisted Q's arm so the switchblade fell out of his hand, dropping to the ground.

Harris charged out from where he'd been sleeping. He saw Violet wrestling with Red and ran over and yanked him off her, then headbutted Red. Taken by surprise, Red tumbled backward and landed flat on his back.

Harris stood over him, waiting to see what Red was going to do. He was so focused on Red that he didn't see Duke emerge from the shadows and creep up behind him. Duke grabbed Harris and slammed him into a headlock with one arm, then pulled his switchblade and pressed it to Harris's neck with the other hand.

Red glowered at Harris as he pulled himself up off the floor.

Duke sneered at Harris. "I don't like it when people don't respect my guys." He looked around for the other members of Harris's group. Seeing that Duke had the upper hand, Jimmy and Violet released Q and turned to face Duke. Lauren inched up behind them.

Duke waved the knife in front of Harris's face as he yelled across the room to Jimmy, Violet, and Lauren. "Gimme all you got or say goodbye to Benedict R. here."

Jimmy raised his hands in the air as he walked toward Duke. "Listen," he said. "We don't have much, but take what you want." He nodded toward Harris. "Just let him go. Surely, we can resolve this peacefully."

Duke laughed hideously. "Peacefully?" He flaunted the knife as he spoke. "You had your chance for that already. You should have just forked over your money and cards, and we might have let you alone. Maybe. But it's too late for that."

Harris cocked his head as far as he could turn it, still in the headlock. "You can have my EBT card," he said. "It's inside in my tent."

Duke nodded to Red and pushed Harris toward him. Red brandished his blade at Harris.

"Go get everything they got," Duke demanded. "Where's the girl you told me about?"

Red followed Harris inside the office while Q grabbed Lauren and dragged her over to Duke.

"Leave her alone," Jimmy said evenly.

Duke paid no attention and took his time

looking up and down Lauren's body, then nodded appreciatively. He moved his face close to hers as he ran his hand through her hair and over her cheek.

"Hmm, she could make some money for us, with a bit of a cleanup."

Jimmy stepped forward to pull Lauren away from Duke's leering eyes, but he stopped short when Duke ran his switchblade along Lauren's cheek. Lauren looked at Jimmy with stark terror in her eyes.

Harris and Red returned with Red holding the EBT card, a few dollar bills, and some other items.

Jimmy and Violet exchanged a look. Suddenly, Jimmy charged at Q and pushed him away from Lauren, then struggled to hold him so he couldn't access his knife.

At the same time, Violet jumped up and grabbed Duke's wrist. She twisted his arm hard to the right so the switchblade pointed away from them and then jammed his thumb viciously with her elbow. The knife dropped to the ground, and Violet grabbed Duke's fingers, yanking them back hard. They all heard the bones break in Duke's hand. He screamed in pain and doubled over, grasping his hand against his chest.

Violet swung down and smoothly snatched up

the switchblade before popping back up.

Harris had also charged Red the moment Jimmy and Violet made their moves, and he wrestled him to the ground.

Violet jerked Lauren's arm and pulled her out the door toward the alley. Lauren looked back anxiously and saw Jimmy still struggling with Q. Jimmy was on top of him and had him pinned to the ground. He looked up at Lauren and Violet and yelled, "Run! Now!"

Jimmy held Q down until he was sure Lauren and Violet had escaped. But with a grotesque-sounding grunt, Q heaved Jimmy off of him. Jimmy rolled over, picked himself up, and sprinted down the alley after the women.

Red and Harris both stumbled to their feet and circled each other. Red lashed out, trying to stab Harris with the switchblade, but Harris dodged it . . . once . . . twice . . . and again as Red lunged toward him.

Looking like a heavyweight boxer, Harris reared back and swung his fist hard, landing a strong blow to the side of Red's head. The man fell, unconscious, the switchblade tumbling out of his hand as he hit the ground. But Q saw it and scooped it up before

Harris could get to it. Q snapped open the blade and chased Jimmy down the alley as Harris took a second to breathe before charging after them.

Q caught up to Jimmy and tackled him. He raised the knife, ready to plunge it into Jimmy's chest, when Harris flew in just in time, slamming Q from behind.

Harris grabbed Q's arm and twisted it as hard as he could, forcing Q to drop the switchblade.

Duke barreled toward Harris, holding his injured hand away from his body, his face crimson with fury. He hit Harris full force, knocking him unconscious in a heap on the pavement. Duke saw the blade and grabbed it. He wielded it over Harris's body, but Jimmy hit him from the side and grasped Duke's arm. They desperately grappled as Jimmy tried to get him to release the knife, but to no avail.

At that moment Red charged back into the fracas, having regained consciousness, and pulled Jimmy away from Duke and threw him against the alley wall. Still brandishing the weapon, Duke took advantage of Jimmy's vulnerability. He turned and viciously stabbed Jimmy in the stomach.

Jimmy cried out in pain as the blade plunged into his body and blood spurted from his belly, instantly soaking the front of his shirt.

Duke stood over Jimmy and laughed a deep, insidious laugh. Then he, Red, and Q took turns kicking Jimmy repeatedly. Jimmy curled into a fetal position as the sounds of grunts and boots stomping filled his ears so loudly, he couldn't even hear himself crying. His raw shrieks of pain pierced the otherwise silent night as the thugs tortured him.

* * * * *

Lauren and Violet had escaped and run toward the Downtown City Mission. They burst into the courtyard and pounded on the door of Gabrielle's apartment at the mission compound.

"Gabrielle! Gabrielle! It's me, Lauren! Help!" Lauren called out.

After a few moments, a sleepy Gabrielle opened the door. "Lauren? What are you doing here?" she asked, rubbing the sleep from her eyes. "What's going on?"

"Call 911!" Lauren shrieked. "Jimmy and Harris are being attacked. The gang. They're trying to kill them!"

Gabrielle reached for her phone and dialed.

Violet looked at Lauren and said, "Okay. You stay here. I'm going back."

"No! No . . . please . . .Violet," Lauren begged, but Violet was already dashing back toward the fight.

Gabrielle returned her attention to Lauren. "Come inside. Are you okay?"

Lauren looked at the warm, inviting interior of Gabrielle's home for a second and then said, "I'm sorry, Gabrielle. I can't stay. I gotta go back!" Lauren turned and ran off in the direction Violet had gone.

Meanwhile, Duke, Red, and Q searched through the unconscious men's clothing, looking for anything valuable as Jimmy and Harris lay bleeding on the ground. A police siren that caught their attention was getting closer.

"Let's get outta here!" Duke yelled to his goons. They dashed out of the alley and disappeared into the night.

Harris regained consciousness but remained curled up on the ground, coughing up blood onto the concrete. He stirred and tried to right himself, and then with great difficulty, he pulled himself to his feet. He looked around for the others and saw Jimmy lying motionless nearby.

Harris hobbled over to his younger friend.

"Son, you okay?"

Jimmy didn't respond. Nor did he move.

"Jimmy. Jimmy," Harris said tensely. He knelt and looked down at Jimmy and started to pray.

* * * * *

Lauren ran down the road leading from the Downtown City Mission back to the alley near the abandoned office building.

Ahead, Red, Q, and Duke rounded the corner running in her direction, but Lauren spotted them before they saw her. She ducked out of sight behind a fence and watched through the slats as they ran past her.

Two police cars careened around the corner, following them before screeching to a halt. Two officers jumped out, guns raised and pointed at Red, Q, and Duke. A third officer pulled his car behind them, got out of the car, and stood next to the open car door, his gun aimed.

"Freeze!" one officer yelled. "Don't make another move!"

Red and Q slowed and raised their hands above their heads, but Duke ran faster.

Gabrielle stepped out of the mission compound just as Duke rounded a corner and headed in her direction. But the third officer was right behind him, and with a giant leap, he slammed into Duke and tackled him to the ground. The officer turned Duke face down, yanked his hands behind his back, and slapped a set of handcuffs on him. Duke howled in pain as the officer tightened the cuffs around Duke's broken hand. The other officers handcuffed Red and Q and guided the three of them into the back seats of their police cruisers.

One of the officers beckoned Gabrielle to join them. She moved toward them, and they spoke for a minute or so, and then the officers got into their vehicles and left, presumably headed to the downtown police station.

Gabrielle breathed a heavy sigh of relief and went back inside the mission.

Lauren waited until the coast was clear before stepping out from behind the fence. She looked up and down the street and then ran to find her friends.

As she approached the building, out of breath and afraid, her eyes searched through the darkness for the others. Her countenance brightened when she saw them still down the alley. But then she gasped in horror to see a crumpled man lying on the ground. As she got closer, Lauren realized it was Jimmy. Harris, badly bruised with his forehead bleeding, and Violet crouched over Jimmy, urging him to hang on.

"Stay with us, Jimbo," Violet said. "We need you around here."

Lauren ran to them and knelt next to Jimmy, trying not to show her fear or worry. But then she saw how badly he was bleeding. His face was purple and swollen and his body was contorted.

"Jimmy!" she cried out. "Oh, God! Please help him."

Violet ripped off a piece of her jacket lining and gently but firmly pressed the cloth onto Jimmy's wound, trying to stop the bleeding. The cloth quickly turned red with blood.

"We gotta stop this bleeding," Violet said. She pressed more of the cloth into Jimmy's stomach. He stirred and squinted at them through one swollen eye, and they all looked at each other with relief.

"Thank God," Harris said. "For a moment there, I thought you were . . ."

"Aw, I've been through worse," Jimmy tried to joke. "Don't worry. I'll survive."

"No, Jimmy," Lauren said, her face tight with

concern. "We have to get you help. You need a doctor."

"Yeah, sure," he said. "I'll just go to the ER with the insurance I don't have. They'll take real good care of me."

"I don't think they would turn you away," Lauren said. "Not the way you are. . . ." Her words caught in her throat as she stared at Jimmy's blood-soaked clothing.

"How much pain are you in, son?" Harris asked with fatherly concern.

Jimmy couldn't resist. "I'm fine. You should see the other guy!"

They all shared a nervous laugh . . . until Jimmy began to cough. The group stared at him, worry and concern clouding their faces.

Jimmy's face scrunched up in pain, his breathing suddenly became labored, and the color drained out of his face. More blood dripped from his shirt.

Lauren looked at Harris and Violet. "We gotta get him to the hospital!" she cried. "Right now! Look at him, he's dying! We need an ambulance!"

"It'll take too long," Harris said. "The hospital is close by. We'll have to take him there ourselves."

"But how?" Lauren asked.

Violet looked around and Harris's and Lauren's gazes followed hers. They spotted a large, empty shopping cart, and Violet jumped up to retrieve it. Then she and Harris carefully picked up Jimmy and set him in the cart as gently as possible.

They took turns pushing him up the street toward the hospital. He looked awful. Now unconscious, Jimmy's clothes seeped blood. Lauren held Jimmy's motionless hand as they pushed on even harder, despite being severely out of breath and struggling.

"He's bleeding out," Harris said quietly to Violet. Harris looked down at Jimmy slumped in the shopping cart. He took over the steering from Violet and broke into a full-blown run, pushing Jimmy down the sidewalk in the rickety cart, Jimmy's body jolting over the bumps on the pavement.

"I ain't gonna let you die on me, kid," Harris gasped as he pushed the cart with all his strength.

Violet ran behind them. "Hang on, Jimmy!" she called out. "You gotta make it!"

Harris wheeled the shopping cart straight into the emergency room reception area at St. Teresa's Hospital with Lauren and Violet close behind him. The clock on the wall showed 5:00 a.m. and the room was crowded with people needing assistance. Harris doubled over, breathing hard.

Some of the people in the waiting area stared in disdain at the homeless people who had barged into the medical facility and created a ruckus when so many others were hurting too. Others turned away and tried to ignore them.

"Can anyone help us?" Lauren pleaded.

The busy receptionist sitting at a desk behind a glass wall looked up momentarily, then went back to dealing with the patient in front of her who was filling out forms.

A woman in nursing attire and sneakers rushed into the room. The name on her badge read: *Kim.*

"Help!" Harris called out to her, pointing at Jimmy in the cart. "He's been stabbed real bad!"

Kim stopped immediately as she saw that the receptionist was busy. More importantly, she noted the expressions of panic on the faces of Lauren, Violet, and Harris. She looked down at Jimmy, covered with blood in the shopping cart, and her eyes widened.

"I need a trauma team right away!" she called out.

Two more nurses ran out and grabbed the cart.

"Stab wound," Kim said to them. They started to push Jimmy toward the double doors leading to the treatment area. Harris, Violet, and Lauren ran alongside them.

Kim stepped in front of the group, blocking them from entry.

"Let them take him," she said kindly but in a no-nonsense manner. "He may need surgery. You need to stay in the waiting area."

"Please," Harris said. "He's family. We need to stay with him."

Kim looked at Harris and raised her eyebrows slightly. "Real family? Actual family?" She paused and cast a quick glance at Violet and Lauren.

"He doesn't have any insurance," Lauren offered with a worried look on her face.

Kim nodded and spoke quietly. "Homeless?"

Harris nodded despondently.

"Okay. Actually, that will be fine. He'll be eligible for aid. Can you help me check him in? We need some information about him."

None of them said a word.

Kim sensed their anxiety and recognized that Jimmy's personal information would not be forthcoming. "It's okay. Don't worry," she said. "Our trauma team is amazing. I work in the emergency department. If you stay around here, I'll try to find out how he's doing, and I'll let you know. Have a seat. I'll be right back." Kim followed the gurney into the interior of the hospital.

Lauren, Violet, and Harris stood motionless, watching as the nurses and the cart with Jimmy in it disappeared from view and the large, heavy hospital doors automatically closed behind them.

Chapter 19

HOURS LATER, the trio was asleep in the hospital waiting room, along with several other people waiting on family or friends. Nurse Kim stepped into the room and softly tapped Lauren on her shoulder.

Her eyes popped open, and she bolted up as if she'd been zapped by electricity. She calmed down when she saw Kim standing over her.

"Is Jimmy okay?" she asked. "Can we see him yet?"

"Not yet," Kim said in a calm voice. "Right now, he's not conscious. He lost a lot of blood, so we need to keep an eye on him. You should all go home and get some rest. You can come back anytime tomorrow. There's nothing more you can do here today."

Lauren looked at Harris and then at Violet. Both had awakened and wore concerned expressions.

"He's gonna be okay, though, right?" Violet asked Kim.

"We still need to run some more scans and tests.

By the looks of it, he doesn't need surgery. We just need to guard against infection. We'll know more in a few days," Kim answered and headed back toward the double doors.

That was not the answer the group had hoped to hear.

"So we just have to go?" Violet asked. "We don't get to see him?"

Lauren burst into tears with deep sobs shaking her body. Violet put an arm around Lauren and squeezed, then Harris wrapped them both in his strong arms.

"Thank you, Nurse Kim," Harris called before she disappeared. "We'll be back. In the meantime, we will pray for Jimmy and trust for the best."

* * * * *

Over the next few days, while Jimmy remained in the hospital, Harris searched for a new place where the group could live. Although he'd heard that the police had jailed Duke and his cohorts, there was no guarantee they would not be back on the streets soon. So Harris had explored less obvious possibilities and discovered what he considered an ideal, isolated location overlooking a river. He couldn't wait to show it to the others.

Violet, Lauren, and Harris viewed the empty patch of grass by the riverbank as if they were considering a luxury home purchase in the suburbs. They pushed two large shopping carts filled with their meager belongings as they walked along the river, searching for a new home.

Harris waved his arms enthusiastically as he looked around. "I don't think we'll do better than this for a good, relatively safe, and remote spot," he said with unexpected gusto.

"Nice, Harris," Violet said with a sarcastic tone. "And we have a swimming pool right on our doorstep." She nodded toward the briskly flowing river. "Jimmy would love this." Violet looked away from Harris and Lauren. "I mean, Jimmy *will* love this," she said.

Lauren's eyes glazed with tears again, and she flopped down on the ground.

Harris leaned over to open his bag and pulled out half a sandwich. He walked over and offered it to Lauren.

"Here, take this."

Lauren shook her head.

"Come on," Harris said gently. "It's been a long day. You need to eat something."

Violet sat beside Lauren and wrapped her arms around the younger woman. "One thing I know," she said softly, "is that God takes care of those who help others. The Good Book says, 'The generous man will be prosperous, and he who waters will himself be watered.' Jimmy's gonna be okay." She hugged Lauren and smiled at her. "And you got us too."

Lauren placed her head on Violet's shoulder and the tough former US Marine held on to her tightly as they listened together to the rippling river, each lost in her own thoughts.

* * * * *

The following day, Lauren headed out to one of the tent encampments she had first visited with Jimmy. She carried a bag of leftover bagels she had secured from the bakery. Several of the homeless men and women sitting outside their tents moved toward Lauren when they recognized her as Jimmy's friend. She gave them all bagels and asked them to pray for Jimmy.

Chrissie popped her head out through her open

Producers Jennifer Stolo and Robert Craig on location in Auburn, CA, for filming.

HEAD

ABOVE: The crew captured drone footage to enrich "Lauren's" backstory.

OPPOSITE PAGE: Film editors Shaun Lupton and Alejandro Guimoye work in close partnership on set, united by their goal to use the power of film to inspire action.

The cast and crew spent weeks filming in the rain, highlighting the true conditions of those experiencing homelessness.

Opposite page: It was a joy to have Ashanti on set as she portrays Violet, a veteran fighting her own war with addiction.

Directing in the rain, Julia Verdin connects with Ashanti and Isabella Ferreira about their scenes as a street family.

Producer Robert Craig converses with Xander Berkeley about the reality of our film's homeless encampment set.

PLAYBOY

Julia Verdin, director, screenwriter, and producer, poses between scenes with actors Spencer Greene, William Baldwin, and Mark S. Allen.

Opposite page: Chris Polczinski, production sound mixer, sets up the sound booth outside the bar scene, where William Baldwin's character is harassed due to his gambling debts.

ABOVE: Director, screenwriter, and producer Julia Verdin shares script updates with William Baldwin.

OPPOSITE PAGE TOP: Associate producer Nikki Vogt has some fun on the first day on set with producer Robert Craig.

OPPOSITE PAGE BOTTOM: William Baldwin, executive producer Robert G. Marbut Jr., and Mark S. Allen pose while waiting on set.

no address
Robert

After recording Ty's interview for the *Americans with No Address* documentary, Julia Verdin, director, screenwriter, and producer, Ty Pennington, and producer Robert Craig pose for a photo.

Film editor Shaun Lupton and director, screenwriter, and producer Julia Verdin on film location in Folsom, CA.

Behind-the-scenes magic! Associate producers Nikki Vogt and Laura Nickowitz team up with producer Angela Lujan during pickup shots, turning moviemaking chaos into cinematic gold.

OPPOSITE PAGE: Angela Womack, department lead for makeup, prepares Brian Cohen for his role as a business owner who denies "Jimmy" a job.

Peter A. Holland led the cinematography team in capturing scenes of the street family celebrating Dora's birthday.

tent flap. "Heard about Jimmy," she said. "He gonna be okay?"

"We all hope so," Lauren answered. "How are you doing?" She passed around more bagels as they chatted.

"They took away our porta-potty," Chrissie complained. "I could sure do without this place stinking so much." She chuckled, but it really wasn't funny. "You give Jimmy our best," she said. "Tell him we all miss him."

"Thanks, Chrissie," Lauren replied. "I sure will."

With Jimmy still in the hospital, the next Sunday, Lauren, Harris, and Violet attended the chapel service at the Downtown City Mission. At the close of the service, they knelt in the pew to pray. Gabrielle saw them and came across the aisle to join them.

"We're all praying for Jimmy," she said. "He's a good kid. He'll pull through. I know it."

"Thanks, Gabrielle," Lauren said quietly. "I'll tell him that if we can see him. That will mean a lot to him." She checked the time and looked at Violet. "Let's go now and see if there's any news."

The trio hurried to the hospital but was met with resistance by the head nurse on the floor where

Jimmy was located. The nurse refused to allow them to see him. They remained in the hallway and waited as one nurse after another passed without paying any attention to the shabbily dressed homeless people. Lauren watched another nurse pass and tried to catch her attention, but she hurried down the hall.

Then Kim entered the hallway and Lauren waved her down.

"Can you get us in to see him today?" she asked.

Kim nodded. "He's in the last room at the end of the hallway," she whispered. "But only one of you can go in at a time. And I should tell you that he still isn't—"

Lauren didn't wait to hear Kim's caution. She was already running toward Jimmy's room. She found it and peered through the doorway toward his bed.

He looked so vulnerable, lying motionless in the hospital bed. His eyes were closed, his face pale, and he was hooked up to an IV with various instruments and monitors surrounding him.

Lauren stared at Jimmy—who at first she wasn't sure was breathing—as she slowly made her way into the room and sat down next to his bed. She sobbed quietly as she fixed her eyes on him, hoping for any sign of improvement. She gently reached over and placed her hand on his.

Jimmy's eyes fluttered open and he looked around groggily. He squinted at Lauren and reached out for her, taking her hand in his. Lauren squeezed his hand and a faint smile appeared. Then he fell back to sleep. Lauren stayed only a few more minutes before relinquishing her visitation time to Harris, then to Violet. Jimmy continued to sleep, but the trio of friends left the hospital encouraged by his progress.

Jimmy remained in the hospital for another week before the doctor assigned to him would even consider discharging him. Even then, he insisted that Jimmy would need to get as much bed rest as possible and, once he left the hospital, he should not engage in any lifting—nothing more than five pounds—with limited physical activity and nothing strenuous.

A few days before Jimmy's discharge date, his friends returned to the hospital to visit him. Jimmy sat up in bed, surrounded by Lauren, Violet, and Harris as well as Gabrielle. A large box of cookies sat on the bed, along with some chocolate brownies in a foil container. "Someone told me that these are your favorites," Violet said, pointing at the brownies. "I'm not a baker, but I did my best. Of course, they might have a touch of peanut butter in them." She smiled.

Jimmy looked around at the group sharing treats and lots of smiles. "I should get injured more often, if it gets me this much attention," he joked.

"No! You shouldn't," Lauren responded, failing to see the humor.

A nurse came into the room and pointed to the clock, indicating that visiting hours were over. Gabrielle, Violet, and Harris waved their goodbyes and stepped outside the room. Lauren started to join them, but Jimmy reached out and caught her hand.

"Are you doing okay?" he asked.

Lauren smiled at him. "Now that you're getting better, I'm good. You had us all really scared." She leaned down and kissed him on the cheek. "Feel better, Jimmy," she said. "I'll be back tomorrow."

"I will," Jimmy said. "I promise." Jimmy watched her leave, smiling as he touched the spot on his cheek where Lauren's lips had been.

* * * * *

Another full week passed before Jimmy's doctor finally consented to discharge him. An orderly presented

Jimmy with a written list of stipulations and admonitions regarding his recovery and then helped him into a wheelchair. The sun shone down on the white walls of the hospital, creating a shimmering, almost crystalline appearance. Harris grinned constantly as he pushed Jimmy in the wheelchair, guiding him out of his room and down the hospital corridors, accompanied by Lauren and Violet and a nurse. At the front exit, Harris handed Jimmy a pair of crutches to assist him in walking with less pain while his wound continued to heal.

Jimmy thanked the nurse and hadn't yet gotten to his feet when Violet's face scrunched up in pain. Her body shook in spasms.

"Ohhh . . . ahh . . . oww," Violet said as she clutched her stomach, clearly in serious pain, and then straightened and shook her head as if nothing had happened. "No worries," she said. "I'm okay."

Lauren, Jimmy, and Harris all stared at her.

"I think something is wrong with her," Lauren whispered to Jimmy.

Harris looked at them nervously.

"What?" Jimmy asked.

Harris paused as Violet grimaced in pain again. He leaned in toward Jimmy and Lauren. "She told me not to say anything, but I'm getting really worried."

Jimmy and Lauren gazed at Harris with quizzical looks on their faces, anxious to hear what he meant. "Come on, Harris," Jimmy said. "Spit it out. What's the matter?"

Harris spoke quietly and somberly. "She's got stomach cancer. We gotta do something for her." His face was pensive. "I can't lose anyone else."

"You're right," Jimmy said. He pointed toward the hospital doors they had just exited. "We need to go right back in there and get her a doctor."

Violet turned around, standing straight and erect, her shoulders back in good military form. She glared at Harris. "Why'd you have to worry them? I told ya, Harris—"

"We gotta get you some help, V," Jimmy said.

"Please," Violet said with resignation in her voice. "If I don't have much time left, I want to enjoy it." She pressed her hand to her stomach as spasms shuddered through her body again. Violet reached for Harris's hand and squeezed it for several seconds.

"Come on," she said when the spasms eased. "Let's just get Jimmy home. I hate hospitals. If my time is up, I'd rather spend it with you guys." Violet started off down the street, walking quickly.

Jimmy wheeled after her and Lauren and Harris followed close behind him.

"No, V!" he called out to her. "We have to go back and get you a doctor!" He kept wheeling after her, but Violet did not turn around. "Please, V. We'll all help!" he yelled.

Violet stopped and whirled around, facing her friends. "No! Please, stop. If you really care about me, then respect my wishes."

Harris tried to embrace Violet, but she pulled away from him and kept walking back toward the river, her head down.

Jimmy watched her go, shaking his head. Harris laid his hand on Jimmy's shoulder.

"I've tried too," he said. "We just have to be there for her right now." He handed Jimmy's crutches to Lauren and then resumed walking up the street after Violet.

Jimmy dropped his head into his hands. "I can't believe this."

Lauren reached over and looped her arm around Jimmy's shoulder. "Hey, she'll come around."

"No, I don't think so," Jimmy replied. "She's so stubborn." He paused and looked up at Lauren.

"Everything is falling apart. Dora's gone. Violet won't— and Harris is getting up there in age. And one of these days, you're going to come to your senses and move on."

"I'm not going anywhere," Lauren protested.

Jimmy looked back at her with true affection. "This family is all I have."

"Come on, Jimmy," Lauren said with a smile. "We're staying together. You're going to find a place for all of us, remember? Maybe we'll start a shelter of our own one day."

He smiled at her. He appreciated her confidence in him. He pushed himself up and out of the wheelchair and took the crutches from Lauren's hand. Lauren nodded approvingly. "Don't worry. I'll take the wheelchair back to the hospital."

"Thanks. I'm sure they'll need it for someone else."

"Um, there is something I need to tell you. Your mom's been asking about you again. She'd like to see you," Lauren said.

"No. Don't talk to me about her," Jimmy said, sadness permeating his voice. "Just don't. Please." He brushed Lauren's arm off his shoulder, leaned on the crutches, and hobbled down the sidewalk.

Lauren watched him go and made no effort to follow.

Chapter 20

SHORTLY AFTER breakfast the next day, Robert, Kim, and Sam walked toward the parking lot where they had parked their car. They had spent the previous night at the Salvation Army and were carrying towels and toothbrushes, and Kim was dressed in her nursing scrubs, holding her handbag containing some personal belongings and basic makeup. As they got closer to the car, fear struck Robert.

Their car was chained to a tow truck.

"No! No, no, no!" Robert yelled as he frantically ran toward the repo man who was about to drive off with all their worldly possessions. Robert pounded his fists on the hood of the truck and yelled loudly, "Whoa! Stop!"

He moved to the driver's side of the truck and banged on the man's window. "Hey!" he shouted. "Please! No! You can't take our car. Come on, man! It's all we've got left!"

Kim stood in the parking lot with Sam, looking

on. The repo man ignored them, and Robert as well. He cranked the ignition and was about to put the truck in gear when Robert yanked the door open and reached across him, trying to turn off the motor.

The repo man pushed Robert away. He looked at Robert's panicked face with Kim and Sam behind him, and for a moment it seemed like he might reconsider.

But he didn't. He slammed the door and threw the truck into gear.

Robert desperately hammered his fists on the truck window, yelling and pleading with the man as the truck began to pull away.

Sam pointed at their car and started to wail. "Daddy!" he yelled. "My dino's in there! Don't let him take him away!"

"Our clothes are in there!" Robert yelled to the driver. "At least let me get the kid's dinosaur out. You can't take our clothes. What are you doing?"

Robert ran after the tow truck, waving his arms crazily at the driver. "Hey! Hey! Stop! Please . . . my kid's lucky dino is in there!"

"Stay here," Kim said to Sam. She caught up with Robert and grabbed his arm. "Stop, Robert!" she cried. "Stop it! Just stop before you get hurt."

"He can't take everything we own," Robert protested.

She shook her head in disgust. "One more bill you didn't pay, huh?"

The tow truck hauling Robert's BMW—as well as Sam's dino—rounded a corner and disappeared into traffic. Robert bent over and put his hands on his thighs, trying to catch his breath. Defeated and dejected, he turned to face Kim.

She spun on her heel and went back to Sam, then crouched to meet his gaze and tried to console him. She looked at her watch and then up at Robert. Her eyes were red with tears.

"I gotta go to work, Robert," she said. "We can't afford for me to lose my job too."

Robert nodded. "I know. I know. I'm sorry, Kim. Go. I'll take care of Sam and look for a safe place where we can stay. Or maybe you can ask around at work?"

Kim looked back at him, gritting her teeth, trying not to explode. "How many times do I have to tell you, Robert?" Her voice rose in intensity and volume as she spoke. "None of my friends has room for us. And if they knew what has happened to us—" She shrugged and shook her head with her eyes closed. "It's humiliating!" she blurted. "If my parents were here, they'd tell me, 'We told you so, but you wouldn't listen.' I should have paid better attention to what they were telling me about you!" Her anger poured out without filter.

"Kim"—Robert waved his hands in front of his chest—"not in front of Sam. Please. Maybe if you'd actually asked—"

"Don't you dare!" she shrieked. "Your gambling and incompetence are what got us here. This is *your* mess. *You* need to fix it!"

Robert flashed her a disconsolate look and nodded toward Sam, who was still bawling. "I will. Okay? I'm gonna fix this, Kim. Just go. I'll figure something out. We'll come back and meet you around five o'clock, right here."

"Yeah," she nodded, looking at the ground, the sky, anywhere but at Robert. Then she turned and walked off in the general direction of the hospital.

Robert crouched next to Sam and pulled him in for a long hug as he stared up at the heavens. "God? If You're up there . . . help."

* * * * *

A few nights later, Jimmy, Lauren, Harris, and Violet sat in a secluded area on an old blanket in front of their tents near the river. A patch of large trees and some high shrubs hid them from the view of curious passersby on the street a few hundred yards away. Lauren had found and lit a candle and set it on a plate in the center of the group. Apple slices, bagels, a large bar of chocolate, and peanut butter sat on plates circling the candle.

Violet broke off a piece of chocolate and dipped it in the jar of peanut butter. A big smile lit up her face as she relished the taste.

"You're a rock star, kid," Violet said to Jimmy. "Thank you for this feast. I'm in heaven right now."

"How's your head doing?" Jimmy asked. "Those painkillers help? What about your stomach? Any better?"

"I'm—" Violet started to answer, but footsteps and rustling nearby captured their attention. Violet's body stiffened. She put her finger to her lips and held up her hand.

Harris quickly blew out the candle. All four stood and peered into the darkness.

Harris nodded toward some barely visible shadowy figures moving in their direction.

"Could those gang guys have gotten released?" Lauren whispered, her voice tinged with fear.

Jimmy stepped forward to find out, but Lauren pulled him back. "Don't," she said. "Please, don't."

"If it's them, I'll . . ." He clenched his fists in anger. Lauren grabbed his wrists and pulled him to her. "Jimmy, no!" she whispered. "You're still healing. Do you want to get hurt again? Take a breath. Count to ten. You don't know . . . it could be anyone out there."

Jimmy looked at Lauren. Even in the dark, he could see the imploring look in her eyes. He took a few deep breaths and counted slowly and quietly. "One . . . two . . . three . . ." He moved around Lauren to take another look. The shadowy figures were gone. Jimmy relaxed his hands and stopped counting.

"I think they left," Violet whispered. "But let's move over there to be safe." She pointed to an open grassy area and beckoned Jimmy and Lauren to follow her as they ducked behind some trees.

"Hey, where's Harris?" she asked.

"He stayed with the tents," Lauren replied.

"All right," Violet said. "We'll catch up with him later."

* * * * *

A half-moon shined down from the sky, giving the river an eerie shimmer as the water flowed swiftly by the grassy area where Jimmy, Lauren, and Violet had taken refuge.

Robert, his clothes now dirty and rumpled, and Kim, carrying her purse and still wearing her nursing scrubs, trudged along a narrow path above the riverbank. Sam trailed behind them, whimpering because he had not been able to attend school.

Kim glared at Robert in the moonlight, clearly annoyed with him. "I don't see a house down here, and it certainly doesn't feel safe wandering around near the river in the dark."

Robert was irritated too. "What do you want me to do, Kim?" he asked sarcastically. "The better motels are all full. So is the shelter. The Salvation Army can't even take us till Tuesday."

Kim's voice softened slightly. "This is just so insane . . ." Worry tinged her voice. "Sam is tired . . ."

"It's just for tonight," Robert said. "This abandoned house I found is perfect. It's clean and even still has the beds in it." Robert looked around, trying to spot the location of the house.

Instead, he saw some tents occupied by homeless people alongside the river. A couple of beat-up shopping carts sat near the tents. Robert squinted into the darkness.

"Maybe I'll be able to see it from over there," he said. He headed toward the tents with Kim and Sam trudging along behind him.

In the tent closest to the river, where he had gone to find some matches, Harris sensed movement even before he heard it. He peered out through his tent flap anxiously and his eyes focused on the backs of three people—a man, a woman, and a little boy. He sighed heavily, grateful that the figures weren't members of Duke's gang out for revenge.

Robert, Kim, and Sam moved closer to the carts, where Robert picked up an apple and began to devour it. Kim looked around nervously, sensing that they were being watched.

"We should leave," she said quietly. "This is crazy. We need to get back to the main road." She heard Robert chomp down on the apple. "What are you doing? That doesn't belong to you. That's their food." She pointed at the tents near the riverbank.

"I'm starving, that's what," Robert said. He handed what was left of the apple to Kim. "Go ahead.

Take a bite. And give some to Sam too."

Nearby, Sam found a half-eaten bagel and stuffed it into his mouth. Kim shook her head and pursed her lips to show her disgust.

Then Harris crawled out of his tent. Robert and Kim backed away when they saw him, shocked that anyone was there. Afraid of the boogeyman, Sam wailed and took off running. Harris ran a few steps after him.

"Hey!" he called. "It's okay. If you're hungry, come on back. We got some more bagels. Stop! It's too dangerous to be running out here in the dark."

Robert and Kim dashed after Sam, stumbling along in the darkness. "Sam!" Robert called out. "Come back! You need to stay close to us."

Harris stopped near the riverbank and looked after them, perplexed, trying to spot them in the dark shadows cast by the trees.

A short distance away, Jimmy, Lauren, and Violet heard the commotion and came out from behind the trees where they had been sitting. To their surprise, they saw a man and a woman running past them.

Still running in the dark, Sam drew closer to the river. He suddenly tripped and went flying, hitting the ground on the downslope, his body rolling over and over as the slope grew steeper closer to the river.

"Argh!" Sam yelled. "Help!"

Robert and Kim panted breathlessly, their eyes searching for him in the darkness, frantically looking in the direction from which they'd heard him call out. But they were too far away. They couldn't see him. There was nothing they could do but wait in horror.

Sam continued tumbling toward the river, attempting to grab bits of sticks or weeds to stop his fall with no success.

"Sam!" Kim screamed into the night.

Then she and Robert heard a sickening dull thud. They rushed to the riverbank and looked over. They both gasped in horror as their eyes took in the steep drop-off below.

"Sam!" Robert called. "Sam! It's Dad. Where are you?" Robert and Kim leaned over the edge as far as they dared and peered down into the darkness. "I don't see him," Robert said frantically.

Kim bent low, looking down toward the river's edge. She screamed when she saw Sam's little body lying on a ledge far below them.

"There he is!" she shouted to Robert. "Sam!"

She turned back to Robert. "He's not moving. I'm going down there!"

"Wait, Kim!" Robert put his arm out to stop her. "It's too dangerous. We need some rope." Robert ran back toward the tents as Kim continued to watch Sam below.

"Sam!" she called. "Honey, it's Mom. Say something if you can hear me." Frustrated, Kim started toward a small bluff closer to the water, tenuously taking a step down.

Jimmy, Lauren, and Violet hurried toward her, and Jimmy hobbled forward and pulled Kim back from the edge. When he saw her face, he blinked in surprise.

"Nurse Kim?" he said. "What are you doing here?"

Kim pointed toward the river's edge. "Our son! He fell . . . He's down there."

Jimmy looked down and saw Sam's frail body splayed out on the rock below. "I know a way down," he said. Without waiting for Kim to respond, Jimmy slid over the side of the embankment and dangled his legs over the edge.

Lauren rushed toward him. "Jimmy! No!" she yelled. "What are you doing?"

Jimmy looked up at Lauren and saw the anxiety on her face. "It's okay," he said. "I've got this." He gingerly made his way down the cliff, grabbing on to rocks and tree branches as he lowered himself inch by inch.

Robert returned with Harris in tow, carrying a rope and a flashlight. "We got a rope!" Robert called to Kim.

"Lauren, take the flashlight, and keep it aimed on Jimmy," Harris instructed.

Lauren grabbed the light from Harris and shined the beam down on Jimmy as they watched him slowly descend. Harris got busy working to create a rope harness.

"Come on!" Robert called to Harris. "Hurry!"

"Be careful!" Kim called to Jimmy.

"He'll be okay," Robert said to her. "Let's go," he said to Harris.

"Sam! Say something!" Kim continued to call out.

Harris tossed the rope down to Jimmy. "Catch, Jimmy!"

Jimmy reached up and grabbed the rope with one hand, then managed to strap himself into the harness, wrapping it around his body as he clung to the slope with his other hand.

"Sam!" Robert called.

No response. Nothing could be heard but the sound of the rushing river and Jimmy's grunts as he carefully chose his steps in the dark and made his way down the embankment, all the way to the ledge, the river only a few feet away.

He crouched by Sam's body and gently touched his arm. "Hey, kid," he said. "You okay?"

Sam made no sound, and he didn't move.

Jimmy looked away for a moment as his heart sank. He looked back at Sam and put his hands on his shoulders. "Hey, kid. Come on," he said.

Still no movement.

Kim and Robert peered down the cliff anxiously. Kim leaned precariously close and teetered over the precipice. Robert pulled her back to safety. She reached out and took Robert's hand as they nervously watched Jimmy trying to rouse Sam.

"Is he okay?" Kim called.

Jimmy didn't answer. Lauren, Violet, and Harris looked at each other with dread.

"Check his breathing!" Kim called.

Jimmy leaned over Sam and pressed his ear to the boy's mouth. He rose to his knees and looked down at Sam again.

Sam's eyes fluttered open. Jimmy turned his head up and yelled, "Yes! He's breathing! I think he's okay." Then he began wrapping the rope around Sam.

"Support his head," Kim instructed.

Jimmy looked down at Sam. "You hurt, son?"

Sam moved groggily and sat up. He looked at Jimmy and shook his head.

"I don't think he's hurt badly," Jimmy called up. He continued to wrap the rope around Sam so he could hang on to him.

"You'll be all right, Sam! We're here. Mom and Dad are here. We're waiting for you," Robert said.

Harris looked over at Robert. "Okay, when Jimmy's ready, get that slack in the rope and hold on to it. Stay behind me and help me pull."

Robert moved behind Harris and grabbed the rope while Violet called down instructions to Jimmy. "Get the kid on your back, Jimmy," she said. "Put his arms around your neck. Just go slow and make sure you are tight in the harness." She paused. "We got you."

Jimmy looked at Sam. "You okay with that, kid?"

"Yes," Sam said weakly.

Jimmy crouched down low next to Sam and

swung the boy onto his back. Sam hung on for dear life, clinging to Jimmy with his arms locked around his neck.

"Get up carefully, son," Harris called down. "Go slow. Real slow."

Jimmy looked back to Sam. "You still okay?"

Sam nodded.

"Okay, here we go. Close your eyes," Jimmy said. "Hold on to me tight and don't let go, no matter what happens."

"Okay," Sam whispered.

Jimmy slowly stood, straining a bit under Sam's weight.

Violet and Harris moved back to pull on the rope with Robert's help as Jimmy slowly started to climb, using the rope as support, searching the darkness for somewhere to plant his feet each step of the way.

Lauren attempted to keep the beam from the flashlight one step above Jimmy to help him decide where to put his hands and feet.

"Shine it just to the left," Jimmy requested, "so the beam isn't blinding me." Lauren moved the flashlight. Harris, Violet, and Robert strained as they pulled Jimmy and Sam higher. Slowly, anxiously, inch by inch, Jimmy rose higher on the cliff wall with Sam on his back.

Near the top, Jimmy hung in place while Harris and Violet held the rope taut and Robert and Kim leaned over to lift Sam off Jimmy's shoulders. With Sam securely on the ground, Harris and Violet pulled Jimmy the rest of the way up and over the edge.

"Oh, thank you!" Robert called to the group. "Thank you! Thank You, God! Thank You!"

Jimmy flopped on the ground, gasping for breath and holding his stomach where the stitched knife wound still throbbed.

With Robert's help, Kim took Sam into her arms and moved him back a short distance from the cliff. She gently laid Sam flat on the ground and checked his pulse and his breathing. Robert got down on his knees, took Sam's hand, and held it tightly while Kim tried to ascertain Sam's condition.

"Are you okay, son?" Robert asked.

Sam nodded weakly.

Robert looked up at Kim with tears in his eyes. "I'm so sorry," he said. "I've really messed up. I've put you and Sam in danger. I just wanted to give you a good life." Tears trickled down his face.

"I know," Kim said. "I know, Robert."

Seeing that everyone was safe, Violet closed her eyes, perspiration pouring down her face, her shirt drenched. She let go of the rope and flopped down on the ground as well.

Jimmy was still bent over on the ground, out of breath but doing better. After a few minutes, he straightened up and slowly walked over to where Robert and Kim were checking on Sam.

Harris shined the flashlight around the area and spotted Violet, her head in her hands, sitting on the ground. He knelt beside her and touched her cheek. Her skin was clammy, and she continued to breathe hard.

"How's my girl doing?" Harris asked. "You need some water?"

Violet looked at him and tried to smile. "In a minute," she said. "I want to see how the boy's doing."

Breathing normally now, Jimmy lowered himself next to Kim and Robert and looked at Sam, who was now sitting up. "Is he all right?"

"Yes, thank God," Kim said. "And thank *you*." She took a deep breath. "I don't know what we would have done if you all hadn't been here. Thank you. We owe you everything."

"Yes, thank you," Robert said, "from the bottom of my heart." He looked at Jimmy. "What you did was really brave. Are you okay?"

Kim looked over at Jimmy too. "Ah, yes. You're supposed to be on bed rest, as I recall," she said, trying to suppress a smile. "How are you doing? No blood, no broken stitches, or anything?"

Jimmy chuckled. "I'm fine."

Harris helped Violet up and, with flashlight in hand, they trudged toward the reunited family to check on them. It was only then, for the first time, that Violet got a good look at Robert's face in the beam of the flashlight. Her jaw dropped and she stopped dead in her tracks as she recognized him.

"Oh no!" Violet said. "No way! Not you!"

Jimmy didn't understand. "Violet, chill. Everything is okay."

"Yeah, V," Harris chimed in. "Easy does it. Be nice. Just be kind."

"No!" she yelled, wrinkling her brow and pursing her lips. She pointed at Robert accusingly. "That's him! That's the guy who wrecked our camp. Remember the water hose and the men in black?"

Harris peered at Robert, looking at him more intently, trying to make the connection.

Violet scowled at Robert and spat out her words. "I can't believe we just saved your kid . . . you dirty—" Violet started toward Robert, her fists raised as if she were going to slug him.

Jimmy jumped in front of her and blocked her path.

"V!" Jimmy said. "What's wrong with you? What are you talking about? Whatever it is, now is not the time, especially in front of the kid. Let's talk this out later."

Violet balled her fists and glared at Jimmy, then slowly backed off.

But Robert did not deny Violet's accusation. Instead, he hung his head low, embarrassed.

"Please, forgive me. I'm sorry," Robert said. "I've made a lot of mistakes. I really wish I could take it all back or push rewind and make it all go away. I'm so sorry."

"Your 'sorry' is too late!" Violet yelled at him. "You rich folks and your fancy words. You think they mean something, but they don't. Not to us." Violet turned and stormed off.

Harris followed her in the darkness. "V, wait!"

Robert looked up at Jimmy, who was still staring at him with a puzzled expression on his face. Robert's eyes were swollen and red as the tears streamed freely down his face.

"I'm sorry," he said to Jimmy, his words tumbling out of his mouth in no particular order. "If you hadn't been here . . . I've made a mess of everything . . . for you"—he looked at Jimmy and Lauren—"for my family." Robert waved his hand toward Sam and Kim. "You didn't deserve this." He gulped hard, his words garbled by his tears.

Jimmy stood there staring at Robert in the dark. His eyes glared at him coldly at first, but then after a few moments, his expression softened and he put his hand on Robert's shoulder.

"Hey, the past is the past," he said. "I'll talk to them. Right now, it's late and your boy should get some rest."

"Thank you, Jimmy," Kim said quietly. "I don't know how we can ever repay you."

"You already have," Jimmy said, gingerly patting his wound and smiling in the dark.

Robert carried Sam, and as Jimmy walked with them toward the road, he paused briefly, then turned to Kim and said, "Actually, there might be something you could help us with."

"Anything, Jimmy," Kim said.

"Our friend Violet—you met her in the hospital when I was there, the woman who got so angry a few minutes ago. She's a tough military vet, but she's got stomach cancer and won't get treatment. Is there anything we can do to help her?"

Kim nodded in understanding. "If she'll talk to me," she said, "maybe I can discuss some options with her. Truth is, the earlier she's willing to do treatment, the better chance she'll have to survive."

"She's a stubborn one," Jimmy said. "But I'll try to make it happen."

Kim hugged Jimmy goodbye.

Robert reached out his hand and said, "You're a good man, Jimmy." He continued to hold on to Jimmy's hand. "Your parents would be proud of you."

Jimmy winced slightly at the reference to his parents, but he said nothing other than "Thank you" in return. He broke away from Robert to hug Sam. "Be good, kid," he said, tousling Sam's hair. "If you ever need anything . . . come find us."

"Thank you, Jimmy," Kim replied. "Please take care of yourself. And please, make sure your friend comes to the hospital. Don't worry. We'll find a program that will cover the costs, but there's no time to lose. The earlier we can start chemo, the better her chances will be."

Jimmy nodded. Kim's admonition made sense to him. Now all he had to do was convince Violet.

Chapter 21

UNCOMFORTABLE IN the seedy part of town, Robert, Kim, and Sam walked quickly past several closed businesses and sketchy-looking street people. Robert spotted a motel set back a short distance off the busy street. "This looks like it might be safe," he said quietly to Kim. "Let's check it out."

He pushed open an aluminum screen door, and the three of them stepped inside a small, run-down motel lobby. A scruffy male clerk sat watching television behind a high counter separating the office area from the foyer.

Kim glanced around the room at the old furniture and well-worn magazines on an end table along with several beer cans and dirty coffee cups. The corner of her mouth wrinkled, and her lips pursed tightly. The place was a dump.

Robert saw Kim's negative reaction and leaned closer to her. He spoke quietly so the man behind the desk couldn't hear. "Hey, this place is close to your work, at least."

Kim stared back at him, annoyed, the look in her eyes throwing darts at her husband. Robert turned away from her and called across the counter to the clerk, who was still absorbed by the screen.

"Good evening, sir," Robert said. "We need a room for one night, please."

The clerk turned and looked at Robert and Kim with skeptical aloofness, his eyes slowly roaming their frames. His gaze fell on Sam and he nodded slightly, then slid his chair over behind the counter.

"Sixty-eight dollars," he grunted.

Robert slapped a credit card on the counter. "Sure."

The clerk took the card and ran it through a machine. Then he handed the credit card back to Robert. "Declined," he said. "Sorry."

Kim flinched when Robert didn't even argue with the clerk. He simply handed him a different credit card. "This one may work," he said. "I mean, I'm sure this one will work."

The clerk swiped the card through the machine. "Same thing," he said, shaking his head and scowling as he returned the card to Robert.

"Run it again," Robert begged. "Please, try it again."

The man obliged, but the result was the same. He handed the second credit card back to Robert.

Kim couldn't take any more. "I've got it." She stepped up and handed the clerk a different credit card, one in her name only. "Use this."

Surprised, Robert leaned toward Kim and sputtered, "Where'd you get that? What account is that?"

Kim didn't bother to answer.

The clerk ran the card successfully, and Kim signed for the room. She took the key, looked at Robert with disdain, and walked out the door.

With the sounds of traffic whizzing by, car horns blaring, and the incessant noise of sirens emanating from the city, the family—tired and defeated—trudged to their motel room. The sleeping area and small bathroom looked little better than the lobby. Once inside, Kim sat on one side of the bed and stared at the wall. Robert hurried into the bathroom.

The sound of the toilet flushing caused Kim to turn her head momentarily as Robert came out of the bathroom and walked silently past Kim to the opposite side of the bed. Both stared into the abyss of nothingness.

"Dad," Sam's voice broke the silence. "I'm hungry. Can we get something to eat? Please?"

Kim got up and crossed the room to where Sam was seated in a chair. "Okay, honey, I know," Kim attempted to soothe her son. "We're going to get something soon . . . somehow. Just be patient." She shot Robert an accusatory look, her lips compressed in anger. She said nothing, but Robert read her thoughts and recoiled defensively.

"Hey, don't look at me that way," he said. "It's not like I'm—"

"Not like you're what?" Kim stood and waved her hand at him. "*You* are the reason we're in this mess, Robert!" she yelled. "Get that through your thick skull."

"Why is this always about me?" Robert railed. He sprang up, facing off with Kim. "You're the one who wanted the bigger house and the nicer car. You can't put all of that on me." Robert's veins popped across his forehead.

Kim's hands flew to her waist. "Really?" she retorted. "This is *my* fault? I'm the one with a job here, in case you hadn't noticed. Where are my thanks for that? Huh?"

"Your thanks? I had a job," Robert responded.

"I've worked nonstop, night and day, for ten straight years."

"For what?" Kim snarled. "Your gambling habit? It certainly wasn't for us. You don't even spend time with your son." Kim pointed at Sam, who was cowering in a corner of the room.

"Stop!" Sam cried. "Stop it. Please, Mom. Please, Dad. Please stop."

Out of breath, both parents turned toward their son, who was sitting with his hands over his face, crying. Kim rushed over to him and wrapped him in an embrace.

"Oh, Sammy, I'm so sorry," she said. "This is not your fault. You didn't do anything wrong. Mom and Dad are sorry." She turned and glared at Robert. He stepped toward them, but Kim waved him away.

"You need to leave," she said. "Go get your life together, Robert."

Robert was stunned. "Come on, Kim. What are you talking about? Where am I going to go? What are you saying?"

Kim let loose of Sam and stood up, facing Robert to confront him. "Just what I said," she answered. "I paid for this room, not you. Get out!"

"What?" Robert shook his head and looked at Sam, then back to Kim. "Don't do this in front of him."

"You heard me. Get out."

Robert stepped forward again, his arms opened toward his wife. "Kim, we can fix this."

"Fix this? Yeah, sure," she said. "You keep saying that. Look at where we are. It's gone too far, Robert. Just . . . get . . . out."

Robert looked at Kim pleadingly.

"Leave!" she yelled. Then her voice softened a bit. "Please, Robert, just leave." A pained expression flooded her face. "I don't care what you do or where you go. Get help or don't get help. I don't care anymore. I'm done."

Kim stood resolute, her arms crossed. She raised one arm and pointed toward the door. "Leave . . . now. Now!"

Robert looked at the door, then back at his son. Nearly in tears, he leaned down and put a hand on Sam's shoulder. "I'm going to fix this, buddy. I'm sorry. I am so sorry."

"Robert! Just go."

Robert picked up his jacket and, with a defeated expression, walked out the door, leaving it slightly ajar. Sam saw the open door and bolted for it, following his father outside the motel room.

"Sam!" Kim called after him, but she was too late. Sam was already out the door and chasing after Robert.

Kim ran after Sam, flying out of the motel room behind him . . . but then she stopped short at the sight that met her eyes. Robert was kneeling in front of Sam, hugging him tightly.

"Sam!" she called. "Sam, come back here right now."

Robert loosened his embrace of his son and wiped tears from Sam's eyes and his own before standing.

"I'm sorry, buddy," he said. "Your mother is right. This is my fault. I don't want you to be upset with her. Okay? I gotta go. Stay with Mom. I love you, son." Robert kissed Sam's forehead and gave Kim a last look, then looked back at Sam.

"I love you, too, Dad," Sam said and turned back toward Kim, who was still standing in the motel room doorway.

"Okay," Robert whispered after him. He blinked hard and walked away.

Kim held Sam close, trying to comfort him, but Sam was inconsolable.

To Kim, the events of the night seemed almost like a sign—the end of a long, sad decline. She wrapped Sam in her arms and together they walked silently back inside the dreary motel room and locked the door.

* * * * *

Robert slowly walked down the street, looking around aimlessly. He reached into his pants pocket, pulled out his wallet, and to his surprise, found a ten-dollar bill—his last. He looked up at a building and saw a sign: *Liquor.*

His fingers fondled the ten-spot as he paused outside the door of the liquor store. He could keep the ten dollars for something important, or he could step inside the door. He shook his head slightly, pulled on the door, walked up to the counter, and stood in line behind a homeless woman. Robert opened his wallet to the cashier and showed him the ten-dollar bill.

"What can I get for this?" he asked, sounding like a kid bartering with his best teddy bear. He pulled out the ten and placed it carefully on the countertop.

The cashier grunted, grabbed a bottle of cheap vodka, put it in a brown paper bag, and pushed it across the counter toward Robert as he scooped up the bill.

"That'll work," Robert said. He pulled the bag to his chest as if he'd been given an achievement award. He hadn't, of course. Quite the opposite.

As soon as Robert exited the liquor store, he stuffed his hand into the bag and pulled out the bottle of vodka. He unscrewed the top and took a long swig of the cheap booze, gagging on its gritty taste. He shook his head hard, turned, and walked on down the street, taking another drink as he meandered from side to side on the sidewalk in the run-down business district.

He continued up the street, guzzling the vodka as he went. When the bottle was empty, he glared at it angrily, as if everything that was wrong was the bottle's fault. Robert cursed it, then reared back and smashed it against the side of a building. In a drunken rage, he kicked a nearby trash can, sending its contents careening across the sidewalk.

He stumbled and wobbled, tripped over the curb, and staggered his way back to the motel and found the room where Kim and Sam were staying. He pounded on the door and yelled, "Kim, let me in! Please! Open the door!"

Inside the room, Kim and Sam huddled together in the bed. Sam clung to his mother as tears trickled down both of their faces.

Robert continued banging on the motel room door. "Please, let me in, Kim! I've got nowhere to go." More agitated, Robert violently beat his fists on the door.

The motel clerk heard the commotion and came out of the front office. When he saw Robert banging on the door, he yelled, "Hey, bud! Knock it off. Don't make me call the cops!"

Robert ignored him and kept beating on the door. Finally, he sank to the ground, his back against the door to Kim's motel room. In his drunken stupor, he sprawled out on the cement in front of the door.

The clerk shook his head angrily and went back inside to call the police.

A few minutes later, Robert saw the red and blue lights of a police car and heard the short bursts of a siren. He staggered to his feet, then fell backward as two officers got out of the patrol car and made their way toward him. Robert blurted a series of expletives at them.

"Take it easy, buddy," one officer attempted to calm him.

But Robert wasn't having it. He hauled back and took a feeble swing at the policeman.

"Okay, that's it!" the officer said as he and his partner wrestled Robert to the ground and pulled his arms behind his back. They slapped handcuffs over his wrists, read him his rights, then dragged Robert to his feet and pushed him into the back seat of the squad car and slammed the door. Robert sat with his hands cuffed behind his back, his face pressed against the glass, ruefully looking out the window, alone and ashamed.

The officers drove Robert to the local jail where they fingerprinted him. They stood him against a wall and a bright lightbulb flashed in Robert's face as he stood against the plain backdrop. "Turn to your right," a voice said in the darkness, and Robert groggily obeyed. "Now, your left." The bulb lit up Robert's face again. "All right, get him outta here."

Another officer led Robert to a small jail cell with a metal commode and sink combination in the corner and a cot along the side of the wall. The door of the cell clanked loudly as the officer slammed it shut. "Sleep it off, man," he said before walking away.

Robert looked back at the man but said nothing. He trudged over to the cot and curled up on it. A thin blanket was folded at the bottom of the bed, but Robert didn't bother covering himself. Within a short time, he was out, fast asleep. He didn't wake until the following morning.

When the deputy came to open Robert's cell door late that afternoon, he found Robert sitting on the cot, holding his hands to his head, hung over, his demeanor that of a defeated man.

"Come on, buddy," the deputy said. "Time to go. You're outta here." He unlocked the cell door and Robert stood, wobbled a bit, then caught his balance. He shuffled out of the cell and followed the deputy through the cement-floored hallway, then through another series of locked doors.

At the front of the jail, the commanding officer looked at Robert, with his disheveled hair and rumpled clothes, and scowled.

"Let this be a warning to you," he said. "I don't want to see you in here again. You know better."

"Yes, sir," Robert mumbled. "I do know better. Thank you."

He stepped outside and shielded his eyes from the late-afternoon sunlight. The glare combined with his hangover was almost more than he could handle. He looked up and down the street, trying to decide which way to go. It didn't really matter. If you didn't know where you were going, any road would do. With his head hung low, he shuffled down the street with no direction at all, looking like a man twice his age.

Late that night, in a desolate part of town, two vicious thugs attacked Robert. They punched him, kicked him, and knocked him to the ground. They stripped him of his warm jacket and stole his phone, his watch, and the maxed-out credit cards. They left him alive, lying motionless on the street. Bloody, battered, and beaten, he had nothing, nobody, and nowhere to go.

Chapter 22

SEVERAL WEEKS after being discharged from the hospital, the knife wound in his side healing well, Jimmy felt strong enough to take a bold step. He humbled himself and went for the job interview he had missed because of the attack.

Dressed in the best clothes he could find, a plaid shirt and tan pants—but not a suit—he walked uptown to a slightly old-fashioned hardware store, tucked between several modern-looking shops on the same street. The hardware store displayed a selection of home improvement tools and other products on racks outside the shop on the sidewalk on both sides of the entrance. A sign—*Help Needed*—was posted on the window near the front door. Jimmy pushed the door open and bells jangled as he entered.

He looked around the colorful store with aisles jammed full of just about anything anyone could need for do-it-yourself home-improvement projects. He approached a cashier at the front.

"Hi, I'm looking for Mr. Mills."

The cashier brushed her long hair away from her face and pointed toward one of the aisles. "He's back there."

"Thank you," Jimmy said and headed through the narrow aisle.

A rugged man, wearing a scruffy beard, a gray T-shirt, and a red work apron, stood on a ladder organizing a Gutter Glove downspout display.

"Mr. Mills?"

"Hello there," the man called down from his perch on the ladder.

"I'm here to see Mr. Mills, the store owner," Jimmy said.

"That's me," the man said. "I'll be with you in a second or two. Hey, can you pass me that box right there?"

"Sure." Jimmy grabbed the box Mr. Mills had indicated and passed it up to him. With his other hand, Jimmy held on to his resume. He took a deep, nervous breath.

"I'm Jimmy," he said. "Gabrielle set up a job interview for me a while back."

"Ah, yes, I remember," Mr. Mills replied. He squinted slightly as he looked at Jimmy. "You're the one who didn't show up."

Jimmy looked down at the floor, embarrassed and somewhat surprised that Mr. Mills remembered the abandoned interview. "I'm so sorry about that, sir," he said. "I made a mistake. I should have called and explained what happened." He stopped talking and simply handed his resume to Mr. Mills when he'd finished adjusting the display.

Mr. Mills eyed the resume as he descended the ladder. He then walked down the aisle toward the back of the store and indicated for Jimmy to follow him.

"I recognize you," he said. "I've seen you helping out at church." He rubbed his chin. "Look, we all make mistakes. I understand, and I believe in second chances." He paused and looked Jimmy in the eyes. "Gabrielle says you're a hard worker and usually quite reliable." A trace of a smile creased Mr. Mills's face but was quickly replaced by a frown as he looked more carefully at Jimmy's resume. "You would have been a good fit for the floor manager job," he said. "But the current opening is for a cashier who has prior experience. Do you have any experience handling a cash register?"

"No, sir," Jimmy answered, shaking his head.

"But I'm a real hard worker and a quick learner. I'll do my best with anything you throw at me."

Mr. Mills looked deeply into Jimmy's eyes. He paused. Unknown to Jimmy, Mr. Mills's father had been homeless due to his heavy drinking. Mr. Mills had experienced firsthand the effects alcohol can have on a family, so he had taken responsibility for his own life at an early age. He became a devout Christian and maintained a Christian lifestyle. Along the way, he developed a desire to help the homeless people in his community and had joined forces with Gabrielle at the Downtown City Mission. A fair-minded, kind-hearted man, he truly believed in giving someone the benefit of the doubt when it came to extending a hand up, rather than a handout.

"I'll tell you what," Mr. Mills said. "I do need some help getting this stuff on the shelves and getting the stockroom organized. Let's see how you do with that. You can start today if you'd like, and I will pay you in cash at the end of the day."

Jimmy's jaw dropped in excitement. "Really?" he asked.

Mr. Mills nodded and smiled. "Really."

"Oh, thank you, sir!" Jimmy gushed. "You won't regret it! I promise."

"Great. Grab an apron up front, and I'll meet you in the stockroom."

In his excitement, Jimmy lunged forward and hugged Mr. Mills. Then he quickly released the store owner, not wanting to overstep his boundaries.

Mr. Mills didn't seem to mind one bit.

* * * * *

It took a few more weeks, but with the help of Harris and Lauren, Jimmy persuaded Violet to return to St. Teresa's Hospital for an exam. His most compelling argument: *"Violet,"* he'd said, his hands on his hips, *"Harris, Lauren, and I* need *you. You are a soldier. It's your duty. You have to do this for* us.*"* Eventually, she'd agreed.

From there, the process took on a life of its own with doctors and nurses offering Violet their insights and expertise. Violet consented to chemotherapy and Kim was there to comfort and assist her each step of the way.

Because of her serious condition, Violet's oncologist suggested she remain in the hospital during the treatments, so Harris, Lauren, and Jimmy visited her there.

Violet's head had been shaved and she lay in bed making a bracelet out of some paracord Harris had given her. She was hooked up to several machines and monitors, but for the most part, she was doing okay. Her eyes lit up when her family entered her room.

"There she is! How's my warrior?" Harris asked. He leaned over the bed and hugged Violet.

Jimmy handed her a small bouquet of flowers. "It ain't much, but . . ."

Violet looked at the bouquet, much like the ones she used to hawk on the streets. "Thank you so much," she said as she wiped a tear from her eye. "What have I been missin'?"

"Oh, you ain't been missin' nothin'," Harris replied with a twinkle in his eye. "But we've sure been missin' you!"

Violet wiped another tear from her eye. "I'm sure happy to see you all." She smiled.

"How are you feeling?" Lauren asked.

"Well, I don't have to comb my hair," Violet quipped.

They all chuckled.

"You're still beautiful to us," Harris said.

"Thank you," Violet said, covering her face and

pretending to blush. "Hey, want to share some of my hospital food? Kim's been sneaking me extra because we knew you'd come." She pulled out an assortment of food and snacks from a drawer next to her bed. The group sat around her, munching, talking, and laughing for a long time until visiting hours were over.

Before everyone left, Violet reached over to Lauren and took her hand. She slid the paracord bracelet onto Lauren's wrist, squeezed her hand tightly, and smiled warmly at her.

Lauren smiled back. "Thank you, sister," she said.

* * * * *

A week or so later, the doctors discharged Violet from the hospital, after she promised she would return regularly for her chemo treatments.

"Oh, she'll be here, all right," Harris assured the oncologist. "We'll see to that."

"I'll get here," Violet said. "But right now, I'm just glad to be going home."

One morning a few weeks later, shortly after dawn, Gabrielle walked down a slope near the river, through the long, high grass where the group was living. She looked around, searching for something or someone. She spotted Lauren by her tent, folding up a sleeping bag. Gabrielle smiled and waved at her.

"Jimmy around?" she called out to her as she approached.

"No," Lauren said. "He should be back shortly, though. He went out for breakfast . . . er, I mean, he's gone to find us some breakfast."

"Sure did!" Jimmy called out as he trudged through the trees behind them, carrying a large bag of yesterday's bagels. He handed the bag to Lauren.

She smiled happily and set the bag on the ground, then rummaged through one of the shopping carts till she found a plate. She emptied the bagels onto the plate and placed it on a battered card table in front of Jimmy. Harris joined them and grabbed a bagel. Jimmy was about to take one, too, when Gabrielle walked closer.

"Hey, Jimmy," she said. "Can I have a word with you . . . privately?"

Jimmy cocked his head and gave her a questioning look. "Sure, I guess so." He followed her a few feet away, back behind some trees.

Gabrielle stopped and turned to him. "It's about your mom," she said somberly.

Jimmy felt his face go pale. "No, please . . ." He turned away from Gabrielle so she couldn't see his face. He put his head in his hands. "He did it, didn't he?" he rasped. "He killed her . . . I knew I shoulda . . ."

A female hand tapped Jimmy on the shoulder. He turned around and, to his complete surprise, he saw his mom standing there, holding a bag of chocolate brownies. Her eyes sparkled, despite an ugly, recent bruise on her cheek.

"I did it, Jimmy," she said. "John is gone. The police came and took him away." She lightly touched her cheek. "And I'm pressing charges against him."

Jimmy wrapped his arms around his mother and held her tightly. Liz leaned back and looked into his eyes. "Come home, Jimmy," she said. "I'm going to get a job and we can continue living in our same home. Please, come home, son."

Jimmy released her and turned to look over at Lauren, who was watching anxiously, along with Violet and Harris—his street family.

"Mom, I . . ." Jimmy paused, not quite sure how to say what he felt. "I met someone . . ." He looked over at Lauren again. "And I have Harris and Violet over there . . ."

Liz turned and took them all in, casting her gaze from Lauren, to Violet, to Harris. She thought for a few seconds.

"Well, we have enough space at our house . . ." she said thoughtfully. "And they seem like good people . . . so there's room enough for them, too, if they want to come live with us."

Jimmy could hardly believe what he'd heard. He wiped a tear from his eye. "Really?" he asked. "Do you mean that, Mom?"

Liz nodded affirmatively and smiled as Jimmy's face lit up. He hugged her again in a tight bear hug, lifting her off the ground, his face buried in her shoulder. For several moments, Jimmy held on to his mom and wouldn't let go.

A few days later, the group gathered at Liz's home—and Jimmy's home—for breakfast. Liz brought out a platter of scrambled eggs and placed it on the dining room table. Wearing a scarf over her bald head, Violet reclined in a comfortable chair in the corner of the room, where she played a game of chess with Jimmy.

Harris placed two of his most recent paintings

of Dora on another table in the room. The paintings perfectly captured Dora's essence, beauty, and sophistication. Harris lightly caressed the edges of one of the canvases with his fingertips as he gazed at the image.

Lauren came out of the kitchen with a pan of sausages. She saw the new Dora paintings and moved over to admire them. "Wow! These are lovely, Harris."

"This is what she looked like in the first movie I saw her in," Harris explained. "And this one . . ." He paused, swallowed, and then smiled. "This one is the Dora we all knew and loved. I guess that's the way I remember her now, winging her way to heaven."

Lauren hugged Harris lightly. "You portrayed her perfectly."

Watching from across the room, Liz smiled. "Brunch is ready," she called out in a happy voice.

The front doorbell rang and echoed through the house. Jimmy hurried over to answer the door and smiled broadly when he saw Gabrielle standing there with a large bouquet of flowers.

"Gabrielle! You made it. Come in, please." They embraced in a quick hug and walked into the living room.

Gabrielle handed the flowers to Liz. "For you," she said.

"Thank you! Perfect timing, Gabrielle," Liz said. "Brunch is ready. Please, come sit down. We have plenty of food. Enough for all."

Liz, Lauren, Jimmy, Harris, Violet, and Gabrielle gathered around the table and took their seats. Before they started eating, Harris stood back up.

"I just want to express my gratitude," he said, "for us all being together . . . and for all that we are about to receive, and all that we have received." He paused as the others nodded in agreement. They joined hands and bowed their heads as Harris led them in prayer.

"For what we are about to receive, oh, Lord," he spoke emotionally, "and what we have received, we are truly grateful. Amen."

Jimmy raised his glass of orange juice in agreement. The others smiled and did the same, clinking their glasses together.

"Dig in," Liz said. "And don't be bashful."

"No danger of that," Violet quipped.

Jimmy smiled. "Thanks for helping me keep our family together, Mom," he said. "It's really a blessing just to feel safe, to have a roof over our heads . . . and to have plenty of food to share. Thank you, Mom."

He looked over to Gabrielle. "I'm grateful to you, too, Gabrielle, and for all of your volunteers who have been there for us." He put his hands together and looked up, still speaking to Gabrielle but also to Someone much higher. "Guide us to what more we can do to help all those still struggling out there." He nodded toward the street.

"Well, I have some exciting news," Gabrielle said as the group began eating. "Remember that abandoned motel I mentioned once before? The one we were hoping to turn into housing for people in need?"

Jimmy and Lauren nodded as Gabrielle continued. "We've finally managed to get a meeting with the mayor about it. Somebody is going to have to raise the money for the renovations, and we're hoping the city will help. But most people on boards and committees have no clue what is really needed." She paused and looked around the table, her eyes connecting with each person. "So, I was wondering . . . would you all be up for coming along with me to meet with the mayor to discuss what needs to happen?"

Jimmy, Lauren, Harris, and Violet exchanged

confused glances. Harris spoke for all of them. "Us?" he asked. "You mean we would get to meet the mayor of the city?"

"Of course, you!" Gabrielle gushed. "Who knows the homeless situation better than you? Your input has been a great help to me in our work at the Downtown City Mission. And the mayor would really like to hear directly from you rather than people who think they know best but would merely perpetuate the problems."

Jimmy's jaw dropped in astonishment. "We would meet with the mayor?"

"Yes!" Gabrielle answered. "The informational meeting has already been set up for next week. Think you can fit it into your schedule?"

The group high-fived one another, nearly jumping up and down in excitement. "You just tell us when, where, and what time," Harris said when his words could be heard above the din. "We'll be there!"

Later that afternoon, Violet busied herself working on a new bicycle repair table and Harris sat painting a landscape scene. Lauren went outside and sat in the sunshine on the front porch steps. After a while, Jimmy stepped outside and sat down next to her.

He seemed nervous. "Thanks for believing in me, Lauren," he said. He reached into his pocket and pulled out a small jewelry box. "It's not much . . . but I got this for you. Maybe if I keep working at Mr. Mills's hardware store, I'll be able to afford a ring someday." He opened the jewelry box and took out a simple but beautiful bracelet and placed it on Lauren's wrist.

Her eyes widened in surprise and her face beamed with joy. "Oh, Jimmy," she said. "I never thought I'd ever be this happy. Thank you!"

Jimmy's smile nearly went from ear to ear. "Me either. I mean . . . I never thought, not you . . . I mean, I never thought that I would . . . aw, you know what I mean."

They laughed together. Lauren leaned her head on Jimmy's shoulder as he wrapped his arms around her, both of them smiling at the growing love they felt for each other.

Chapter 23

AT THE MEETING the following week, Lauren, Jimmy, Violet, and Harris gawked in awe at the oak-paneled walls of the mayor's elegant office, decorated with photos of significant newsmakers and other celebrities with whom the mayor had met. Opposite the photos, a large American flag covered almost the entire wall.

"Come in and sit with me," Gabrielle instructed, pointing to some open seats around a large conference room table. Dressed in their best clothes, the group still looked out of place as they sat down at the table.

The mayor, a man in his early forties, wearing a sophisticated gray suit, sat at the head of the table, surrounded by various city officials vying for his attention and several administrative aides. A model of the motel and various plans and blueprints were laid out on the table.

The mayor welcomed the group and then asked

each of them to tell their story—a bit about their background and how they came to be homeless. He then welcomed their suggestions regarding the needs of people living on the street and how the city could best address the issues. Drugs, crime, mental health, trash, and the various "nuisance factors" involved with encampments taking over areas of downtown all entered into the discussions that followed.

"What can we do to help alleviate these issues while maintaining the dignity of every person?" seemed to be the question that arose from the city officials. "We don't want to hurt anyone, but we can't allow our public parks and other areas of the city to be turned into rubbish-covered, drug- and crime-ridden sections of town," one official said.

They asked for Harris's and Violet's opinions as well as Lauren's and Jimmy's regarding what could really make a difference. They also asked numerous questions of Gabrielle, as someone who had been working on the front lines, helping homeless people for years. The officials listened spellbound as the group described the conditions that had contributed to their homeless experiences, as well as the many needs of others still on the streets.

"My story pales," Jimmy said, "when compared

with the horrors experienced by many of the teenage girls living on the streets, alone and afraid with nowhere to go. They are easy targets for every sort of predator." Lauren nodded in agreement.

The model of the renovated motel, offering low-cost or free housing to homeless people who needed a fresh start, as well as healthcare and mental health services, seemed to make the most sense. The group discussed ways homeless people could access such a place through organizations such as the Salvation Army and the Downtown City Mission that were already working with many people on the streets and knew the issues firsthand. They also discussed how hygiene standards could be established, if or how rent could be paid, and how the renovated motel could be maintained.

After a long while, the mayor stood up. "Well, this has been quite an illuminating and productive meeting," he said. "Thank you, Gabrielle, for introducing our experts here." He nodded toward Harris, Violet, Jimmy, and Lauren. "Your input has been very valuable." He looked to some of the city officials and said, "We should have done something like this a long time ago. It makes sense to have this group involved in this project."

He turned and smiled at Jimmy, Lauren, Violet, and Harris before continuing. "We understand that we have not done enough to help solve these issues in the past. You have provided us with some good suggestions about where we can improve—including comprehensive wraparound services for mental health and addictions, along with safe, decent housing that can move people off the streets and into a better environment. Your ideas make sense for everyone."

The mayor paused and let his eyes move from person to person around the table. "Let me see if I can get this pushed through quickly," he said. "We know the system has let a lot of people down. Hopefully, with your help, we will be able to take the right steps and do better going forward."

Everyone erupted in spontaneous applause. The mayor raised his hand and smiled as he exited the room, followed by several administrative aides.

* * * * *

It took several months of hard work and cooperation between the city and local groups working with the homeless, but the big day—the opening day of the renovated motel—finally came. Jimmy and Lauren held hands as they stood looking up at the large sign on the roof. The sign read: *Haven for Hope—Services and Housing*. Jimmy wore a badge that said *Manager* and Lauren wore one with *Program Coordinator* on it.

Lauren looked at Jimmy with obvious pride. "I always knew you could do it, Jimmy," she said, making no attempt to hide her affection for him. "I knew you were destined to do incredible things."

Jimmy smiled at her and then looked back at the building. "We did this together," he said. He gazed tenderly into her eyes and said, "I couldn't have done this alone."

A minivan filled with homeless people pulled in front of Haven for Hope's office. Jimmy chuckled when he saw Harris in the front passenger seat. He smiled even bigger when Violet hopped out of the driver's-side door and opened the side panel door for a middle-aged Latina woman carrying a baby. Violet reached out and helped the woman out of the van. Two Black men in their early twenties followed the Latina woman, and a disheveled elderly white man inched out after them.

Harris pulled a wheelchair out of the back of the vehicle and brought it around to the side door. He climbed inside the van and lifted the remaining passenger, a female military veteran, into his strong arms. Harris carried her out, gently placed her in the wheelchair, then wheeled her over to the front entrance.

Jimmy, Violet, and Lauren grabbed the garbage bags filled with the new residents' few possessions. All three understood what those items meant to the people getting out of the van.

"This is the last group for today," Violet said. "I'll see ya later. I'm off to start my new job at the bike shop."

"Good luck," Lauren said. "Nah, you don't need it. You'll do great!"

Violet smiled. "Thanks for that vote of confidence." She hopped back into the van and headed off to work—for a real salary.

Gabrielle came out of the Haven for Hope office, and with a bright smile on her face, she called out to the newcomers, "Welcome! We're so glad you are here. Welcome home!"

Jimmy stood back and watched as Gabrielle and Lauren led the new residents inside the building.

Harris stepped over and patted him on the back. "We've come a long way, son."

"I know," Jimmy said, as much to himself as to

Harris. "Who would have thought?" He smiled at Harris. "Thank you for teaching me how to fight—and more importantly, when not to. And for teaching me to hold my temper and only fight for what really matters. Most of all, thank you, Harris, for modeling for me what it means to be a real man of God."

* * * * *

Later that evening, Lauren served as a volunteer helping to hand out food from the Salvation Army food truck. Near the railroad tracks, she spotted a woman sitting on the ground next to a large boxcar with a blanket wrapped around her. A duffle bag and a black plastic bag filled to the brim sat next to her. Lauren approached her cautiously but confidently and crouched in front of her.

"Hi," she said with a warm smile. "My name is Lauren. You really shouldn't be out here by yourself at night. I have somewhere safe you can go, if you'd like to go with me."

The woman looked back at Lauren as if trying to figure out her angle.

"It's okay," Lauren said. "I was on the streets before too. I know what kind of stuff happens out here. But the Salvation Army is safe, I promise. And they have hot chocolate."

The woman smiled, and Lauren helped her to her feet. Together, they walked to the Salvation Army. Lauren led the woman inside, where a Salvation Army officer was waiting.

"This is Major Meechem," Lauren said, "and he is going to take good care of you."

The major came over and offered her his hand. "Welcome. We're so glad you are here," he said. "Let me get you some hot chocolate."

He led the woman toward the interior of the mission, but not before she looked over her shoulder at Lauren and smiled.

Lauren grabbed a box filled with several more bags of sandwiches from the food truck and headed back out onto the streets, giving the food away to any homeless person she found. She saw a dirty, disheveled man pushing a shopping cart filled with other people's cast-off junk—now *his* junk, the sort he used to mock people for holding on to in the homeless encampment.

Lauren didn't recognize Robert. He hadn't shaved in days, and he wore a filthy, frumpy coat and a warm red cap that covered his head except for some greasy hair sticking out around his forehead and ears. Lauren watched as he stopped a well-dressed man walking in his direction on the street.

"Can you spare a buck or two?" he asked. "Or even some change?"

The well-dressed man grunted something and walked on by—much like Robert himself might have done a year earlier.

"No?" Robert slumped next to the shopping cart and sat on the curb. He clutched a photograph of Sam in his hand and looked at it longingly.

Still oblivious to Robert's identity, Lauren approached cautiously, carrying several Salvation Army sandwich bags. She stopped in front of Robert and leaned toward him.

"Hi, I'm Lauren," she said. She reached into the bag and pulled out a freshly made sandwich. "Do you want a sandwich?" she asked, stretching her arm toward Robert.

"Sure," he muttered. He reached out and received the food.

"I know somewhere safe . . . and warm, where you can go. The people there are great, and they'd really love to help you."

Robert shook his head slowly. "Nobody wants

me," he said. "I'm disqualified. I've messed up too badly."

"I know that feeling," Lauren said. "I was on the streets for a while too. It seemed like nobody cared. But I discovered that's not true."

Robert turned his eyes up to look at Lauren's radiant face.

"Hey, we've all fallen short," she said. "And lost our way . . . lost ourselves, our jobs, our homes, our stuff . . . our loved ones . . ."

Robert flinched at her last words and pulled the photograph in his hand closer to his chest.

"If you are feeling lost and alone, like I once was, just know that God hasn't given up on you. He's here for you." Lauren waved her hand in a sweeping motion toward the shopping cart. "Even here. And He has a plan for you too. Miracles are possible. I'm living proof of that. So don't give up. Don't give up on God, and don't give up on yourself. Love and faith conquer all. With Him, life is full of endless possibilities."

"Why are you talking to me?" Robert asked. "Why do you care what happens to me?"

"Because I've been there. And when I got back on my feet, I promised God, 'The next time I see someone in need, I'm going to ask how I can serve that person. I'll do what I can to show hope and love and compassion to others.' So I tell myself, *Have faith. He might be working a miracle through you to bring someone home for good.*"

Lauren paused and looked directly into Robert's eyes. "And tonight, maybe that someone is you."

Robert chomped down on the sandwich. "Maybe so," he said. "But not yet."

"Okay," Lauren said. "No pressure. I understand. But just so you know . . ." she pointed heavenward. "He's ready when you are."

Robert nodded and watched Lauren move on up the street.

* * * * *

Once up and running, Haven for Hope provided housing for homeless people, as well as support services and job training. Each day, Jimmy and Lauren looked for fresh opportunities to help others. Gabrielle offered them valuable tips she had learned over the years in her work with the homeless, and they incorporated many of her ideas into Haven for Hope. On most days, Harris and Violet volunteered with them.

Harris set up a large whiteboard at the far corner of one room, announcing *Veterans Support Group*. Each week, he met with war-torn veterans, some of whom had been severely wounded or suffered PTSD or other issues as a result of what they had experienced in their military service. Some had drug and alcohol issues, many relived the horrors of war over and over in their nightmares, and most had anger issues.

Harris understood those needs all too well. "You just gotta breathe," he encouraged the vets. He demonstrated his breathing techniques, taking four-count deep breaths and then slowly exhaling, counting to ten before responding to conflicts, and other simple but effective coping practices.

Like Jimmy and Lauren had experienced, many of the people who showed up at Haven for Hope had no address, nowhere they could call home. When they came to Haven for Hope, they received more than a new address—they found acceptance and love, and, most of all, hope.

Jimmy and Lauren couldn't help everyone . . . but they could help one person . . . and then another . . . and another.

* * * * *

A year or so later, still painting nearly every day, Harris decided that rather than show his work in a gallery downtown, he would host a gala exhibition at Haven for Hope. His paintings—many of them of Dora, Violet, Jimmy, and some recently done of Lauren, as well some wood carvings and self-portraits—hung on the walls all around a small makeshift art gallery.

Harris beamed proudly as he moved through the crowd and shook hands with the art lovers who showed up for his unveiling. Violet was decked out in a formfitting black outfit, highlighted by large earrings, several pearl necklaces, and a circular pearl belt buckle. After chemo, her hair had grown back fuller than before and was now pulled back and cascading down over her shoulders. Lauren wore her favorite lavender-and-purple sweater-and-skirt combination with darker lavender shoes, and Jimmy wore his comfortable flannel shirt and tan pants. Both smiled as they watched Harris receiving accolades from the art aficionados sipping drinks and moving from one piece of art to another in admiration.

"This is even better than we could have imagined," Jimmy said to Lauren.

Lauren nodded and embraced him warmly. She looked into his face and smiled. "And we've only just begun," she said. "God sure works in mysterious ways. I never thought I would have such a sense of purpose . . . and acceptance and significance." She reached out and took Jimmy's hands in hers.

"I thought God had abandoned me," she said. "But He didn't. You and Mama were right. God really does hear our prayers. And He answers—in His own way and time."

"Wow! Since when did you get so spiritual? Is this my same Lauren?" Jimmy asked.

Lauren playfully punched him in the arm. "It is! And it *isn't*. I've been changed, Jimmy. You know what I mean. For those of us who have been down and out, with no address, when hope dies, it is hard to find it again. But miracles can happen. It just goes to show that you never know why things happen the way they do in life. But through it all, I found God. And I found you. I found my family—and *love* found me."

A Note from the Author:
What Can I Do to Help?

KEN ABRAHAM spoke with Dr. Robert G. Marbut Jr., chief consultant for the movie *No Address*, regarding what one person or group can do to help thwart the overwhelming problem of homelessness in America. Dr. Marbut served as the executive director of the US Interagency Council on Homelessness from 2019 to 2021. He is the founding president of Haven for Hope, a highly praised food and shelter program in Texas that helps large numbers of homeless people every day. He is a welcomed source of knowledge concerning homelessness in many cities across America.

Unafraid to challenge the status quo or to confront programs that are not working well in their efforts to alleviate the struggles involved with homelessness, Dr. Marbut offers advice that may surprise you.

A NOTE FROM THE AUTHOR

When we encounter the problem of homelessness, it is so overwhelming that we tend to think, *What can one person do? How can I help find food, lodging, and mental health services for all those people who are living on the streets or in encampments?*

Or we may ask, "Is it really safe for me to get involved? I've heard about the alcoholism and drug addiction associated with many homeless people. Not to mention potential robberies, rapes, or other dangerous behaviors. When I encounter people on the streets or in encampments, I see people who are poor and destitute, but I also notice numerous unsavory-looking individuals. Do I dare get near these people?"

For most of us, it's not that we don't *want* to help, but we simply don't know how or where to do so.

Dr. Marbut suggests we begin by getting a better game plan.

Myths abound about the causes of homelessness, but one of the major mistakes many people make is to assume homelessness is rife with recreational drug usage. That assumption confuses the *cause* with the *effect*. Yes, drug use is rampant in homeless encampments and the results are horrific, with many addicted people living and dying together in dangerous, trash-strewn, needle-ridden environments.

But drug usage among the homeless population is not the primary *cause* of the problem; we have the causality backward. Most individuals don't become recreational drug users and then become homeless. That may happen 6–8 percent of the time, but according to Dr. Marbut's studies, approximately 76 percent of homelessness can be traced to untreated mental illnesses that lead to addiction, that lead to homelessness.

More often, a person begins self-medicating and then becomes addicted. For a variety of reasons—whether erratic behavior, incompetency on the job, failing to show up at work, uncontrolled or unwarranted outbursts of anger, domestic violence, or other issues—the person gets fired from his or her job, loses income, and eventually cannot or will not have enough money to pay the mortgage, rent, or basic housing expenses. Not surprisingly, that person often resorts to living on the streets. But it isn't because they are a recreational drug user. Far from it. The mental illness has taken over and evolved into a serious addiction. We have it backward, and until we understand that basic dichotomy and straighten out those mistakes, it's going to be hard to successfully address the issue.

But that complicates matters even further. Why?

Because most individuals and even most church congregations feel totally inadequate to deal with untreated mental illness in a loved one, much less an unknown person.

What can we do?

One of the best things most good Samaritans and church groups can do is to support organizations such as the Salvation Army, Citygate Network, and similar groups that have chosen to deal with mental illness and substance abuse issues head-on. These organizations have been confronting alcoholism and drug abuse for years and have developed programs to help individuals who are addicted. In recent years, they have poured even more time, resources, and money into providing opportunities for homeless people to enter a program that works, that will help them with food, medicine, treatment, and other matters.

Some of the larger, better-operating rescue missions and some independent missions have addressed these issues but not on a collective, nationwide basis, as the Salvation Army has done.

Here's what churches or other faith communities can do even in places where homelessness seems out of control. First, financially support the people who know what they're doing. Critics might say, "Well, it's much easier to make a donation than to go meet a homeless person face-to-face," and that is true. But in this case, providing financial support to an organization that knows the needs of the homeless and how to meet them is invaluable.

Second, step up and help those places and organizations as a volunteer. Go help the Salvation Army. Go help a rescue mission. Go help a Family Promise site or a Citygate mission. Go help a Catholic Charities agency or a St. Vincent de Paul group. They always need volunteers. By volunteering, your presence will often release a professional staff person to better help the people you are trying to serve. Moreover, by volunteering, you will discover that you often receive more of a blessing than those you are hoping to bless.

Third, look for the road less traveled, the opportunities less taken. Most charities and organizations feeding, clothing, and providing medical resources and programs to the homeless attract numerous volunteers during Thanksgiving week, the Christmas season, Easter weekend, and other religious holidays. But they also need volunteers on May 25, February 10, and August 20. The need for help is year-round. Look for times and locations where your volunteer efforts can have the greatest impact and make the most difference.

What should you *not* do?

Don't do something that enables a homeless person to stay right where they are and merely perpetuates the problem. Dr. Marbut suggests that we consider this radical concept: Every sandwich delivered to a homeless person helps kill people. Why? Because every sandwich delivered to them helps them stay away from recovery.

This is something many well-intentioned people do every week. These sincere, godly, spiritually-minded people would most likely be appalled if you asked them to harm a homeless person, but by giving the homeless person a quick bite to eat, yes, we are helping them survive another day, but we are actually enabling that person to continue living on the streets or in an encampment. We are perpetuating the cycle rather than encouraging the homeless person to seek help in a program that will actually make a long-term improvement in his or her life.

That may sound cruel at first glance, but people who work day in and day out with the homeless know the hustle and know that a homeless person will often stay on the street and avoid treatment, whether for addiction or mental illness, as long as possible. So that sandwich is like a Band-Aid on a bullet wound, and enough sandwiches will take the person out by helping them avoid finding a program that provides the services and encouragement they need.

Can we do both—provide for immediate needs and encourage people who are homeless to get into a long-term program? Yes!

How?

We must *engage* rather than merely *enable*. Enabling keeps an addicted person out of recovery. Engaging—talking, building a relationship with the person, and pointing them toward a program that can help them—is far more difficult but much more essential and effective in the long run.

"Let me show you how many tents I gave out," one minister once said, "and how many sleeping bags we've distributed to the people living in the park."

This pastor was appropriately pleased that the

congregation had stepped up with compassion to help the homeless by providing tents and sleeping bags for them. But tents, sleeping bags, and sandwiches are temporary. They are useful, but they do not change the person or solve the problem. If anything, they may exacerbate the problem and prolong the agony.

Can we force people to seek help?

Probably not. But you can make it less convenient for them if they are unwilling to seek programs that can truly make a difference in their lives for the better.

But who are you to say what is good for a person?

Common sense tells us that food and shelter are basics life needs. Add in medical support for those who are addicted or are suffering from mental issues, and the need becomes obvious.

The truth is, some homeless people do not want help.

"You're saying you want to stay in the woods?"

"Uh-huh."

"Well, okay."

But that doesn't help. Granted, it's easier to let a homeless person stay in the woods than to attempt to get that person to seek help at a Salvation Army or a Haven for Hope that offers real treatment and recovery. But it is worth the effort to try. Many will refuse; some will find health, hope, and a new life.

Dr. Marbut advises: "Encourage your volunteers to go serve a meal at a rescue mission. Serve a meal at a Salvation Army. Go serve a meal at Haven for Hope or one of the independent rescue missions. But don't go feeding homeless people in a park or on a curb. If you do, you are perpetuating the problem, and you might just be part of killing people."

Rather than simply passing out a sandwich, or even a meal, as helpful as that might seem, it would be more effective to take portable tables to the homeless encampment or to invite the homeless person to share a meal with you at a nearby picnic table, or better yet, at a Salvation Army center, where you can build a relationship with them. Tell the person, "We're not going to do this often, but I'd like to eat lunch or dinner with you. Would you please be my guest?" It is important to emphasize that you are not going to do this every day or even every week, so the person does not become dependent on you. Seek to build a relationship with that person across the table. Pray for an opportunity to offer more long-term help.

"Can I take you to a place that can help you with your addiction?" Or, "May I take you to our vision clinic that can provide eyeglasses for you?" Or, "Can I take you to the dentist? Or a doctor who can offer psychiatric care?" The key is to point toward getting the person into a long-term program that can help them.

Does that mean Christians and other spiritually-minded people should not distribute food and clothing to people in need?

Of course not.

Jesus said, "Truly I say to you, to the extent that you did it to one of these brothers of Mine, even the least of them, you did it to Me" (Matthew 25:40 NASB, 1995). We know that even a cup of cool water given in the name of Jesus will not go unnoticed in heaven or unrewarded. But when a church group or a civic organization merely distributes food to a homeless person, without providing long-term alternatives, they are really saying, "It's okay. Just stay where you are and don't come in for treatment or recovery. You can keep up all your bad habits, and I will continue to bring you food."

This kind of generosity—although well-intentioned—is bad for the homeless person, it is bad for the community, and, because this sort of program often uses Styrofoam cups and plates and plastic eating utensils, it is often bad for the reputation of the faith community. Why? If there is not a trash pickup element in the program, much of the trash ends up discarded, creating another mess and a negative impression of those trying to help. Ironically, it becomes a negative message about the faith community that is trying so hard to help. Instead, their reputation is often trashed by the garbage left behind after the program to feed homeless people. "You're just making the problem worse," critics assail many benevolent Christian ministries and others who give of their time and resources, hoping to make a positive difference.

No doubt, God honors even our feeble and foolish efforts to help feed, clothe, and assist the poor and needy, but maybe there is a wiser, more effective way for good-hearted, spiritually-minded people to serve the people we are trying to reach. Rather than passing out food near an encampment, the faith community can say, "We're going to help feed hungry people, but we're going to feed people *inside* the rescue mission or a facility such as Haven for Hope, and we're going to clean up afterward."

Another important question that many spiritually-minded civic leaders are asking nowadays is: "What about the encampments? We cannot simply allow these dangerous, ragtag, makeshift tent enclaves, rife with drugs, alcohol, mental illness, and trash, to flourish and take over whole sections of the community."

What can people who are trying to help people who are homeless do about the encampments?

Dr. Marbut's team has developed a plan to help both communities and the residents of homeless encampments. The encampments must be broken up and the people brought in to a more permanent, better setup, but we can't just go in with bulldozers, plowing over the tent communities. A pre-conditioning process is necessary.

Dr. Marbut says, "We go to the encampment and inform the residents, 'In ten days, the police will be coming through here, and bulldozers and dump trucks will be clearing out this area. You must prepare. We love you and we have a good place for you to go.'

"A few days later, we return and emphasize that the plan is in place. 'Hey, we just want to let you know that seven days from now, the bulldozers are coming, so you need to be prepared to move, and we have a good, safe place where you can go.'

"Then a few days later, we return and say, 'Get ready to move. We have a much better place for you.'" This approach allows the residents to realize that the evacuation of the encampment is really happening. It also offers hope for a fresh start.

"Of course, part of that solution involves having housing and services ready to accommodate the people who are displaced by the renovation process. It is counterproductive to break up the encampment if there are no facilities available with enough capacity to house the displaced people. Those living in tents will simply pull up stakes and move to another location.

"When the bulldozers show up at the encampment, social workers need to be on the scene to help the people who have been living there. That's when the rescue mission or the Salvation Army or Haven for Hope must be ready to receive the homeless people and take them in for services.

"Certainly, some homeless people will simply move on to the next city or location where they will begin all over again. But if enough cities take the same proactive approach, we can make a considerable difference for the better. This process must be implemented with care and respect, and our attitude must be, 'We love you too much to allow you to remain in the encampments.'"

One caution: It does little good to move people from an encampment into a hotel. People who are addicted will not do well and may possibly die in that environment. They must be taken to a rescue mission with rehabilitation facilities where they can actually find help for their issues. Certainly, Christian groups should encourage faith-based facilities, but even those that are not spiritually-oriented can be helpful.

Obviously, there is a need to build facilities or renovate existing structures such as old motels, as was done in the movie and in the book *No Address*, where individual housing units can be secured. But merely having a roof over a person's head is not sufficient. There must be full-time treatment and training available to help them get a fresh start in life. In addition to the need for physical housing locations, we also need qualified, caring, well-trained caseworkers who are willing and able to work with the people seeking help.

As noble as many city mission services

are—gathering people off the streets, giving them a meal, a shower, and a bed, and then making them leave the following morning—that, too, is simply a bandage. Life is a full-time deal, and treatment and rehabilitation for homeless people requires a twenty-four-hours-a-day, seven-days-a-week approach, including food, shelter, safety, hygiene, and cleanliness, as well as education and honing of skills. It takes a program. It takes plenty of beds, plenty of food, plenty of volunteers, and plenty of prayer, as well as professionals who have the necessary skills to deal with mental illnesses, addictions, and depression.

This is not a quick fix. Experts who have actually worked with centers to help give people a hand up, rather than merely a handout, estimate that it takes at least eight to ten months for a person to recover from homelessness. Some people will need additional long-term care, especially in cities where they have not had any sort of care previously. The good news is that for nearly 75 percent of people who experience homelessness, real recovery is possible with the proper treatment.

Let's pray together that God will raise up people who have the heart to help homeless people find the resources they need, and, most of all, that they might find faith in Jesus Christ, who provides hope for a better life now and an eternal future.

For more information on
how you can get involved
in helping to alleviate
the problems of homelessness,
please contact:
noaddressmovie.com.

HOMELESSNESS COULD HAPPEN TO ANYONE

WILLIAM BALDWIN
BEVERLY D'ANGELO
XANDER BERKELEY
ASHANTI
ISABELLA FERREIRA
LUCAS JADE ZUMANN

no address

Robert Craig Films
www.NoAddressMovie.com
ROUGH DIAMOND PRODUCTIONS

Americans With No Address

THE DOCUMENTARY

Investigates the homeless crisis in our country and captures the untold stories of those experiencing homelessness.

A 90-minute documentary that investigates the tragic homeless crisis across America with an unbiased mission, identifying which solutions are working and which are not. The producers of the feature film *No Address* interviewed top experts on homelessness by spending four weeks touring the country, interviewing CEOs, executive directors, politicians, and those experiencing homelessness to get the truth of what is causing the crisis in America.

Robert Craig Films

Where To Watch

For viewing options visit www.NoAddressMovie.com

Robert Craig Films has a big heart for finding ways to reduce homelessness and wants to give 50% of net proceeds from The Big 5 to nonprofits.

1 **MOVIE**
No Address is a unique drama about a group of individuals who fall into homelessness unexpectedly, bond together as a family, and navigate the challenges of not having a physical address in the hopes of getting their lives back.

2 **DOCUMENTARY**
Americans With No Address is a documentary that uncovers the grim reality of homelessness in America and the unbreakable spirit that thrives in the face of adversity.

3 **BOOK**
New York Times bestselling author Ken Abraham wrote the *No Address* novel based on the award-winning screenplay.

4 **INTERACTIVE STUDY GUIDE**
No Address: An Interactive Study Guide, containing contributions from industry leaders nationwide, provides education and structure for how to best approach, engage, and serve individuals who are experiencing homelessness.

5 **MUSIC**
The *No Address* soundtrack was created in partnership with Grammy Award-winning artists, writers, and producers.

Robert Craig Films

APPLY NOW for a **donation** or host a **red carpet screening** by using this QR Code or visit us at **www.NoAddressMovie.com**